comes a red horse

Robert C Marsett

comes a red horse

There comes a red horse and on him sits war — or is it vengeance?

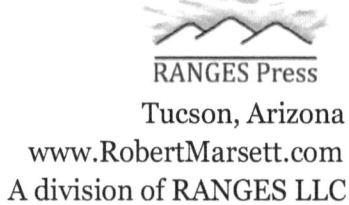

RANGES Press

Tucson, Arizona
www.RobertMarsett.com
A division of RANGES LLC

First printing 2020

The characters and events in this book are fictional, and any resemblance to actual persons or events is coincidental.

ISBN-13: 978-0-9841030-1-0
ISBN-10: 0-9841030-1-5

Dedicated to all punchers, buckaroos, soldiers and the women who put up with them.

PROLOG

The young man stood staring at the carnage before him. He seemed to be studying the blood, the bone fragments and the brain matter but without much interest. Sensing his horse nervously switching his tail disapprovingly and leaning back as if to say, it's time to go, the young man gave his get down rope a slight tug reminding the horse to stay put. He sighed and asked himself, "How the hell did I get here?"

CHAPTER ONE

September, 1971

"She's the finest elephant dog in Cochise County." Bob Hasett

Bob Hasett walked across the tarmac and into the terminal at Tucson International Airport. He had just flown in from the East coast where he was visiting his folks. Bob was fresh out of the Army having returned from Vietnam two weeks earlier. Now he was looking forward to spending some time punching cows while he figured out what he would do next. After a couple of weeks of extreme boredom back home, failing completely to reconnect in any meaningful way with his twenty-year-old, now college student friends, he was glad to have something to focus on.

"Why howdy, Bob, it's good to see you made it back in one piece," said the big man under the big hat as he stuck out his hand. Bob took his hand, noticing the hard-calloused nature of it and wondering if a bear's paw was this big.

He answered back a little self-consciously, "Hi, Uncle Jack. It's good to see you, too."

"How're your folks, young fella?"

"They're fine. They wanted me to give you and Aunt Maria their best."

Jack Barnes, Bob's uncle, grinned at this. He was in his mid-fifties, well-tanned, and weather beaten from years of working outdoors. Even though he was a couple of inches shy of six feet, he appeared taller. Perhaps it was the easy and confident way he carried his two hundred pounds. "I bet your mother wasn't as keen on her good wishes for Maria as you let on."

Bob hesitated a moment and then said, "No. She was sincere. I think Mom has finally given in to the idea that you and Aunt Maria are married."

"Well," Jack boomed with a laugh, "she should. It's only been thirty-four years. I don't think Maria is going to change into a Gringa or a Methodist at this late date."

Bob chuckled, "I expect you're right, Uncle Jack. Is she still strong on the Saints?"

"That she is; sometimes she isn't quite sure if it's the old ones or the Latter Day ones she is fondest of, but I figure a saint's a saint and don't much care either way so long's she's happy."

Bob started to ask if Uncle Jack was still butting heads with the LDS bishop of his local ward but hesitated. Jack noticed Bob had started to say something but stopped so he asked, "What is it, Bob?"

"Oh, nothing...it's none of my business."

"You're sure?"

"Yes, sir, I'm sure."

"Okay, have it your way."

As they walked from the gate to the baggage claim area. Jack asked about the family back East. Bob filled him in on the latest news and then asked, "How are things at Tres Cruces?"

"Oh, the ranch is doing fine. We had a good winter followed by a good monsoon. The country has haired over real good. The cattle are fat, and prices aren't too bad. As my Papa would have said, 'We're sittin' in tall cotton'. You got here at a good time. We won't start fall works for another ten days or so. That will give you plenty of time to get settled in."

"So, did you stick me with the rough string, all broncs and snides?" Bob asked smiling.

"No, I cut you a decent string of horses. I managed to hold Crestnut in the rest-cavvy for you. That wasn't easy; everybody wanted that old pony, but I told them he was yours not the ranch's. That quieted things down some." Crestnut was a big sorrel that had speed, strength, good cow sense, and most important, an honest disposition.

"Uncle Jack, he's not mine. He's yours. I appreciate your holding him out for my string, but you needn't have gone to the trouble."

"Bob, I decided that if you came out here when you got back from Vietnam, that red horse was yours. You always seemed to get along well with him."

"Thanks, Uncle Jack. Crestnut was always my favorite. I remember you put him, Mumford, and old Pete, to babysitting me back when I first came out here for the summers. I was fifteen then ... that was what, five years ago? Crestnut always took good care of me. Lord knows, I needed it. I mean it, Uncle Jack, thank you very much. It means a lot to me."

Jack smiled, "You're welcome, Bob. A man needs a good horse. Think you can remember which end to hang the feed bag on?"

"Yes, sir, the end without the tail."

"That's right; we might make a hand out of you yet."

"Yes, sir, you might. Is my old saddle still in one piece?"

"You bet; that old stamp out will serve you a while longer."

The luggage was coming out now and Bob started looking for his. There were a few duffel bags coming out mixed in with the civilian luggage. Most of them looked pretty new, only one had the worn look of canvas that had been dragged around the world and steeped in tropical heat and humidity. The other duffle bags, the fresh bags, belonged to GIs heading to Fort Huachuca or Zoomies going to Davis-Monthan Air Force Base.

Bob walked over and checked for his name stenciled on the side of the worn duffle bag and grabbed hold, finding the right balance as he hoisted it onto his shoulder, a maneuver that only came with practice. Whoever had designed the duffle bag had a sense of humor. Why else would you only put one shoulder strap on a bag designed to carry seventy to eighty pounds?

Bob watched briefly as a group of young rookies struggled to hang their duffle bags by that single strap on their shoulders. "Excuse me, Uncle Jack. I'll be right back."

Bob strode over to the group and said, "Look here. That piece of shit will never carry that way. Just throw it up on your shoulder or carry it by the handle. You guys headed to Fort Huachuca?"

"Yes, sir."

"Don't sir me; I was just a puke like you. There should be a shuttle bus running down to the Fort. Check at the information desk to see what the deal is."

One of them spoke up, "Johnson just went to find out what's going on."

Just then a GI walked up. "They don't know anything about a shuttle. I guess we have to try and hitch a ride."

"You don't want to do that. It's about a seventy-five mile hump," said Bob.

Just then Jack walked up. "You boys need a ride to Fort Huachuca?"

"Why, yes, sir, I guess we do," answered one of them.

"Okay, we can help you out if you don't mind the back of a pickup."

They all began to answer at once "Thank you sir that would be great. No sweat, the back of a truck is fine."

"Okay, okay, boys," Jack said raising his hands to quiet them down a bit. "Bob, can you get them herded out to the curb while I get the truck?"

"Yes, sir, Uncle Jack."

As Jack Barnes headed out to the parking lot, Bob rounded up the young GIs and lead them out to the curb. One of them asked, "He your uncle?"

"Yes."

"Is he a cowboy?" Asked the GI.

"Yes, he has a ranch down near the border."

"No shit, a ranch, like in the movies?"

"Well, yes, sort of like the movies. The Tres Cruces is one of the largest outfits in southern Arizona. He runs cattle on a little better than eighty thousand acres." Bob answered.

"That's huge; does he use horses?"

"Yeah, that's the only way to work this country. Here he comes; police up your shit."

As Jack pulled up to the curb, Bob saw Scooter, Jack's Queensland Blue Heeler, riding in the bed of the truck. This was her domain, and she ruled over it with the determination that was the hallmark of her breed. When she saw Bob, she perked up her ears and began wagging her tail. She greeted Bob warmly but was not about to give up any dignity by yapping or jumping up and down; that foolishness was for other dogs, not her.

Jack got out of the cab for the sole purpose of letting Scooter know that the young GIs were allowed in her truck. He spoke to them kindly and told Scooter that it was OK. She looked askance at her traveling companions but then decided that, like the cows, they were just something else to guard as part of her job.

As the GIs loaded their bags and themselves into the bed of the truck, Jack smiled and said to Bob, "Finest elephant dog in Cochise County." Bob grinned and nodded.

One of the GIs looked at Bob and asked, "Elephant dog?"

"That's right, elephant dog," said Bob.

"I don't get it."

"Tell you what, we're going to travel through fifty or sixty miles of Cochise County today on the way to the Fort. You keep your eyes open, and if you haven't figured it out by the time we get you to your company, I'll fill you in, OK?"

The young GI looked doubtful but said, "OK."

As Jack pulled away from the airport he said, "Bob, we need to head over to Manuel's and pick up your saddle. I took it in for a little tune up, you know new treads on the stirrups, new fleece, and the like."

"Uncle Jack, you needn't have gone to all that trouble. It would have been OK."

"No, it needed some work, if you don't notice the difference, the horses will."

Bob was a little embarrassed by this. A cowboy never rode a saddle that sored a horse's back. "Oh, I don't want to be galling any backs."

Jack just smiled and nodded, "Don't worry, you won't."

† † †

Jack pulled into the gravel covered yard next to the adobe outbuilding that served as Manuel's workshop. Manuel had several acres of irrigated pasture on Tanque Verde Wash, east of Tucson. There weren't many folks this far out of town, but to Jack Barnes, it was still in town with small holdings of ten to twenty acres up and down the wash all the way back to the edge of the city.

The fact that Manuel's nearest neighbor was a big dude ranch only a quarter-mile away just confirmed Jack's notion that this country was too crowded. Looking at Bob he said. "It won't be long before they pave Speedway all the way out here and start building subdivisions, country's filling up fast."

"Maybe not so soon, Uncle Jack, it's still quite a ways to the city."

"I hope you're right."

As they walked up to the door of the shop, it opened and a small old man appeared with a big grin on his leathery brown face. "Hola, Señor Barnes ¿Como esta?"

Clasping Manuel's hand and pumping it, Jack answered, "Bien, Señor, muy bien ¿y usted?"

Seeing the young man with Jack and the soldiers in the back of the pickup, Manuel dropped the Spanish switching to English in the interest of good manners, "I am fine, too. You are here for the saddle, yes?"

"Yes, sir, we are. This is my nephew, Bob Hasett." Jack motioned towards Bob. "He's fresh back from the war and just out of the Army. He is going to be working for me, so he needs a decent saddle."

Bob put out his hand and said, "Mucho gusto, Señor."

Taking the young man's hand and pleased with his attempt at Spanish, Manuel replied, "No, the pleasure is mine. I'm always glad to welcome home a GI. Come inside for something to drink and bring in the others, they may be thirsty."

As they all stepped into the cluttered shop, Bob was aware of the pleasant smell of leather and oil. Looking around he could see saddles in various stages of completion along with the tools of Manuel's trade. There were completed saddles on sawhorse-like stands, rawhide covered saddle trees hanging from the ceiling, and pieces of leather laid out on the large work bench.

While Manuel and his wife, Nellie, busied themselves with drink requests of ice tea, coffee, and sodas, Bob wandered around the shop looking for his old factory-made stamp out saddle. He couldn't find it, but that did not surprise him; with so much stuff in the shop, it could be missed.

While Poking around, his attention was drawn to a new saddle. It was a beautiful piece of craftmanship, and Bob let out a little whistle of admiration. One of the GIs had wondered over and was looking at the saddle, too. He noticed Bob's reaction and asked, "What's so special about this one?"

Bob smiled and started pointing out the details of this saddle. "This is a no shit buckaroo rig. It is a slick fork, see no swells in the front below the saddle horn. It has no townie padding on the seat, just smooth leather, so you can spend a day in it without rubbing your butt raw. It's basket stamped." Bob said as he rubbed his hand over the intricate pattern that resembled a basket weave.

"It has a big four-inch saddle horn and a five-inch high cantle board." Said Bob placing his hand on the cantle board that acted as a seat back. "And see here Bob said pointing at the brass ring molded into the saddle skirt, "It's three-quarters, flat plate rigged. That means the ring is in the skirt, not suspended from the tree, and it is three-quarters of the distance back from the saddle horn to the cantle board."

Bob then lifted the stirrups to show the GI the tapaderos. "These things that look like boots are tapaderos. This particular style is called bull dog taps. They fit over the stirrup and are there to protect your boots from the brush." This was a fine piece of work. Just the sort of stick Bob hoped he would own someday.

Manuel walked over, "What do you think of this saddle?"

"I like it. You do beautiful work. What kind of tree is it built on?"

"It's a Visalia 3B that I made special for this saddle."

"So you make your own trees."

"I do when it's a special saddle, and this one is special."

"Yes, Sir, it is."

Just then Jack Barnes walked over and said, "What would you change if it was yours, Bob?"

"Bucking rolls are all I'd add."

"What about a mule hide wrapping for the horn?" Asked Jack.

"I like mule hide on the horn."

Looking at Manuel, Jack said, "Bucking rolls and mule hide horn wrap it is, Manuel. Is that a problem?"

"No problem, I can have it ready in a few minutes. Why don't you two go drink your ice tea while I take care of it?"

Bob was confused by all this, so as he followed his uncle over to the counter where Nellie was pouring out drinks, he asked, "Uncle Jack, why is he really putting bucking rolls on that saddle? It's not because of what I said, is it?"

"Why, yes, it is, Bob. You should have what you want on your new saddle." Jack was grinning big now.

Bob was taken aback by this. "Uncle Jack, are you saying that saddle is mine?"

"Don't you like it?"

"Like it? I love it, but I can't afford a custom-made rig like that."

"Your aunt told me that if she had to watch you ride out on that old Monkey Wards stamp out one more time, she would start adding a lot of those Hatch green chilies to my food, and she meant 'a lot'. I remember how you admired my old slick fork, and as I recall when you rode Al's Buckaroo rig, you said it was the most comfortable saddle you had taken a seat in. So Maria and I got you this as a welcome home gift."

"But a saddle like that costs a fortune. I can't let you do that."

"Yes, you can and you will. Just do us the honor of accepting the gift in the spirit it was given."

Bob felt a little ashamed. "Uncle Jack, I can't thank you enough for this. It is much more than I can ever repay."

"GI, you already paid."

CHAPTER TWO

It has a stark beauty all its own.

They had left the Sonora Desert with its iconic big saguaro cactus somewhere near Benson and were now headed south on Highway 90 towards Fort Huachuca. Bob looked back at his brand-new custom saddle in the bed of the pickup. Scooter had tired of sampling all the air that blew past her and was relaxing on the pad and nice wool blanket that Manuel had thrown in for free saying, "A good saddle needs a good pad and a pretty blanket." Bob was feeling pretty good about things.

"You admiring your new stick?"

Bob smiled, "Yes, Uncle Jack, I am. I can't wait to try it out."

"Well, tomorrow you can tack some shoes on your string and do just that. Manuel already twisted and stretched the stirrup leathers for you. She's ready to go."

"Sounds good," said Bob as he stared out the window at the San Pedro Valley. It was a broad, open valley stretching from Mexico in the south to the Gila River, a hundred miles or more to the north.

This part of the valley was bordered on the east by the Dragoon Mountains with the prominent rock outcrop of Sheep's Head and the sandstone boulders and cliffs of the Western Stronghold. The Dragoons were an impressive bit of western landscape with a history to match.

These mountains and the Chiricahuas farther to the east had been the base of operations and hideout for the Chiricahua Apache band led by Cochise for fifteen years. It was said that Cochise Stronghold in the Dragoons was where Tom Jeffords brought General Oliver Howard to negotiate a peace treaty with the Chiricahua Apache, ending a decade of fighting.

The valley sloped down from the Dragoons on a broad alluvial fan before reaching the San Pedro River that gave it its name. The verdant green of the cottonwood along the river course was quite visible, even from Bob's vantage point of several miles away. The valley then sloped up to the west on another alluvial fan that spread out from the Whetstone Mountains. Moving his gaze from the lower elevation on the left near the river up to the higher elevation on the right in the mountains, he saw Chihuahua Desert shrub change to upland grasses and then evergreen oak mixed with juniper. He imagined he might even see some ponderosa on the slopes of Apache Peak. His gaze had just traversed an elevation change of four thousand feet.

It seemed pretty barren to outsiders, but Bob knew it teemed with life. It had a stark beauty all its own. What a difference from his surroundings just three weeks ago. This country hadn't changed much in the past year and a bit. Maybe it had never changed. The old timers did talk of more grass in the old days, but that was before Bob's time. Jack started to say something but then decided it would be better to leave Bob be.

Thirty minutes later, they pulled up to the north gate of Fort Huachuca. Bob leaned over towards the driver's side and said to the MP, "We are taking these troops to the Student Company; is it still over on Jeffords Street?"

"Roger that, is that all you're doing on post today?"

"Yes, that's all. We picked them up at the airport in Tucson. We're headed over toward Douglas after we drop them off."

"Then you will want to go out through the main gate. I'm going to let you in without a vehicle pass so long as that is all you're doing."

"That's all we're doing," said Bob, "Thanks, Sarge."

"No sweat, GI. Don't let any of those rookie maggots fall out and get hurt."

Bob smiled, "Affirmative."

As they drove off Uncle Jack asked, "How'd he know you were in the Army?"

Bob shrugged, "Ears."

"Ears?" asked Jack.

"Yeah, not enough hair to cover my ears. Jody's ears don't show ... too much hair."

"Who's Jody?"

"Civilian guys are Jody."

"I'm a civilian."

"That's true, Uncle Jack, but you're way too old to have long hair, and besides you're a veteran. You're no Jody."

"Is that a good thing...not being Jody, I mean?" Jack asked with a smile.

"Damn good thing, better to have a sister in a whore house than to have Jody for a second cousin."

As they parked in front of the company, Bob got out of the truck and said, "OK, you guys, that's the Orderly Room. There should be a CQ on duty to sign you in."

The young GIs all shook hands with Bob and Jack, chattering away and thanking them for the ride. Bob then asked, "Did you figure out why Scooter is the finest elephant dog in Cochise County?"

"No," they all answered.

One guy said, "There are no elephants in Cochise County."

Bob looked incredulous, "Not now!"

They all groaned at the joke and nodded approval. While this was going on the screen door of the Orderly Room opened and the CQ, a staff sergeant, stepped out dressed in khakis. He watched for a while then approached the pickup. Bob was surprised to see it was Danny, one of the guys from his company in Vietnam.

Danny looked at Bob and then a big smile of recognition crossed his face. "By God, it's you, Hasett. How the fuck are you?"

"Alive."

"And that in itself is a surprise, not to mention the fact that you're not doing the long course in the stockade, either." Then looking at Jack, he asked, "Is this the uncle you told me about?"

"Yes, it is. This is my uncle, Jack Barnes."

Danny grasped the old rancher's hand and shook it vigorously. "This nephew of yours was quite the hot dog in the Nam, but a fine troop." Then looking back at Bob, "So you decided not to re-up."

"That's right. I decided to get out."

Scribbling on a page of his memo book and tearing it out, Danny handed it to Bob, "Well, Hasett, you call me, and we'll go have a beer if you're old enough."

"Not old enough yet; we'll have to go to Mexico, or you can take me to the NCO club."

"No sweat GI; Viva Mexico." Danny then turned to the young GIs, "What the fuck is your major malfunction, standing around like a bunch of half stepping zoomie fucks? Get your sorry butts in the Orderly Room so I can assign you bunks."

Danny then herded them towards the Orderly Room door; looking back over his shoulder towards Bob, he nodded before returning his attention to his charges and said, "I bet you dumb fucks didn't even know that Hasett, that ugly fuck riding in his uncle's truck, is a fucking war hero. Now that's no bullshit, a genuine fucking war hero. Maybe someday if you're lucky and don't crash and burn first, you'll be worthy enough to carry toilet paper to him in the shitter."

† † †

As the pickup headed out the main gate of Fort Huachuca and started east on Fry Boulevard, Jack looked over at Bob and asked, "What was he talking about, you being a war hero?"

"Nothing, he was just giving the newbies a hard time."

"Bull. Your mother said something about you being put in for some big award, but she didn't know the details."

"It's no big deal. I didn't get it anyway."

"Get what?"

"I was put in for a Distinguished Service Cross, but it isn't going to happen."

"What do you mean it isn't going to happen? What are you talking about? A DSC is no small deal."

"I pissed some folks off, and I imagine the recommendation was lost in the circular file."

"You want to tell me about it?"

"What, the DSC or pissing off folks?"

"Both."

"Maybe later, it's a long story."

"OK, but I want to know about the DSC, so you have to tell me sometime."

"No sweat, Uncle Jack. I'll tell you over a beer one of these days."

As short as this conversation was it was long enough to get them to the city limits of Sierra Vista, a small town of about six thousand inhabitants. Most of whom Bob thought lived in Garden Canyon Trailer Park. "This place hasn't changed much."

"No, it hasn't, but rumor has it that it will in the near future."

"Why's that?"

"The Army is moving the Intelligence School to Fort Huachuca."

"No shit! Why the hell would they move the Intell School out here from Baltimore?"

"I don't know, but folks are expecting it to have a big impact on the local economy. They say it will double the size of the post population."

"I don't doubt that. This is a small post population-wise. That's one of the good things about it. If it doubles in size, the chickenshit level has got to increase."

"Well, that may be, but folks are thinking it will be good for the local economy."

"So, what do you think, Uncle Jack? I thought you liked being away from the crowd."

"I do indeed; as the song goes, 'I love my fellow man, but prefer it when he's scattered out some.' In the end I guess it doesn't matter much. It's a good long piece from Sierra Vista to the Tres Cruses."

"Yes, sir, a good long ways."

They drove up and over the Mule Mountains, through the tunnel passing through Bisbee where the normal crowd of about a dozen folks stood at the chain-link fence. They were looking into Lavender Pit, an open-pit copper mine, waiting for the three twenty-five p.m. blast conducted daily by Phelps Dodge. "When do you suppose they'll reach China with that hole?"

"As long as the copper prices stay high, they'll keep digging, but I expect China is safe for a while yet." Jack grinned then added, "There's a job there if you want it."

"I'll pass. I don't have any desire to dig a big ditch."

"It's a hole not a ditch, and the pay's good. Cruz's boy is some kind of boss there, and he could get you on."

"I appreciate that, but I don't want any boss more than is necessary. On the ranch, I figure to get a fair bit of time on my own." Bob said that hoping his uncle would get the hint and gave him a glance.

Jack smiled. This time it was a big toothy grin. "Bob, I was thinking the same thing. I expect you don't need a lot of folks in your road these days, so I decided to put you up at Mountain Camp with Cruz until the fall works, and then we'll see. I was thinking Desert Flats. You'd be keeping an eye on the first calf heifers, and I expect pulling a calf now and then, but you'd be pretty much on your own."

"I would like that, thanks."

† † †

After leaving Bisbee, they drove east through Double Adobe and continued on to Highway 666 where they turned north.

"You can be sure the local Stake President is not real fond of the name of this road," said Uncle Jack.

"Is Stake President a Mormon Church thing?"

"Yep."

"I'm surprised he hasn't had it changed."

"He's tried, but so far it stays 666."

"I remember the first time I rode on this stretch of road with you. I thought it was the road to hell or through hell. Quite a change from other places I'd lived."

"What do you think now?"

Bob thought about this for a second, "I've been to hell, and it doesn't look like this." Bob continued to look out the window at the passing countryside and added, "This old desert country grows on you. It's hard ... but I like it."

"I need to stop in the store up here at McNeil and grab some things for Maria. Give us a chance to stretch our legs. Do you want anything?"

"I think I'll grab a Coke and maybe a candy bar."

"I'm sorry, Bob. I forgot to even ask about lunch, or maybe you'd like a beer. We can go over to the Idle Hour for a cold one."

"A beer sounds good, but I don't want to go into a dive to get it. Maybe we should just pick up a six pack for the road."

"Good idea, I'd rather do that. Think one six pack is enough for both of us?"

Bob looked as though he was thinking hard about this. "No, we'd better get two."

Jack smiled, "That should last us through the drive and dinner."

"Is Aunt Maria going to get upset?"

"She accepts my slips into sin from time to time. It's okay as long as I don't make a habit of it. Besides this is a big deal, you're home from the war. She'll be so tickled to see you that she'll give us a pass on this one."

As they pulled away from the store and onto Highway 666, Bob popped the caps off the bottles using his ring and handed one to his Uncle Jack, "Salud."

"Salud," answered Jack, "neat trick, no opener."

"Comes in handy sometimes," then looking out the side window, "we're hell bound for sure, Uncle Jack. Here we are on the devil's highway, drinking the devil's brew." Raising his bottle to the outside world, Bob growled, "Fuck 'em if they can't take a joke."

Worried, Jack shot a quick glance over to Bob but decided to let it be. "Yeah, fuck 'em if they can't take a joke," he said under his breath.

Passing through Elfrida, Bob was nearly done with his second beer, staring out the door at the irrigated farm fields of cotton and corn when they passed a Cochise County Sheriff's deputy sitting at a stop sign waiting to cross the highway. Bob gave him a casual salute raising the long neck bottle to his hat brim, "Good afternoon, officer."

Jack caught this out of the corner of his eye. "That should give him something to think about."

Bob seemed to snap out of a daydream, "Sorry, Uncle Jack. I wasn't thinking. That was stupid." Then turning to look behind them, "Is he following us? Oh, shit, yes, he is." Bob then looked at his uncle and began to apologize but was cut off.

"Here finish your beer and take mine. It would be better if I'm not holding an open bottle when he stops us."

Reaching over to take his uncle's beer, "Yes, sir, I've got it." Bob was chagrined. He didn't mind a little scrape with the law, but this was different. He had put his uncle into it, and that was unacceptable.

The deputy sheriff did pull up behind them and flashed his brights. "It's Tommy. He wants me to pull over. Tommy's a good guy; let me deal with him." Jack looked at Bob with that no shit expression and added, "You behave; a lot of yes, sirs and no, sirs would be in order."

"Yes, sir," he replied with a sheepish grin.

Jack grinned at this. He knew the boy was not trying to be an asshole, just having a bit of fun. After all, how could he take this seriously? He had just returned from a year at war. This was no big deal, just beer.

"Howdy, Jack, I thought it was you."

"Howdy, Deputy Judson."

"Oh, cut the bull, Jack. It's still Tommy. Do you know why I pulled you over?" The last was said as he looked across the truck at Bob.

"I expect it was because this cuss decided to salute you with his beer bottle."

"Yes, sir, that's it." Looking at Bob, he asked, "Who are you?"

"Bob Hasett, sir."

"Have you got ID?"

"Yes, sir." Bob pulled out his wallet and produced his Virginia driver's license.

Looking it over, Tommy Judson raised his eyes and said, "This is a Virginia license; it says your twenty years old, too young to be drinking that beer, and it's expired. Can you explain any or all of this?"

"Why, yes, sir, I can explain all of it. I am twenty, and therefore, underage so that's no mystery." Jack shot a warning look at Bob, which Bob ignored. He was starting to feel a little pissed. "I just flew into Tucson today, so I haven't had a chance to get an Arizona license yet. As for it being expired, I just got out of the Army two weeks ago, and I was told I had ninety days to get a new license." He was looking the deputy square in the eye, no malice, no joy, no nothing, and the deputy was returning a hard stare of his own.

Jack spoke up now, "Tommy, this is my sister's boy, Bob. He just got back from Vietnam. He'll be working for me at the ranch."

Tommy's eyes were still locked onto Bob's, but now they softened a little. "Welcome to our neck of the woods, young man. Be safe, Jack, and keep the beer out of sight. There's a state trooper patrolling this road, and he's not near as nice as me."

"We'll be more careful, Tommy, thanks, and tell Louise and the kids hi."

"Sure will. Adios." He waved over his shoulder as he returned to his patrol car.

Jack put the truck back in gear and pulled out onto the highway. He was concerned about Bob. He had just seen a glimpse of something in him; he had not seen before, at least not in Bob. He had seen it in others; after the fight on the Shuri Line in Okinawa, both marines and soldiers suffered from it. It was not so much what was there as what was not. It was a hollowness, a void. "You OK, son?"

"Yeah; I'm fine." Bob took another beer from the six pack, opened it, and started to drink it but stopped; he looked at it and then poured it out the window. "I'm no drunk, Uncle Jack."

"I know; it's fine. We'll be at the ranch soon and get you some dinner and a good night's sleep. Tomorrow you can try out that new saddle."

"That sounds good." Especially the good night's sleep, thought Bob. He hadn't had a decent night's sleep in a couple of weeks.

A few miles north of Elfrida they turned east and before long had left the irrigated fields of the valley floor. This was no longer the San Pedro Valley. They had crossed the Mule Mountains at Bisbee and were now in either White Water Draw or Sulpher Springs Valley. Bob could never figure where one began and the other ended.

As they were crossing the desert grassland that ran up to the foot of the mountains, Bob recalled that it wasn't too far now, perhaps twenty miles. He was hungry and looking forward to a big supper, and he liked Aunt Maria. It would be nice to see her again. He would also enjoy seeing some of the cowboys he knew, especially Cruz, but he was hoping this evening would be no big deal. He was tired, and he didn't feel like socializing much.

He was not keen on answering a bunch of questions about the past year. It wasn't that he minded talking about Vietnam, he just didn't have the energy to deal with it right now. Looking straight ahead at the Chiricahua Mountains he sighed and let his mind wander, remembering the times he had spent up in the high country with Cruz. He began to relax. Until then, he hadn't even realized he was tense.

After dinner, Bob and his uncle walked over to the barn and into the saddle house. Opening the old refrigerator, Jack reached in among the vaccines and antibiotics removing two beers. "No sense in getting your aunt all humpy and on the prod. We'll just keep the beer out here."

Bob opened the bottles, and they took a seat on the step. Looking across the corral, Bob glanced toward his right at the mountains and was taken by their beauty. They were big, rugged, and glowing pink with the reflected light of the sunset. He then looked toward the west and was treated to one of those brilliant sunsets that Arizona is known for. "Wow, that's something." Turning to look back to the mountains he said, "Uncle Jack, I see more color from the sunset looking east than most people in the world see when looking directly at it."

"You don't mean it."

"Yes, I do." Nodding towards the mountains as he stood up, "Look at that," he said facing east. "You can stand with the sunset at your back and see a pretty good show in the wrong direction. Folks back East would call *that* a brilliant sunset." He said pointing towards the Chiricahuas. Now he turned around, "Then you look to the west, and the sky's on fire. You don't see that everywhere." Pointing, he added, "mountains topped off with waves of clouds glowing yellow, orange, pink, red, and even purple."

Bob paused for a moment lowering his head and thinking he must sound stupid talking about glowing colors and waves of clouds. "Sorry, Uncle Jack." He paused again then looked back at the magnificent sunset. "It's just that I didn't think I would ever see this again. Hell, I wasn't even sure if I remembered it right or was just making it up in my head."

Jack followed Bob's look to the west. "Young fella, I know what you mean. I felt the same way once a long time ago. It's good to know your memories are true," then raising his beer to the sunset, "Salud."

"Salud, Uncle Jack," Bob answered and took a deep drink from his bottle.

CHAPTER THREE

"... these people no derecho" Cruz

The air was cool, but the sun was bright, so Bob was glad of the shade provided by the old Emory Oak as he put shoes on his string. As much as he hated shoeing horses, the morning had gone pretty well. All the horses stood as they should, and except for Mumford trying to take a bite out of him from time to time, and Crestnut leaning on him to nap while Bob was rasping his front feet, there were no problems. These horses had been turned out in the rest-cavvy for a while; running around barefoot on the hard soil and rocks had kept their hooves worn down as if they had already been trimmed.

Bob had decided to put a few miles on each of the horses in his string today. He wanted to get to know them and find out if there were any snides feeling fresh after their rest. He started with Crestnut, not because he needed to check out his disposition, but because he wanted to start with an easy ride on a horse he liked. It was mid-morning, and he figured he could get that ride in before lunch.

After brushing off the worst of the dirt from Crestnut's back, Bob led him over to the door of the saddle house where he had left his saddle and pads on some old feed bags; this was a brand new, high-dollar saddle, and he wasn't going to have it laying in the dirt just yet. He hobbled Crestnut and removed the halter, hanging it on a hook inside the door. He folded the new wool blanket over the pad, placed them on the horse's back, and got them centered. As he lifted the saddle in place, his Aunt Maria came into the corral. "Oh, I see you are done with the shoes."

"Yes, Aunt Maria. I'm all done. I thought I'd go for a short ride to get the feel of it again."

"And try your new saddle, eh, sobrinito?" She smiled a big genuine smile.

"Yes, there is that." He said with a smile of his own.

"Wait here, and I will bring you something for lunch; then you won't have to hurry back."

"You don't have to do that. I'll be fine," he called after her. She was already headed back to the house and had apparently grown deaf. Bob just shook his head and chuckled to himself while getting on with the task of putting his new saddle on his favorite horse. He adjusted his off billet, a half breed of fine latigo leather, so the cinch would be centered under his horse. He then ran his latigo through the cinch ring three times and drew it snug but not tight and tied it off with a buckaroo latch.

With the headstall in his right hand and the bit in his left, Bob hooked his right arm over Crestnut's head while he slipped his old Kelly and Crockett ring snaffle into the horse's mouth. As soon as the horse felt the sweet steel against his teeth, he opened his mouth and accepted the bit without complaint while Bob pulled the crown piece and throat latch over his ears. He smiled. It was a pleasure to work with this horse.

After checking the position of the bit and fastening the throat latch, he put the looped reins over his horse's head and laid them on his neck before tucking the horse hair get-down rope of his mecate under the front string of his leggings. All that was left was to remove the hobbles and thread them through the back-cinch ring of his saddle.

He led Crestnut around the corral a bit, checked his cinch and decided he was ready. Just then his Aunt Maria came through the corral gate, "Bob, here is some lunch for you. It is not so much, but I think you will like it."

Bob took the small canvas bag, and as he tied it behind his cantle board he said, "Gracias, Tia Maria. I'm sure it will be very good."

"De nada, sobrinito." Maria then turned and went back to the house.

With that, Bob stuck his left foot in the stirrup, grabbed the horn with his left hand and swung up. Sitting in the new saddle, he shifted his weight around a little checking the feel of the seat and getting comfortable. So far, so good, he thought. Then he gently pulled back on the reins, and as he felt Crestnut shift his weight to the rear, he turned his horse towards the gate and untracked him with a cluck and soft tap of his spur.

At the gate he leaned over, unlatched it, and pushed it open; after riding through the gap, he grasped the gate, turned Crestnut sideways to it, and the horse sidestepped, closing the gate so Bob could drop the latch back in place. "Yes, indeed," he said to himself, "this is one fine horse."

† † †

Bob put Crestnut into an easy trot as they left the corral and headed southeast up the cow trail in Headquarters Draw. He was in full costume now and feeling pretty punchy. His jeans were shot-gunned into his tall, black and red boots; he had a big, yellow, silk, wild rag tied around his neck and bat wing chaps with big silver conchos made from Mexican pesos. There was a holster sewn onto the chaps, and it held a forty-five pistol. There were two pigging strings laced through the ring on his chaps, as well. He wore a darkish tan, canvas brush coat over his white shirt, and the biggest black hat he could find. His spurs had been made for him by Cruz a few years ago. They were a modified Chihuahua style with a slight turn down on the shank and big, two and a half inch, eight-point rowels that were well tempered with lots of ring. And if that weren't enough, he had his brush cuffs. He couldn't help it; every now and then he would check his shadow as he rode. Yep, he thought, pretty punchy.

He had covered a couple of miles before topping out on a low saddle looking out over Burro Canyon. Across the canyon, the Chiricahua Mountains began to rise in earnest with row after row of peaks and ridges. Bob would be back in those rough mountains in a few days, gathering the cattle off of their summer range. He was a little apprehensive. It was tough country to work, and he didn't want to make any mistakes.

After taking in the view for a few more minutes, Bob decided he may as well eat some lunch. He stepped down from his horse and untied the lunch sack from the saddle. He didn't bother to remove the saddle after such a short distance on a cool day. He just loosened the cinch; he didn't hobble Crestnut either he just sat down on a large rock keeping the mecate tucked into his leggings. Maria had done well for him with two big beef and bean burritos with lots of green chilies and some cookies for dessert.

As he finished his lunch, he noticed some dust rising by a watering point on the canyon floor. He couldn't see it, but he knew it was there because of the little thicket of trees around it. Must be cattle, he thought. Stuffing the lunch sack in his pocket, he tightened the cinch and swung back up on Crestnut's back. He decided to go have a look at the dirt tank and check on the cattle. Might as well, he thought. I'm here and it's only a mile or so away.

Crestnut had hit his easy shuffle of a low trot, and pretty soon they were more than halfway to the water point. Bob decided to pull off the trail and go up the side of a low hill to get a better look. He thought he could hear someone whistling and whooping. The last thing he wanted was to get in somebody's road and cause a wreck with spilled cows and a mad cowboy. Better to see what was up and offer help, if needed.

Sitting his horse on the hillside next to an oak tree where he had a good view, he could see Cruz and a couple of dozen cows with nearly as many calves. The whistling and whooping had stopped; everything was pretty quiet now as Cruz watched over them while they watered. Bob continued to watch. He could see that some of these girls looked a bit wild, and he thought he could tell that one or two were hobbled. He decided to let Cruz know he was there.

Bob rode away from the tree into the clear and gave a loud whoop followed by a couple of whistles. Cruz looked up and seeing him waved casually, acknowledging the signal. Then he sat up straighter in his saddle and waved excitedly as he recognized Bob. He's waving me in, thought Bob.

Staying wide of the cattle, Bob circled around behind the tank and joined his friend. "Oh, Roberto, como estas?" Cruz blurted out with a big smile as he leaned over and took Bob's hand, pumping it up and down vigorously.

"I'm fine, estoy bien, y tu?"

"I am good, too. Jack told me you be coming soon. I am glad you are here. We have much work to do, and you can help with this thing."

"Okay, I look forward to it. How are Isabel and the kids?"

Now Cruz lost his smile. "Isabel, she's not so good. She has the Lupus. She has very much sore in the knees, and her eyes not working so good."

Lupus was a disease Bob had heard of but knew nearly nothing about. All he knew was that it was bad. "I am very sorry, Cruz." And then for the old man's benefit, "I will go to the church and light a candle for her."

"Thank you, she will be happy for this."

"De nada, Cruz, it is the least I can do. And how are the kids?"

"They are good. Freddie is still at the mine in Bisbee. Suzie is in college in Douglas, and Mike is in Tucson working construction."

"Sounds like they are all good."

"Si, they are good." Then looking at the cattle Cruz said, "I told you one thing, these cows are a little bit loco. I bring them all the way from Sunset Springs, and they try to run and run a lot-a-much, but now they are tired. I don't want them to rest too much; I want to get them to Headquarters, better to go now."

Bob understood that Cruz wanted to get these girls moving and get them penned up. Looking them over, Bob could see that these were indeed some pretty wild cows. One of the young cows, maybe a two-year-old, was a slick, long ear, meaning, no brand and no ear marks. These cows must have been back in some really rough country to be missed for a year or two. Then he noticed that there was more than one slick in the bunch. In fact, most of the calves were unbranded long ears; at least two of the young cows were long ears, one of which had a calf of her own. There was even a young unbranded bull; he was a long yearling or two-year-old.

At that point, Bob realized he didn't recognize the brands as belonging to his uncle. "Cruz, these aren't Tres Cruses cows."

"Si, they are not Jack's cows. They are Indian Springs cows. That is the brand for this ranch," said Cruz, pointing at the Crown F brand. Turning in his saddle and pointing to some dust on his back-trail Cruz said, "There some Tres Cruses cows, they coming too."

Are they following us in?"

"Si, I not put them with Indian Springs cows because," Cruz paused and thought for a moment. "Maybe these cows sick and have piojos." With this, Cruz pointed to an old spotted cow that was obviously ridden with lice. "Look at that old pinto cow. She has piojos lota much."

"Oh, piojos are lice?"

"Si."

"That's strange; old Bill Foster is a better hand than that."

"He is no more the owner. He sold the ranch two years ago, mas o menos."

"Who has it now?"

"I don't know, and I tell you this. I not see the cowboys in the mountains for long time."

They were pushing the cattle off the water now and getting them back on the trail, headed to Headquarters. One old cow kept trying to slip away from the bunch with her half-grown calf, but she had been hobbled by Cruz and never got far before being headed off and turned back. A few of them tried to break free a time or two, but Cruz had knocked most of the wild out of them by pushing them hard over several miles of rough mountain trails. It didn't hurt that he had two of them hobbled and a pair of yearlings that were just plain crazy tied together at the neck. The two yearlings were fun to watch. They could never get it together. If one wanted to run, the other did not and vice versa so that they kept pulling against each other to no avail.

From the looks of these cattle, the Indian Springs Ranch was having some problems handling its livestock. It was not good to have unbranded yearlings, but it did happen now and then in the rough country, but slick two-year-olds was just plain bad. He managed to get a rough count and came up with four Crown F cows, two of which were being sucked and drawn down by big slick yearlings, and two of which had no calves. Last, there were the two young heifers and the young bull. All of them were slick, and one of the heifers had a small calf. What the Crown F and slicks had in common was poor condition and bad attitude.

The cows were moving along pretty well now. The country was easy. The cows were tired, and two cowboys could easily keep the wilder ones in check. Pretty soon they were approaching a small coral. It was really the water lot at Ajax Well, not a working corral. It sat on the fence line between the pasture they were in and the holding pasture. Cruz circled wide around at an easy gallop, went into the fenced lot, and closed the gate leading out the other side. When the cows reached the gate, Bob let them take their time, and before long they had all entered, all that is except the two that were necked together. After a little encouragement from him and Crestnut, they decided to join the rest.

Cruz and Bob sat in the gate, looking at the Tres Cruses cows that had followed them. Cruz said, "We have to bring them through. You hold the gate. I bring them in." Once the Tres Cruses cows were in the water lot, Bob closed the gate and walked his horse over to Cruz, who was looking the cattle over with a critical eye. "What now?" asked Bob. "Do we sort our cows from the others?"

"Si, we put the Tres Cruses cows on the other side of the corral by the holding pasture, and the others stay aqui on this side of the corral"

Cruz stepped down now, loosened his cinch, reset his saddle, tightened his cinch and was back in the saddle almost before Bob could make up his mind whether to check his cinch or not. "My horse is young and not know much. Maybe better for you to sort the cows, and I will watch the gate. Crestnut know the cows."

"OK, just let me check my cinch," said Bob as he stepped down.

They pushed all the cattle into the section of the corral that was furthest from the holding pasture. Cruz then placed himself in the gate opening between the two halves of the corral and waited for Bob to bring some cows.

Bob picked out a Tres Cruces pair at the left end of the bunch and headed Crestnut towards them, staying a bit to the right. The cow and calf soon moved a few steps, and Crestnut eased behind them, staying a little to their left and walked them down the fence to the open gate. Cruz had backed his horse out of the way, and as soon as the cow and calf went through, he walked his horse back into the opening acting as a living gate.

The whole operation went pretty smoothly. The Tres Cruces cows were fairly gentle and knew where they were, and the wild cows were not asked to go anywhere — just stay put and out of the way, which they did.

This was a small corral but a stout one with a six-foot fence, so they removed the hobbles from the two bronco cows and untied the two yearlings that were necked together. They got it done without any major mishaps, just a bruise or two for Bob from cow kicks which he failed to anticipate. Soon Bob and Cruz were on their way back to the ranch headquarters.

As they were entering the headquarters corral from the back, they saw the ranch truck pulling into the yard and parking by Jack's house. When Jack stepped out of the truck, he saw Cruz and Bob and motioned them to come over. Cruz immediately put his horse into a trot to cover the one hundred yards separating them quickly. As they rode up to Jack Barnes, Cruz stepped down and pulled off his hat. Jack tipped his own hat in response, then stuck out his hand to Cruz and said, "Buenas tardes, old friend. What brings you down from the mountain?"

"I bring some bronco Indian Springs cows from Sunset Tank. Some Tres Cruces cows follow us in." Pulling his tally book from his shirt pocket, he read off the list of what he had found, telling Jack the number, sex, age, and brands of the bunch. "Jack, something not right at Indian Springs Ranch, too many long ears, and many of their cows every place. I see more bronco cows today but no chance to catch them, very crazy these cows." Cruz always pronounced chance with an extra syllable at the end.

"Were they Indian Springs cows?"

"I told you one thing; they are not Tres Cruces cows. More like corrientes. Si, I think Indian Springs."

"Where were the Tres Cruces cows?"

"They were at Government Trap."

"You think they are the ones you saw tracks for last week?"

"Si, I think so, but no chance for be sure."

"OK, where are the cattle you brought down?"

Cruz told Jack the cattle were penned up at Ajax Well, explaining that he had segregated them but not turned the Tres Cruces cattle into the holding pasture in case Jack wanted to look them over. He had not brought any of them into the headquarters Corral because the Indian Springs cattle were looking pretty poor and had lots of lice and tics.

Jack agreed with Cruz's actions. He told them he had something to take care of and would be over to the corral in few minutes. He instructed Cruz to get the sprayer hooked up to the truck and mix up enough spray to handle the bunch in the water lot. Then Cruz and Bob were to ride back over where they had penned up the cows and wait for Jack, who would drive the truck over with the sprayer. He didn't want a bunch of parasite infested cattle on his place.

After they had finished spraying the cattle and turned the Tres Cruces bunch into the holding pasture, Jack told Bob that he needed him to get a couple of bales of hay to the penned up Indian Springs Cattle. They would stay in the water lot until Indian Springs sent somebody to pick them up. Jack had looked them over carefully and talked to Cruz about the situation on the mountain. "Cruz, I don't like it. Something is not right over on that place."

"I think these people no derecho." Cruz said.

"Si," answered Jack, "they're not straight. I think they're as crooked as a dog's back leg." Jack then turned to Bob, who was about to ride back to Headquarters and said, "Bob, I was hoping to keep you down here at Headquarters for a few days, but it looks like Cruz could put you to better use at Mountain Camp. After you get the hay to these girls, I want you to trailer Cruz back to his camp. I also want you to take your string and stay up there to help him for the next three or four weeks.

"Yes, sir."

Now Jack turned to Cruz. "I want you and Bob to prowl the mountains good. If you can fix the fence between them and us that would be good, but what is most important is to get their cattle off our country and continue getting the Sabino fence ready. We will be starting the fall work in four weeks. We should be in North Sabino in five or six weeks. I may bring Bob back here for a few days, but he will mostly be with you until we start working North Sabino. Then he will join us for the fall works. I don't want you to worry about the fall work. You stay on the mountain and be sure it's ready for the cattle after we wean and ship. If you can put their cows back on their country that would be best, but if you need to, go ahead and bring them down here."

"Have they done any work on the fence yet?" Asked Jack. "I sent posts and wire to them over a year ago. They were supposed to get right on it. Last time I talked to the manager over there, he gave me a hat full of excuses, but said they would get right to it." Jack was getting hot.

"The fence is very bad. I see no fence work from them. I do this sometimes when I find a very bad place."

"Cruz, I'm not blaming you. You know the deal. I sent them over three thousand dollars worth of fencing. They were to provide the labor and let me know when and if they needed more. It's not your fault."

"Si, I understand."

CHAPTER FOUR

These gringos, especially the young ones, did not always understand.

Bob and Cruz were nearly to the Mountain Camp. They had seen nothing unusual on the way up. Where there were supposed to be cows, there were cows and where there were supposed to be no cows, there were no cows. They had driven up the broad canyon leaving the open country of the headquarters behind and were now in that classic Madrian Woodland that made up so much of the mountain vegetation.

There were evergreen oak, pinyon pine and juniper on the slopes, scattered in some places and dense in others. There was lots of grass on the slopes and even more in the flat open areas. Large stands of cottonwood and sycamore dominated the riparian strand along the creek. As they climbed higher they began to see huge Arizona Cypress and ponderosa pines. "Bob, you remember what call these trees?" asked Cruz pointing to one of the big Cypress trees.

"Yes, they're Sabino."

"Si, si, you not forget."

Bob smiled, glad he had remembered. "I didn't forget everything you taught me. Some things I remember."

"Ah, you remember lotta much."

Bob thought, they must be a mile or better above sea level. The air had a little bit of a bite to it even though it was a good hour before sunset. It promised to be a cold night; there might even be a frost. Fall was definitely in the air. The sycamore and cottonwoods along the creek were showing signs of changing to fall colors, and when he looked up towards the tallest peaks, he could see patches of light green with a bit of gold. That must be the aspen beginning to turn, he thought.

What an amazing piece of country, Bob said to himself. You can travel from Mexico to Canada just by going up the mountain. There were antelope in the desert grassland below the headquarters as well as mule deer. There were whitetails in the mountains, and the little pigs called javalina, peccary actually, were everywhere except up high. Besides that there were coyotes, coaties, foxes, mountain lions, and bobcats scattered around with plenty of black bears thrown in. Cruz even claimed there was still a jaguar or two that passed through on occasion, but he said he had not seen a wolf in many years.

"Mira!" Cruz was pointing to the right front.

Looking to where Cruz pointed, Bob saw a whole band of coatimundis scamper across the road with their ringed tails held straight up like warning flags. They looked something like raccoons, but a band of them reminded Bob of a troop of monkeys. He smiled.

Cruz turned into the front yard of the Mountain Camp. A couple of yard dogs came running up to greet the truck barking at first then wagging their tails as they saw Cruz whom they greeted enthusiastically.

Once Cruz and Bob had unloaded the horses and put up their saddles, they each caught up a horse for the next day, put them in a holding pen and turned the rest out to pasture. Leaving some hay for the two night horses, Bob and Cruz headed to the house.

The house was like many of the old ranch houses in the mountains of Arizona and New Mexico. The outer walls were mostly stone, but use had been made of the abundant timber nearby for the roof and interior walls. The house had a rather modest living room with the kitchen and dining area to one side and a hallway on the other leading to three bedrooms and a bath. There was a covered porch on the south, east, and west sides of the house with a sleeping porch on the north that opened into the living room and the master bedroom. The house had propane gas for heating and utilities. The only electricity was provided by a small welder that doubled as a generator. It was only run about an hour every day or two to charge up a small battery bank for the CB radio and small appliances.

As they walked through the front door, Cruz called into the kitchen telling Isabel that they had company. She came out wiping her hands on a dish towel, and looking over towards them, she said. "¡Oh, Señor Bob, bienvenido!" She gave him a hug and motioned to the easy chair. "Sientese, por favor. "¿Que querie beber, cafe, te, cerveza, o Coke?"

"Just water, uh, agua solamente, gracias."

"Bien, agua solamente."

Speaking to Cruz, she told him that Maria had called on the radio to let her know Bob would be staying at the camp for a while. She would have dinner on the table in another half hour so they should relax for a while. With that she returned to the kitchen.

Cruz and Bob relaxed and caught up a little until Isabel called them to dinner. As Bob walked into the kitchen, Isabel motioned him to the chair at the head of the table, "Sientese aqui por favor."

Bob was not comfortable taking Cruz's chair. He looked at him and started to protest, but Cruz just smiled and said, "Please sit down. Tonight you are the guest."

"OK, but tomorrow I am just another hand. OK?"

"Si. That is OK, but maybe Isabel not like this thing."

"I expect you can fix it." Bob was really hungry, and there was lots of food on the table. He looked at Cruz and Isabel to see if they were going to say grace, and they looked at him just as quizzically. Of course, he thought. I am at the head of the table. It is my responsibility. Bowing his head, he went for the quickest blessing he thought he could get away with without being rude. "Lord, we thank you for this food and all our many blessings." Casting a furtive glance around the table he could see he was not yet off the hook. "We thank you for good friends, good weather, and good health. In the name of the Father, Son, and Holy Ghost, amen." He even crossed himself hoping that would help, but he wasn't sure he had done it right.

"Amen." Answered Cruz and Isabel as they crossed themselves.

After dinner Cruz and Bob were sitting on the porch enjoying a beer and the sunset. After stuffing himself with beef burritos covered in green chilies, refried beans, rice and lots of extra tortillas, Bob was enjoying the peace and quiet. Cruz seemed to be enjoying the quiet too, and Bob was glad. He didn't want to make conversation just now. Finally, Bob stood up and said, "I need to get my gear into the room in the barn and get my bedroll laid out."

"No, you sleep in the house. Isabel fixed the boys' room for you."

"You know that's not necessary."

"Si, I know this, but it is better. You sleep inside."

"OK, well, I'm going to get my duffel bag out of the truck before it gets too dark."

"One more cerveza?"

"Yes, I would like one more. I'll get my bag."

Bob had put his duffle bag in the bedroom and rejoined Cruz on the porch. A coyote howled a ways off. "It's been a while since I heard that."

"No chance for coyotes in Vietnam?"

"No, no chance."

Cruz thought about this for a little while. "I would not like it if no coyotes. I like to sing to them."

Bob looked at Cruz a little surprised. "You like to sing to them."

"Si, but I not tell many people this thing. The cowboys ..." here Cruz searched for an English word but gave up, "the cowboys think I am loco if they know." Now Cruz was looking at Bob.

"Your secret is safe with me."

"Mande?"

Bob looked Cruz in the eye and gave a warm smile, "I won't tell anybody, viejo. It is our secret."

With that, Cruz smiled and asked, "You like to hear?"

"Yes, sir, I would like to hear that."

Cruz sat up straight in his chair, cupped his hands around his mouth and began the high-pitched howls and staccato yips of a full-fledged coyote party. Isabel came out onto the porch to watch and listen, surprised that Cruz was sharing this with Bob. She knew he kept it close. These gringos, especially the young ones, did not always understand the animals and might think her husband was loco for singing to them. Perhaps this young man was different. She smiled to herself and went back inside. Pretty soon Cruz had at least two other coyotes answering.

Bob said, "That's something else. If you keep that up, every coyote in the canyon will be singing back to you." After listening a bit longer and enjoying the concert, he said quietly, more to himself than anyone else, "I really missed this place."

CHAPTER FIVE

"My dance card is open." Bob Hasett

In the morning they were dressed, fed, and trotting out by sunrise. Cruz led a pack horse with fencing supplies in his panniers. The air was crisp and still. As the sun rose, the pink retreated from the sky to be replaced by the most brilliant blue. Bob said, "I can't believe I'm getting paid for this."

Cruz chuckled, "Maybe you believe more later after we catch some bronco cows."

Well, maybe, Bob thought. He would probably agree after a hard day, but as hard a day as it might be, the cows weren't armed, and that was a good thing.

About that time Bob's horse, Nobody, decided to fight his head and run backwards a little. Bob got him under control, but Nobody was as humpy as Kokopelli's back. Bob had not had the chance to take any of the fresh off him the day before as he had planned, and now he would have to do it while trying to get a day's work done in the mountains.

"Your horse is a little bronco this morning."

"Yeah, he has an attitude problem. I hope it improves. Any advice?"

Cruz thought about this for a minute. He wasn't sure he understood the question, but he guessed Bob had asked for suggestions on how to deal with the horse. "Si, stay on top."

"Very funny, viejo."

"Si, I think so," Cruz laughed.

They had been traveling for two hours when they got to the fence that separated their allotment from the Indian Springs allotment. This pasture, Northeast Pasture, was one that Tres Cruces rarely used. It was very rough country, much of which was at 8000 to 9000 feet elevation, made up of high mountains and broken ridges with deep canyons and sheer cliffs of hundreds of feet. Jack, therefore, was in the habit of holding it back for those years when feed was in short supply. He said it wasn't the worst place in the world to run cows, but you could see it from there.

Northeast Pasture was about fifteen sections, nearly 10,000 acres. It was northeast of Sabino Pasture in which Mountain Camp was situated and ran along the northeast border of the ranch. This was US National Forest land and open to the public, but the grazing rights were exclusive to whichever ranch held the allotment and paid the lease. Of the 80,000 plus acres that made up the Tres Cruces Ranch nearly half was in the Coronado National Forest. The rest was divided about evenly between state trust land and private land. That meant in addition to about 60,000 acres of public lease land, Tres Cruces had around 20,000 patented acres. That was a lot. All this meant a total of 125 square miles or sections.

Cruz looked up and down the fence line and told Bob, "We go south on the fence. We looking for places where the fence is down. Looking for the cows también. If Indian Springs cows, we put on other side. There is a gate three miles." Here Cruz hesitated. "A la sur."

"To the south." Said Bob.

"Si, to the south." If we find Tres Cruces cows, we take them to Mountain Camp. Maybe we cannot do this thing if the fence is too bad or the cows are too bronco." He thought about this for a while. "OK, we do what we can. You ready, cowboy?"

"Si, I'm ready, estoy listo."

The fence was a mess. There were places where trees had fallen on it, and the fence was down for several yards with broken or bent posts, twisted stays, and broken wire. The wire was so old it was thin and brittle. You could not twist it very tight without risking it breaking. It became apparent that if they put any cows through that fence, they would be back on this side before long.

After fixing a thirty-foot span of downed fence, the third big break they had come across in a mile, Cruz said, "This fence is no good. If we find Indian Springs cows, better to put them in the corral east of Red Rock. It is Indian Springs Corral, maybe two miles on other side."

"Is it on the same trail as the gate?"

"Si."

They did not expect to see any of their own cows in Northeast Pasture, as the fence separating it from Sabino Pasture was in good shape, and the natural barriers were substantial, but they were seeing lots of tracks. It seemed the Indian Springs cows were eating lots of Tres Cruces grass.

At midday they were sitting on top of a ridge taking a lunch break. As they finished, Cruz pointed to a spot below in the next canyon and told Bob there was a spring there where he expected they would find cattle. He wanted to take them south if they would go that way, hoping to pick up any others that may be at the spring at Red Rock or along the trail. Cruz estimated they had already seen the tracks of twenty or thirty cows and calves, and they were mostly headed south.

As they descended the ridge, they faded to the right, away from the fence. This was so they would be in position to prevent the cows from bailing out to the west. The idea was to hold them against the fence and then take them south. Of course, this assumed that the fence would hold them.

The going was tough. It was steep, and they were off the trail, side hilling down the wooded slope. The horses were gingerly picking their way over ground covered by pine needles and rocks, some of which had a propensity to roll or slide. This did not make for good footing, thus the horses were blowing rolls and switching their tails nervously. If that weren't enough, the odd downed tree had to be dealt with just for good measure.

Bob's horse, Nobody, was sweating heavily and more than once he slipped and sat back on his haunches. He was a decent horse and knew his business when it came to cows, but he never had been known for his calm demeanor. Instead, Nobody had a tendency to get flustered when things didn't go just right, and he was getting flustered now.

Bob hoped he would not revert to one of his no shit blow ups, the cause for his being named Nobody, since nobody wanted him in their string. One thing for sure, Nobody did not respond in any way but negatively to harsh treatment. Bob patted his neck and talked soothingly to him letting him have his head and pick his own way. Bob knew there would be only one winner in a battle on this hillside with Nobody, and it would be the horse.

They were nearly to the bottom when Cruz stopped and motioned Bob to come up beside him. Then very softly he said, "You take the pack horse." Handing him the lead rope he continued, "There is the trail that goes back up the canyon to the spring. I go push the cows south." Then pointing up the canyon a hundred yards or so he added, "The canyon very skinny there. You go there and keep the cows from going down." Then pointing the other way, down the canyon to a broad spur coming down from the ridge to the south, he said, "There is a trail for you. When the cows go south you go up and meet me. Watch for more cows on top, very good country. If you see cows, push them to me."

"OK, are you going to signal me when the cows are moving south?"

"You can see this from the skinny place."

"OK, see you on top."

With that, Cruz worked his way back to the east staying north of the canyon bottom, while Bob dropped on into the canyon and followed the trail up the narrows. Here he found a spot where he thought he would be able to see Cruz moving cattle to the south.

Before Cruz would have been in place, three cows and a calf came trotting down the trail towards Bob. He didn't make a big show or whoop at them to stop; he simply moved Nobody a step or two forward and raised his arm to get their attention. That was enough to stop them. He stayed put and assumed a relaxed pose, acting as if he was not much interested in them; in response, they seemed to relax a little. Soon he could hear Cruz whooping and knew he was on the cattle. Bob then squared up in his saddle making eye contact with the cows. He slapped his leggings, clucked once or twice. and untracked Nobody, who was all business now. They walked slowly towards the cows which turned around and started to trot back up the trail. With this, Bob gave a loud whoop so Cruz would know he had cattle at the narrows.

Bob kept his horse at a walk as they moved up the canyon. His only concern was not to let the cows go up the hill to the north, away from the gate at Red Rock. Pretty soon they scrambled up a game trail that led south out of the canyon. That was OK with Bob; it was the right general direction. He stopped where he was waiting for any other strays that may be headed his way.

Soon he saw Cruz coming back towards him, staying uphill a bit on the north side of the canyon. Bob waved and got his attention and pointed to the cattle on the game trail headed south. Cruz saw them, waved at Bob, and turned back to the spring. Bob held his position until he saw several cows heading south about where the fence should be followed shortly by Cruz.

After backtracking and finding the trail, Bob, Nobody and the pack horse had arrived at the edge of the broad ridge after a steep climb. Nobody was a lot more content now having had fairly good footing for the past mile, but both horses were winded. Bob stepped down, checked his saddle and the pack saddle.

After swinging back up, he looked around for sign of cattle, and then headed towards the southeast. He was seeing fresh sign and expected to come across cows at any time. Before long, he came across them. Up ahead he saw about a half dozen, but they didn't see him. They were, in fact, looking to the east. Something had their attention. Bob held up where he was waiting to see if something developed. It did.

A brown and white cow that reminded Bob of a paint horse turned and started towards him. The others began to follow, but when the paint cow saw Bob and the horses, she froze. It was only for a second; then she threw her tail over her back and took off like a deer, more south than east but still in the right general direction. Bob put Nobody up into a high trot, keeping the cows to his east while trying to put a little pressure on them to turn more towards the fence.

It became clear that the cattle were on a trail, and Bob hoped it would take them where he wanted. The trail faded to the east, and Bob started bending his course in that direction as well. The ridge top was fairly flat but had quite a few scattered pine and fir trees that reduced visibility and had to be dodged while trying not to fall too far behind.

Bob had his hands full, trying to keep the cattle in sight, avoiding low branches and keeping the pack horse from going the wrong way around one of the trees. He was getting exasperated when Nobody decided it was time to act up. The horse started to fight his head, trying to turn back towards the north. Bob took his eyes off the cows that were still a little to his left to concentrate on the problem in hand. What he saw ahead and to the right was air and nothing but air; it was a steep cliff. While the cliff was only a few yards to the right, it ran on a line not quite parallel to Bob's, and in a matter of several seconds Bob's course and the cliff would merge.

He turned Nobody hard to the left which required no effort, but the pack horse turned even sharper and managed to get the lead rope rim fired up under Nobody's tail. This was all Nobody needed to decide it was time to just plain break in two.

He bogged his head, bucked straight up in the air and landed stiff legged like a pick ax hitting a flat rock. Bob felt his teeth jar when his butt hit the saddle, and he knew he didn't have too many of these left before he was on the ground. Dropping the pack horse's lead rope, he pushed his free hand against the horn forcing himself against the cantle, while he pressed his thighs up against the bucking rolls and got ready for more. Nobody gave him two or three more jumps that Bob rode out, and he was beginning to feel pretty good about his bronco twisting when Nobody took him under a low branch with his last jump. That was enough.

Bob hit the ground on his butt like he usually did, and he managed to hit a relatively soft spot missing the rocks. Nobody had stopped bucking when he dumped Bob but was still intent on leaving the country. Grabbing his mecate, Bob managed to keep hold of Nobody and stopped him while getting to his feet rapidly. The horse stood quivering, blowing rolls, twitching nervously, and surveying his surroundings with wide eyes and ears that seemed to be pointing in every direction at once.

It was then that Bob noticed the pack horse was in a rodeo of his own. One wreck at a time, thought Bob. I'll deal with that idiot after I get this one calmed down. Slowly walking up to Nobody and talking calmly, Bob gently placed his hand on Nobody's shoulder and then carefully brushed it up to his neck where he stroked the nervous horse while speaking to him in low reassuring tones. Bob then led Nobody to a small clear area, watching him closely to see if he could detect any injury and saw none. Here he loosened his cinch and raised the back of the saddle and pads; he stood next to the horse with his upper right arm resting on Nobody's back while his elbow bent at a right angle, thereby letting his forearm act as a vertical support, holding the saddle up allowing air to cool the horse's back.

Bob took this opportunity to check his own condition and that of his gear. He found that other than a sore butt, everything seemed to be OK.

The same could not be said for the pack horse who had finally stopped his battle with unseen equine dangers and was standing in the middle of a jackpot a few dozen yards away. He was a sorry sight with panniers hanging askew from the pack saddle and dumped fencing material and tools scattered all around. To top it all off, he had done a credible job of hobbling himself with the lead rope. He seemed to be resigned to his fate and stood stoically awaiting it.

"Nobody, I want you to have a look at one sorry sight," said Bob pointing to the pack horse. "That poor bastard just went plumb loco, scared the piss out of himself, dumped his load, and hobbled himself all while running from a for sure equine eating bugger bear. Hell, he didn't get more than a hundred yards from where he started. No wonder they named him Mumford." Nobody ignored all this, but Bob didn't care. He often talked to the horses when alone. "Well, I guess we'd better go and get him straightened out."

Bob lowered the saddle back down onto Nobody's back but didn't bother to tighten the cinch and led him over to a spot near the wreck. He took the hobbles from his saddle and put them on Nobody's front legs. Pulling off his saddle and pads and placing them on the ground, he thought it was going to take some time to fix the mess with the pack outfit, and Nobody could use a short break.

Taking his rope over to the pack horse, he spoke softly to Mumford stroking his neck and slipping the loop of his rope over his head. Now he could untie the lead rope from Mumford's halter and try to get things sorted out, but first he had to get the panniers off and out of the way. The pack saddle was knocked a little cockeyed but was still on top and pretty tight so Bob decided to leave it for last. Once the panniers were off, he took his pigging string and hobbled Mumford for real and went to work getting the lead rope untangled. When he finished with the lead rope, he retied it to the halter, removed his rope, and pulled the pack saddle off.

After a quick check, he could see the sawbuck pack saddle was okay, but he would have to rig some sort of fix for the panniers as each of them had broken a strap. No sweat, he thought. I can rig something up with a pigging string.

Half an hour later, Bob had resaddled the horses, packed the scattered fencing in the panniers, and was ready to get back to the job of finding the cows and catching up to Cruz.

✝ ✝ ✝

It wasn't long before he was on the trail the cows had taken. It was well used, indicating that these cattle had been up here for some time. He put Nobody up into a low trot feeling for any signs of discontent on his horse's part. Once he felt comfortable with everything he began to whoop, as much to let Cruz know where he was as to keep the cattle moving.

He had been traveling this way for less than thirty minutes when he caught the faint sound of Cruz's long, high-pitched whoop. It was more of a call than whoop that Cruz used to locate people. Bob stopped and answered back. Cruz responded immediately, and Bob knew Cruz had heard him. Better yet, the sound was coming from the direction Bob was headed.

Shortly, Bob could hear Cruz whistling and whooping as he worked the cattle. He seemed to be at the bottom of the canyon Bob was descending. It was not nearly so deep as the one where they found the first bunch of cows, but it boxed up pretty well downstream with some sheer walls, as Bob and Nobody had learned. Fortunately, at the upstream end where they were, it was reasonably wide and not very steep.

As he got closer, Bob could see Cruz had his hands full. He had a couple dozen head, some of whom were pretty wild. They were working their way across a dry stream bed in the canyon floor. It was not deep, no more than six or eight feet, but it had vertical or near vertical sides with only a narrow trail to cross on. The cows were bunched up here. Some were taking their time descending the steep trail and then scrambling up the other side. Cruz was sitting back not putting any pressure on them, which would certainly have resulted in a wreck and probably an injured cow or two.

Bob noticed that a few of the cows were taking this opportunity to slip down the canyon bottom in the stream bed. He turned his horse back to the west, staying above the cattle and headed for a place where he thought he could head them off. He had a bit of a lead on them, and they had not seen him so it should not be too difficult.

It all worked about as he had hoped, even though he had lost sight of them as he worked his way around. He was confident he had managed to get ahead of them. Sure enough, when he got to the stream bed, he could see no fresh tracks. He turned Nobody back up the stream bed towards Cruz and the rest of the cattle. In a very short time, the brown and white cow from the ridge top came around a bend and stopped dead in her tracks. The others piled in behind her, and she tossed her head at them in annoyance.

Bob watched all this with interest. She could not go left or right as the stream bed was still boxed in with steep sides. Her only choices were to turn back from where she had just come or blow by Bob and continue on her way. She started to turn back but then heard Cruz as he worked his bunch across the stream. That stopped her; she turned back to face Bob. She tossed her head a few times and snorted, slinging a little snot. Bob imagined she was trying to build up the courage to make a run past, over, or through him. "Bullshit!" he hollered as he slapped his leggings, pushed his horse forward, and began to whoop and holler in earnest.

She dropped her head and threatened to charge, but now Bob was mad. "You no account paint bitch." He hollered. "Get, get up, turn your sorry ass around and get the fuck out of my way." Nobody was closing the distance between them. It was getting to be shit or get off the pot time. She got off the pot.

With the normal amount of foolishness that cows can display in a tight spot when they want to run but are stepping all over one another, they finally got themselves sorted out and started back up the canyon just as precipitously as one would expect. "What a bunch of dumb fucks," Bob said. "You know what, Nobody, I think that bunch could teach the Three Stooges a thing or two about stupid." Bob, Nobody, and Mumford followed the cows back up the canyon without further incident.

Before long, Bob was sitting his horse watching his bunch of cows climb out of the stream bed and fall in with the rest. Cruz greeted Bob as he rode up, "Good work, cowboy. I have no chance for catch these cows," said Cruz referring to the bunch that had gone down the stream bed.

"No problem. I just happened to be in the right place. Glad I could help."

They rode out of the stream bottom and followed their charges at a distance, trying to avoid putting too much pressure on them. Cruz looked over the pack saddle and said, "What happen this thing?" He could see the fixes Bob had made with his pigging strings.

"We got into a wreck. Nobody got spooked when we got close to that cliff back there," Bob said, pointing up at a steep rock escarpment of some 200 feet over his right shoulder. "He started bucking and dumped me on my butt. That got old Mumford worked up, and he decided to have a rodeo of his own. When it was over, he had broken the straps on the panniers."

"You OK?"

"Yeah, just a bruised butt and ego."

"Mande?"

"Si, I'm OK, just a sore butt."

There was no more excitement as they covered the remaining distance to the gate. They had seen more downed fence, but Cruz decided it was best to get the cows across and not risk losing them while mending fence.

Before they got to the gate, Cruz had circled wide to get ahead of the cattle, so he could turn them. Bob just continued to follow and kept them pointed south. The gate opened into a small water lot. The drinker in the water lot was fed by spring water piped from just up hill. The small wire pen was split in the middle allowing both Indian Springs and Tres Cruces cattle to use the water. Cruz was watching the cattle file by as Bob followed the last of the stragglers up to the water lot. Cruz motioned him through the gate, and as Bob passed in front of Cruz, he excused himself by saying, "Con permiso,"

To which Cruz responded, "Si, pasale."

Bob had learned that these seemingly little bits of range etiquette were important to the cowboys. Manners were essential.

Cruz stepped down from his horse and shut the gate behind them. He then opened the gate to the other side of the lot and had Bob block it while he went to the far side and closed the gate that led to the Indian Springs side. Then swinging back up onto his horse, he and Bob pushed the cows to the other side of the water lot.

Both Bob and Cruz were standing in the open gate that separated the two sides of the lot. "Bob, Mumford stay here; we take these cows to the other corral."

"OK, I'll unsaddle him. Do you want me to hobble him or leave the gate to Tres Cruces closed?"

"Leave gate closed. Maybe some cows come here for water when we come back. Then we have chance for catching them."

"Sounds good." Bob stripped off Mumford's pack saddle and halter, closed the gate between the two halves of the pen, and swung back up on his horse.

Cruz then opened the gate to the Indian Springs side and went out first so he could point the cows east to the trail. He didn't want them going north up the easy slope. The steep slope to the south should be enough to keep them from going that way. Bob would bring up the drag, keeping them moving.

The next couple of miles went without significant problems. There were a few attempts by some of the cows to break loose from the bunch, but Cruz managed to keep them in line without much effort. Wild as some of these cattle were, they were getting tired. Even though they had only traveled two or three miles to the gate, there were some steep canyons that had been crossed. The cows were feeling it, but the worst off was an old bull who was keeping Bob and Nobody busy at the back of the bunch.

Pushing the cows up the long pack trail to the Indian Springs corral gave Bob plenty of opportunity to study this bunch. While he did not consider himself to be an expert, in fact, he knew he was a long way from it, he knew enough to be unimpressed. There were a few old Herford cows, which was the breed old man Foster had preferred, but the rest looked like a mixed bag of spotted and brindle Corrientes. The bull was a non-distinct cross of indeterminate parentage. He was no youngster, and his age was working against him. Being a bull, he was in no hurry and when he wanted, he just stopped. Annoying as this was, it was better than having him trying to run off.

The problem Bob had with these cattle was their poor condition. They were well fed, but some looked to be lousy. At least one had a bad cough, and there was more than one runny nose. Aside from the fact that this bunch had its share of slicks, like the bunch Cruz had picked up yesterday, their generally poor condition and the bad state of the fence told a story. Something was not right at Indian Springs.

They were up pretty high now, crossing the saddle over a high ridge. It was open park ponderosa forest with a few Chihuahua pine and Douglas firs thrown in for good measure. Cruz had dropped back and was riding beside Bob. The cows were all headed down the trail at an easy walk now that their climb was over. Even the bull was swinging along at a decent pace. "Maybe one more mile," said Cruz. "Soon the corral."

"Good, I don't think Nobody's got much left in him. He seems to be near bottom."

"Nobody's a little loco, but he has deep bottom. Maybe he is a little lazy and try to fool you."

"Maybe so, maybe it's me that's running near empty."

Fifteen minutes later, they were almost to the corral. The pack trail was a jeep trail now, and it appeared to be pretty popular. There were lots of tire tracks. They put the cattle into the corral, which like the one at Red Rock sat on a fence line separating pasture. It was, however, a working corral with separate pens and an alley. They penned the cows in a side lot that had access to water.

As they were checking their cinches and stretching their legs, they heard the sound of a vehicle coming towards them. That was not particularly odd, but this vehicle was coming from the direction from which they had just brought the cattle. They had seen no sign of a vehicle up that way except on the trail near the corral. Of course, the trail did come in from a side tributary that joined the main canyon a quarter mile back. Maybe that was where the vehicle was coming from. They tightened their cinches and swung back up into their saddles and waited.

† † †

A Jeep pickup pulled up to the corral. A young man stepped out from the passenger side looking incredulously at Bob and Cruz. He demanded, "Who are you? What are you doing here?" While Cruz tried to answer his questions, Bob decided to keep quiet and stay in the background and keep an eye on things. He was behind Cruz and turned his horse a little to the left to block the Jeep's view of his pistol. He tried to look dumb and uninterested.

Cruz was trying to explain that they had brought down a bunch of Indian Springs cattle. The man standing next to the Jeep was not buying it. He was suspicious and nervous. He spoke no Spanish and Cruz was losing his English fast in the frustration of the growing argument. A genuine brouhaha was in the making.

Just then the driver got out, assumed a threatening pose, and joined in the argument. Bob watched this a little longer and could see that things were about to get nasty.

These two soon crossed the line when they threatened Cruz. Bob rode up beside Cruz, reached over and touched his arm. "Con permiso, compadre, I'll take care of these chingados." With that Bob rode to the front, leaned forward on his saddle horn with his hand near the now obvious holstered pistol and began to speak. He didn't yell, he didn't get excited, he didn't show any emotion at all, his voice was calm but very cold.

"I don't know who you think you are, but I'm not impressed. You demand to know who we are without so much as a howdy-do. That's just plain rude. Then you try to browbeat this old man instead of thanking him for busting his ass to bring you a couple dozen of your own cows. That's just stupid and way beyond bad manners. Since you seem to think of yourself as a genuine bad man, here I am, go ahead and try to browbeat me, or better yet, if you're feeling froggy then jump. My dance card is open."

"So what are you going to do, shoot us?" growled the passenger with contempt.

"Only if your partner reaches under his jacket. It will be him first and then you," said Bob nodding towards the driver, then back to the passenger. "Do you work for Indian Springs?"

"Yes."

"Well, these are your cows. They were trespassing on Tres Cruces country, and we decided the neighborly thing to do was bring them back to you rather than keep them for ourselves."

"You can't keep our cows."

Bob smiled and said sarcastically, "How the fuck would you know? Is there a cowboy left on this outfit, or is it all gunzles, dinks, and wannabes?"

"I'm the cowboy here."

Bob looked hard at this man. He was a hard case for sure but no cowboy. He looked like a city boy trying to pass. His jeans were too tight and high above his ankles. He was wearing cowboy boots, but they were the town version with real pointed toes and walking heels. His shirt was OK, but he had the hat from hell on his head. It was a cheap straw that looked like it had been wadded up and shoved in a rat hole for the past year. Bob guessed that was how he tried to make a drugstore cowboy hat look real. To top it all off, he was wearing a red cotton, paisley print snot rag around his neck as if it were a wild rag. All in all, this guy was no hand of any kind. "Bullshit. There appears to be no cowboy at this camp. Get word to your boss that he needs to get up here to collect and doctor these cows. Somebody needs to work on that boundary fence while you're at it. Tres Cruces sent over three thousand dollars worth of fencing materials for just that purpose better than a year ago."

"You don't tell me what to do."

Bob rode Nobody up closer and leaned over the passenger. He had that empty, nothing look in his eyes. "Fuck you, asshole! Pass the word to your boss about the fence and stay out of my way." Then turning to Cruz, he smiled and said, "Compadre, vamanos a la verga. Let's get the fuck out of here." He then winked at the others as he and Cruz kicked their horses into an easy gallop and started back up the trail. Bob threw a quick look back to be sure they weren't going to be shot at.

He had enjoyed that little adventure. He hated bullies and liked to call their bluff. After going around a bend in the trail a couple of hundred yards from the corral, they brought their horses back to a slow trot. "Bob, you give him very bad time. This is a bad man. I think you need be careful."

"Fuck him, he's nothing out here. He may be a badass in town but not out here."

"Si, I think you are right but be careful anyway. This man is dangerous."

"OK."

Cruz was curious about what was up the side canyon where these men had come from. He had his suspicions but kept them to himself. Not wanting to go right up the road leaving horse tracks, he and Bob continued the way they had come, staying on the pack trail when it veered off the jeep trial. Not far up the slope, Cruz turned off on a game trail that ran, more or less, parallel with the jeep trail fifty or a hundred yards off. Before long, Cruz stopped and waved Bob to come alongside him. "Mira," said Cruz pointing to a clearing on the canyon floor, "marijuana."

Bob looked where Cruz pointed and saw tall, green plants growing in a thick patch. "That's marijuana?"

"Si, you never see before?"

"Not like that, not growing. Now what?"

"We go tell Jack this thing." With that they worked their way back up over the ridge, collected Mumford, and returned to Mountain Camp.

CHAPTER SIX

"My decision, I say no." Jack Barnes

When Cruz and Bob had returned to Mountain Camp, Cruz had called Jack on the CB and told him he was headed down to Headquarters to see him. Jack told him to stay put as he already had planned to visit Cruz that evening,

Now they were sitting on the porch, and Cruz had told Jack about the condition of the fence and the cattle they had gathered and returned to Indian Springs. The conversation was in Spanish, and Bob could only follow parts of it. After a time Cruz said in English, "Better that Bob tell you about the two men." Both men then looked at Bob expectantly.

"They weren't cowboys or even rosin jaws for that matter. They had accents like from back East. They were seedy and at least one of them was packing concealed. The guy that seemed to be in charge is mouthy and trying to pass as a hand, but he's a city boy for sure. The other was quiet, but I think more of a threat. He wasn't showy, but he watched everything. I think they're both crooks."

"Were they white or Mexican?"

"White."

"Cruz said there was an altercation."

"Nothing much, no blood was spilled," said Bob with the hint of a smile.

"You need to be more careful with these people. They could be dangerous."

"No guts, no glory, Uncle Jack." Bob could see this did not go over well so he added. "I'll be careful. I'm not looking for a fight, but I hate rude behavior. They were making some pretty serious threats to Cruz. It might have gotten ugly."

Jack could see Bob was not being stupid or rash. "OK, let's just keep an eye on things and be careful. I guess I better go over there and talk to whoever's in charge."

"Don't go alone, Uncle Jack. Take me when you go or that deputy, Tommy."

"What pretext do I have to take a deputy."

"I don't know, the marijuana patch maybe."

"No, I'm keeping that under my hat for a spell. Maybe the two you met have nothing to do with the ranch."

"Shit, let the law sort that out."

Jack answered firmly, "My decision, I say no."

"You're the boss."

Bob had an idea. "I know. Some of the cows looked pretty poor maybe you could get the brand inspector to go with you. Say you're worried about disease getting into your herd."

"I'll think on it."

"Uncle Jack, I'm dead serious. Don't go alone, at least take me. I can cover your back."

"I called last night about the cattle Cruz picked up yesterday and told the manager to come get them. He hasn't showed up yet. Maybe I'll deliver them myself. Bob, I will let you know." Jack stood up. "I better be getting back. Cruz what do you think about trying to clean more of their cows out of Northeast Pasture?"

"Well, you know what best, but I think only a few left. Maybe up at the north end. The fence is very bad. No chance to keep them out if we only put them through. Have to take them to that same corral like today."

"No, I don't want you going back over there. You saw some in the Sabino country yesterday, right?"

"Si."

"OK, see if you can get them penned up and check the fence between Sabino North and Northeast. That's more important right now. I'll take up the perimeter fence issue with Indian Springs."

"OK, we do this," Cruz answered.

Jack stood up and said, "Bob, follow me to the truck. Then shaking Cruz's hand, "old friend, buenas noches."

"Buenas noches, Jack, vaya con Dios."

"Gracias."

When they got to the truck Jack leaned against the door and said, "Bob, I think we have the potential for a big problem with this bunch to the east. The last thing I need is a war with some dope peddling neighbor. There has been some talk about the Indian Springs crowd. Folks don't trust them. You and Cruz stay clear of their country."

Jack stopped here and seemed to be about to leave so Bob said, "Uncle Jack, tell me what's going on."

"I don't have all the facts, just a bunch of gossip."

"OK, tell me the gossip."

"I don't want to spread rumors and get folks all worked up over what may be nothing."

"I met two of those assholes and may have the misfortune of seeing them again. I need to know what I may be up against. I can filter rumint well enough."

"Rumint, what's that?"

"Rumint is rumor intelligence. It means BS."

"OK, I'll fill you in, but keep it to yourself. It may all be nothing. The talk is that this is a dope ring. Some folks think they are Mafia. I don't know about that, but here is what seems to be true. There are quite a lot of folks working over there, at least half a dozen, maybe more. Indian Springs is a four hundred cow outfit. For many years Bill never had a full-time hand only a day worker or two; he only went to one full-time when he was over sixty years old. Hell, he never put on more than four or five for the spring and fall works. A half dozen full-time hands will break the bank of a four hundred cow outfit right quick.

"There's a lot of going in and out at night. Vern, over on the Bar SB told me there are trucks and cars going in there all hours of the night. He said he sees headlights up in the mountains pretty regular. None of that is consistent with running cows. One other thing, Indian Springs has not taken any cattle to the sale in Willcox in nearly two years."

"Has anybody met a cowboy from there?" asked Bob.

"They had a few hands come and go pretty fast after Bill sold the place, but nobody has seen a cowboy from there in a year or more."

"What did the cowboys say when they left?"

"Nothing, they just rolled their beds and left the country pronto."

"Smart," said Bob, "We'll be careful."

"Goodnight, Bob, see you in a couple of days, or sooner if I need you to ride with me over there."

"Good night, Uncle Jack. See you soon."

CHAPTER SEVEN

"Careful con the Hoya." Cruz

Bob and Cruz were sitting under an oak near the corral at Government Trap taking a break and giving their horses a much-needed rest. They had just finished a particularly hairy morning of fighting wild Indian Springs cows. This had not been a gather but a catch. As goofy as the bunches on Tuesday, Wednesday, and Thursday had been, today's were the worst. It made sense that they would be the hardest; they were the last to be caught. There were only fifteen head in the bunch. They were much the same as the others — a few branded cows, some calves, and several yearlings, and two-year-old slicks.

As they rested and let the cattle settle down a bit, Cruz said, "Bob, I tell you joke."

"OK"

"President Nixon go to Alaska and visit the Eskimo people. When he walk to . . ." here Cruz searched hard for words, "snow house?"

"Igloo" said Bob.

"Si, igloo, when he walk to igloo of chief, the Medicine Man pointing at him and shake a rattle at him lotta much and sing over and over hoya, hoya, hoya. President Nixon like this thing. He think it is a good thing. After meeting with Eskimo chief, he and chief leave igloo and walk out. The chief point to some dog shit in the path and say, "Careful con the hoya.'" Cruz laughed at this. It tickled him. Bob laughed a little and told Cruz it was a good joke.

He looked over at the corral and asked, "Do you think we can get the trailer up here?"

"Si, no problem, we do this."

"Good, I don't want to have to fight with these girls all the way to Headquarters." The cows in the corral were a wild bunch for sure. Bob had had to shake out a loop more than once today, heeling for Cruz on a couple of occasions, and once, when he found himself alone, having to rope and trip a big two-year-old that was all bad attitude. Twice he had tripped her and stepped off his horse to tie her when she had gotten back on her feet in spite of Crestnut's keeping the rope taut, and once she had taken a run at Bob, who had found a handy tree to get behind. He had just about decided to end the contest with a forty-five caliber rope if it happened again when he had an idea. He had heard of tying wild cows to trees but had never done it and was not sure how it was done, but he figured it was worth a try. In the end, he sorted it out and had her tied hard and fast to a ponderosa pine.

While Bob, Cruz, and their horses rested, Bob asked. "Cruz, do you think that bronco cow will be OK tied to that tree?"

"Si, she is OK, maybe not so loco later." With that, Cruz got to his feet and said, "I think it time for us to go to Mountain Camp. I call Jack and see what he want do with these cows."

Jack drove up to Mountain Camp with a stock trailer. He had Bob hook up the other stock trailer to the old truck and back it up to the loading chute. After loading fourteen of the sixteen head of the Indian Springs cattle that were penned up at Mountain Camp, Jack told Bob to take them to the same lot as the other Indian Springs cows by Headquarters. He was then to return to get the last two calves as well as three of his string of horses. He would see him at Headquarters. Jack and Cruz were going to Government Trap to spray those cattle and haul them to Headquarters.

"By the end of today we will have gathered, sprayed, and fed thirty-six head of Indian Springs cattle. That doesn't count the twenty-three you took over to them on Wednesday. That's what, fifty-nine head? I need to send that bastard a bill."

Cruz told Jack that there were still a few strays running around. He was going to go and close some of the water lots and set the triggers on the rest to try and trap them. "How many do you think are left in Sabino Pasture?" asked Jack.

"Not too many, I think, maybe ten. More in Northeast I think, but no chance for catch them before fall work. I start checking fence between Sabino North and Northeast tomorrow, be sure no bad places."

"OK, you do what you think is best. This makes me mad. I'm going to have to call Philly about this."

"Philly Orlando," asked Bob, "the brand inspector?"

"Yeah, that Philly. It's one thing to have a few strays from time to time. It happens to all of us, but this is unacceptable." Then as he got into the truck he said, "Bob, tonight I want you back at Headquarters. It will only be for a week or so. Tomorrow we'll make that trip to Indian Springs. Don't mention our worries about Indian Springs to Maria, you know, the drug stuff. She knows something is not right, but there is no need to get her upset."

"OK, Uncle Jack," then to both Jack and Cruz, "see you at Headquarters."

† † †

Bob had slept as well as usual, which meant not well at all. He fell asleep quick enough but then woke up dripping wet. The sheets were soaked in sweat and wadded up in a ball at the foot of the bunk, so now he was freezing in the cool evening air. It was so bad he had to get up and flip the mattress before digging out a fresh set of sheets and remaking the bed.

He didn't remember any dream, but he felt a dread deep inside bordering on panic. But why? He thought. Why does this keep happening?

Once he finished changing the sheets and got into some dry boxers, he crawled back into bed. As he got comfortable, he said, "This shit has got to stop sometime." As he tried to go back to sleep, he thought, oh, well, fuck me if I can't take a joke.

Morning came real early. That was the way it was with not enough sleep. Bob crawled out of the warm bed into the cold air and rushed into the bathroom where he turned on the gas heater before starting his morning ritual of a piss, a shave, and tooth brushing. He didn't bother to go into the cookhouse and make any coffee as he was having breakfast with Uncle Jack and Aunt Maria. She would already have the coffee on so Bob hurried to get dressed and walked over to the house.

"Good morning, Sobrinito," said his aunt as he walked through the kitchen door.

"Good morning, Tia Maria," answered Bob as she gave him a hug.

"Sit down; Jack will be in soon. I'll get your coffee, black no sugar, right?"

"Yes, that's right, thanks."

Jack came in, poured himself a cup of coffee, and took a seat at the table. "Philly will be over this morning to have a look at the Indian Springs stock. I don't have much for you to do except to catch up one of your horses and have it ready and hook up the big stock trailer to the new truck. That way when Philly gets here we'll be ready to trailer over to Ajax Well. Depending on what he has to say, we will probably load up as many as we can and carry them over to Indian Springs. Since I'm going over there anyway, I want to get the worst of that bunch out of here and off my feed bill."

"OK, Uncle Jack," said Bob standing up and starting for the door.

"Not now, sit back down. After you eat breakfast will be fine. Philly has to drive out here from the town. He's not likely to be out here before eight or nine o'clock."

Bob had filled up on breakfast and knocked down a couple of cups of coffee. The morning was crisp. There was no frost on the ground, but it wouldn't be long. When he got to the corral, he was disappointed to see that the cavvy had not come in to water yet. He was not surprised, as they normally did not come in until late afternoon, but he was disappointed just the same. He would have to go find them. He decided to hitch up the trailer first on the off chance the horses would come in while he was doing that. They didn't.

He caught up Pete, the night horse, one of Jack's reliable old babysitters, and headed out into the horse pasture to jingle in the cavvy. Everybody involved, horses and man, knew the drill. The cavvy was as far from Headquarters as they could get in the small horse pasture of two and a half sections or 1600 acres, and they showed no inclination of getting off their feed until Bob and Pete had done their bit. Once Bob was around behind the band of horses, he started Pete towards them at a trot and gave a few sharp whistles and whoops. That was the signal. The horses turned towards Headquarters and started that way at an easy gallop. There was a little splintering and rejoining of the group as they jockeyed for position with a kick or nip here and there, but they soon found the trail and once the pecking order was sorted out with each horse in his assigned place, based on some sort of horse seniority. All went smoothly as they swung down the trail at an easy lope. Bob always liked jingling the remuda. There was something exciting yet comforting in it.

As they approached the corral, Bob pulled up to a walk. It was a bad idea to run horses through cramped openings. As if on cue the rest of the horses slowed to a walk as they passed through the gate. Bob followed and closed the gate behind him.

It was Mumford's day in the barrel. He had been off since Wednesday and even then he had been packing just a couple of light panniers, so he was fresh, but he was perhaps the dumbest horse on the ranch. Bob would be sorting cattle in the pen, so he needed a horse with some sense. Nobody had worked hard on Wednesday, but this would be an easy day so Bob caught him up, grained him, and got him saddled. There was nothing to do now but turn out the rest of the remuda and wait.

† † †

Bob was back at the bunkhouse where he had gone to get a book. Reading was a good way to occupy the time while he waited. As he was starting back to the corral, a car pulled up in the yard. Looking over to see if it was Philly, two young girls got out. One waved and called out, "Hi, Bob." It was Suzie Solano, Cruz's daughter. Bob didn't recognize the other girl.

He walked over towards them and said, "Hi, Suzie, how are you?"

"She took his hand and gave him a quick hug, "I'm good. I don't have to ask how you are, you look good." Then turning to indicate her friend, "Bob, this is my good friend, Angelina Slaughter."

"How do you do?" asked Bob. He did not offer his hand as his mother had taught him to wait for the lady to offer hers.

Angelina put her hand out, "Nice to meet you. I have heard a lot about you from Suzie here."

"That can't be good." Bob had treated Suzie like a little sister, something she was not too fond of. "Don't believe everything she said."

Now Suzie interjected, "Oh, Bob, it was all good." Then looking down at his book, she asked, "What are you reading?"

"I'm trying to read *Moby Dick*. I don't know if I'm going to succeed or not."

"*Moby Dick*. We read that in my English class last semester. It was tough at first, but stick with it. It's worth the effort," said Angelina.

"Thanks, I will." Then to Suzie, "Are you here to see your folks?"

"Yeah, we're going to spend the weekend with Mom and Dad. Mom isn't doing too well, and I thought it would be nice to spend a little time with her, you know."

"Yeah, I get it. She'll like that."

"Angelina lives in town. She's never been up here before so I thought I'd show her around a little. Maybe you could stop by later and keep us company."

"Maybe. I just spent the best part of four days up there helping your Dad. I expect your folks could use a break."

"Well, we'll see. Right now, I need to go see Mrs. Barnes. See you later, Bob."

"OK, later."

Angelina looked at Bob and said, "It was nice to meet you. I hope to see you again."

"Uh, yeah, me too, nice to meet you," Bob was stumbling for words. "I hope to see you again, too."

As the girls walked to the house, Bob watched them, thinking: that is one nice looking woman. Too bad I tripped all over my tongue and acted the fool. Even though they'd only been talking for a short time, it was enough time to notice how well she was put together. She and Suzie were about the same height, but where Suzie was too thin, Angelina was just right with curves in all the right places and those big green eyes. Bob shook his head. Enough of that. He picked up the book and tried to concentrate on the words.

Bob had not read more than a few pages when he heard another vehicle pull into the yard. He closed the door to the saddle house behind him and went to see if it was Philly. Seeing the brand inspector entering the door to the ranch house, Bob went back to the corral to collect Nobody.

Leading Nobody out of the corral and to the trailer, Bob saw the two girls were about to get into the car. Suzie saw him and said something to Angelina. Both girls then looked at Bob, smiled, and waved. He smiled and waved back. "Maybe I didn't screw it up as bad as I thought. She still smiled and waved," Bob said to himself. As Nobody stepped up into the stock trailer, Bob draped his mecate around the horn and closed the gate behind him.

Soon Jack and Philly came out of the house and walked up to the truck and trailer where Bob was waiting. "Bob, you remember Phil Orlando." Filiberto Orlando was one of those people unique to this border country, or the Frontera, as the Mexicans called it. He was born near Cananea, Sonora. His family was about half on the American side of the line and half on the Mexican side. They had been here for generations.

His grandfather had been a rancher with quite a bit of land bordering the Green Cattle Company in northern Sonora. He had not been a true Haciandado, but he was certainly known as Patron by his vaqueros. The Mexican revolution had ended all that when the large land holdings were confiscated by the government and redistributed as small holdings and communal ejidos.

After the loss of the family ranch, Philly's father had found work as a cowboy in Arizona. He moved the family across the line in the late 1930's when Philly was a young boy. As it was with many folks along the border, Philly was equally comfortable speaking Spanish or English, and he was equally at home in either Sonora or Arizona.

After working as a cowboy for a few years and getting a few community college courses under his belt, he was able to land a job with the state as a Brand Inspector or Livestock Officer. In Arizona, Brand Inspectors were law enforcement officers with arrest authority. They were few and far between in Arizona and were viewed as either allies or enemies depending on one's propensity for violating the rules.

Philly's country covered all of Cochise and Santa Cruz Counties. He had a few subordinate deputies in his area, but he was in charge. Philly was an important man in these parts.

"Yes, of course, how do you do, Mr. Orlando?"

"You're a grown up man now, call me Philly. I'm doing well, how about you?"

"I can't complain. Everything is good."

"That's good, young man. It's good to have you home. How did you find Vietnam?"

"Hot and sticky."

"I can imagine, hot like our desert but very humid."

"Yes, sir, that about sums it up."

"Well, like I said, welcome home. Did I see those two pretty young girls flirting with you?"

"Oh, I doubt it. Suzie is just pulling my leg, and I didn't make a very good impression on the other one."

Both men laughed at this. "That's not how it sounded inside," said Jack. "Suzie and her friend were talking to Maria, and Suzie let it be known that if she didn't have a boyfriend already, she would be setting her cap for you, and then the other girl, Angelina, said *she* had first dibs."

Bob was a bit surprised and pleased, but he tried to hide it and just laughed, "We'll see."

Philly then turned to Jack. "I'll follow you up to the corral."

"OK, Bob, are you ready?"

"Yes, sir, all loaded up."

"Good, you drive."

After looking over the cattle, Philly and Jack were discussing the options while Bob sat his horse and kept watching the cows. There were three in the bunch that looked like they could be trouble. Two young cows and a young bull were slick and sported pretty good sets of horns. They were already acting hooky just from having to put up with folks in the corral. Once it looked like a cow was going to take a run at Philly, but Bob, who was horseback, got between them, and she backed off. It wasn't going to take much to get them on the prod when he started the loading.

"Good-bye, Bob, I'll see you around. Take it easy on the girls around here. We don't have too many to spare."

"No sweat, Philly. I'll be good."

"That's what I'm afraid of," he laughed. "Buena suerte."

"Gracias, vaya con Dios, Señor." With that Philly got in his truck and left.

Bob rode over to Jack and waited to hear his instructions. "Philly will notify Indian Springs of their stray cattle on my country. If they don't pick them up immediately, he will take possession and sell them in fourteen days. We are going to carry this load over to them, though, as a good will gesture. Now back to business. Bob, you've got some problem children in that bunch. How do you want to handle them?" Jack asked this because he wanted Bob to sort out the problem and learn from it.

"Which ones do you want loaded?"

Jack answered, "Everything that's branded or sucking a branded cow, and those three biggest slick bulls. We'll see what kind of room we have left after that."

"OK, I would like to sort off the ones that aren't being loaded first and put them in that side lot."

"That's a good plan. Do you want me on the gate?"

"Yes, please, Uncle Jack."

It wasn't long before Bob had sorted the cattle the way he wanted. Jack then backed the trailer up to the loading chute and set the trailer gate. Once this was done, Bob opened the gate from the corral to the loading chute. He hoped he could get the whole wad to load in one fell swoop. If not, then the rank bull that was in this bunch could be a problem. He was glad the two hooky cows were in the side pen and not being loaded with this bunch.

It didn't go quite as well as he hoped. There was the normal amount of hesitating before stepping into the unfamiliar trailer that happens with wild cattle, and more than once the whole mess came boiling back up the chute with their hearts set on escape, but they were stopped by Bob and Nobody. Bob was working a long quirt overtime on the cows, and Nobody had taken to biting any cow that got too close; it worked to good effect. They all turned back, and finally, on the third try, they loaded.

After a quick survey, Jack said, "I think we have enough. We could fit one or two more, but I don't want to run the risk of having them all spill out. Go ahead and leave the others in the side lot. They've got water, and it's big enough for them now that these are leaving. I'll meet you back at Headquarters."

† † †

They were turning up the long drive leading to the Headquarters of Indian Springs Ranch. The trip over the mountain had been uneventful, and it was now early afternoon. "Bob, you understand that I will do the talking."

"Of course, Uncle Jack."

"Are you carrying?"

"Yes, I have my pistol in my waistband under my jacket."

"OK, I expect no trouble, but I don't know these people, and I don't know what to expect. Just keep an eye on things and watch my back."

"No sweat, Semper Vigilantes."

"What," asked Jack?

"Semper Vigilantes. It was my unit motto in Vietnam. Always Vigilant. What was that lepto and vibrio you and Philly were talking about?"

"Leptospirosis and Vibriosis, they are venereal diseases that cattle get. They cause the cow to abort. It is often spread through a herd by the bulls. We were discussing whether we should have tested the Indian Springs bulls for them."

"But you didn't test them."

"No, since they were running only with Indian Springs cows, I don't think there is much chance they could have spread it to our herd, even if they are infected and being young bulls, there is not much chance of that. I just wanted to plant the seed with Philly in case it does become a problem."

Jack slowed down here and watched in his rearview mirror, waiting for Cruz. He wanted them both to arrive together. Mid-morning, Cruz had called on the radio to say he had trapped four head on a water hole, and Jack had told him to go ahead and load them in the camp trailer and follow him over the mountain to Indian Springs. They didn't spray the four head Cruz was bringing because Jack wanted whoever was running Indian Springs to see the sorry state of their cattle. When Jack saw Cruz swing around the corner, he sped up, and they continued to the Indian Springs Headquarters.

The two trucks pulled up in front of a new ranch house, and Jack exclaimed, "That's new. Old Bill lived in that adobe over there," pointing to an old adobe ranch house that was typical of the area. Then looking at the new house, "This place is huge."

They got out of the truck, and Cruz came over. "Jack, that house new. I never see before."

"Me neither. Old man Redfield said they were building a new house up here, but he didn't tell me any more than that."

"There's a lot of money coming here from someplace, and it's not the cows," said Jack. "Now let's keep it close, act just like everything is normal."

Both Bob and Cruz said, "OK."

The three Tres Cruces men were walking up the sidewalk to the main house when the front door opened. A well-dressed man in his thirties stepped out and greeted them. "Hello, can I help you?"

Jack kept walking and said, "Well, yes, we can help each other. I'm Jack Barnes your neighbor to the west. I have the Tres Cruces. We have brought you a bunch of your cattle that were on my forest lease." Jack could see that none of this was of much interest to the man.

"Good to meet you, Jack, I'm Vince. I own this place. What is it we can do for each other?"

Bob wondered if Jack had caught the slight smirk on Vince's face.

"First, I need you to come have a look at these cattle we brought over."

Vince looked mildly amused, "OK, let's have a look."

As they walked around the two stock trailers, Jack pointed out the fact that there were several slicks that were well past branding age. Vince's only response was, "So, what's the problem? They're my cows. I don't have to brand them if I don't want to."

Jack looked incredulous at this. "Yes, you do, if you want to keep them. Are you aware of the fact that any weaned bovine critter that is not branded belongs to the first person to put his iron on it?" There was no response from Vince so Jack continued. "It's mavericking, and while it's frowned on, it's not illegal. I could have branded twenty-five of your slicks, that's unbranded cattle, and they would now be mine, but that's not what neighbors do."

"I appreciate that." Vince was paying a little more attention now. Not because he seemed to care about the cattle, but because he could tell Jack was a man of substance and to earn his enmity could complicate things. "We'll take care of getting them branded. Is there more?"

Pointing to the cows Cruz had brought over Jack said, "These girls are lousy."

Vince looked blankly at Jack but said nothing.

Exasperated now, Jack tried to stay calm. "They are infested with lice, see?"

"Oh, yes, of course. We will call the vet and have them treated."

Bob looked at Cruz and rolled his eyes.

"Where do you want us to put them?"

"Anywhere except on the lawn."

"How about we put them in the corral? That way, they're all caught up and ready to brand and doctor. The ones in the big trailer have already been sprayed. We sprayed everything we caught except these four from this morning and the two dozen we penned up for you on Wednesday."

"Why, thank you. It wasn't necessary for you to spray my cattle."

"Yes, it was necessary. They were on my country, they were infested with lice and, I don't want lice in my heard."

Sensing Jack's rising anger, Vince was beginning to get a little warm himself. "OK, it's all taken care of now. Just put those cows in the corral. What do I owe you?"

"Vince, that's not all."

"What else?"

"There are still twenty-six head of your stock in one of my corrals. We have been gathering your cattle off my forest allotment for the past week. There are still a few more up in the high country. We have gathered a total of sixty-three of your cattle that have been feeding on my grass and expect to gather another dozen or so. I don't want your damn money. I want you to take care of your cows and keep them off my place."

Vince checked himself at this point, obviously holding back his anger. He took a deep breath and said, "Jack, it seems we have gotten off on the wrong foot, and I don't want that. Have your men unload the cattle in the corral, and you and I can go inside and work this out." Then he looked at Bob and added, "I'll send out my foreman to assist you."

Nodding his head towards Cruz, Bob said to Vince, "Tell Cruz, He's senior to me."

Vince repeated to Cruz what he had said to Bob.

"Si, yo comprendo. That is a good thing." Answered Cruz.

Jack thought about this a little and said, "OK, but I want Bob and Cruz to be in on the conversation. They are responsible for the country that borders yours, and their insight could be useful. It also saves me the time of having to repeat everything."

"That's fine. I will have my foreman join us as well. Now why don't you and I go inside and have some coffee while they take care of the cows?"

Cruz and Bob waited by the trucks where they were joined by the Indian Springs ranch foreman. As he was walking up, Bob looked him over carefully. This was no hand. He looked like a caricature of a B movie singing cowboy, and he was not comfortable in this role.

"Howdy, boys," he said with a definite nasal accent that Bob figured to be New Jersey or New York.

Bob looked at Cruz and said, "Careful con the hoya."

Cruz smiled, "Si, mucho hoya."

"Howdy, I'm Bob Hasett, and this is Cruz Solano" replied Bob to the Easterner.

"OK, I'm the foreman. My name's Alf." He put out his hand, and Bob shook it thinking it was pretty soft for a cowboy.

"Nice to meet you," said Bob. "Just show us where you want these critters, and we'll get them unloaded."

"Just put them in the corral, I'll get the gate."

Alf opened the gate, and Bob and Cruz drove the trucks in making wide turns, so they would be headed back out when they were done. After closing the gate the foreman came over. "OK," he said. "I guess we're ready."

"Not quite," answered Bob. "We need to close that other gate or this bunch will be out of here pronto, and you'll have to catch them again." Then pointing to the small trailer, "Do you want to segregate these lousy cows from the rest. We could put them in that side lot."

It was obvious that Alf had no idea what Bob was talking about, but he had a role to play. "Yes, that's what I was thinking. Go ahead and do that." Wisely, he stepped aside and watched as Bob and Cruz backed the trailer, set the gate and unloaded the four louse-infested cows. Remembering what Bob had said, Alf closed the back gate to the main corral.

Cruz and Bob then turned their attention to the cattle in the gooseneck trailer. In the normal fashion of half wild stock, they came bumbling and charging out of the trailer, glad to be free of the tight space. There was a lot of slipping on the slick, shit covered trailer floor, followed by some ridiculously long leaps out to solid ground. Bob was always amused by some of the actions of cattle, and this need to set long jump records when clearing the rear threshold of a trailer was one of them.

The cattle trotted about, darting one way and then another, looking for a way out of the corral, but finding none they settled for getting as far from the trailer as possible.

That is all except the young bull. He decided it was time to start trouble. After a bit of pawing at the ground, he started towards the trailer with bad intentions on his mind. Scooter took the challenge and immediately raced past Bob and Cruz with her sights set firmly on the bull. Cruz said, "Watch this thing. Scooter is very good with the broncos."

Soon the dog was firmly attached to the bull's nose. Her feet were off the ground as the bull tried to sling her off by tossing his head about, but she hung on, growling and shaking her head.

When Cruz thought the bull had had enough, he called off the dog who promptly returned to the truck and jumped in the back, her job done. The bull went to a far corner of the corral and found shelter amongst the cows. Bob looked at Scooter with new found respect and said. "Yep, that's the finest elephant dog in Cochise County."

"Si." Said Cruz. "I think in Sonora, too."

While all this was going on Bob was aware of the fact that Alf had crawled up on top of one of the stock trailers. He nudged Cruz and gave a slight nod towards Alf. Cruz looked at Alf then back at Bob and said under his breath, "No juevos."

"You can come down now. We're done here, if you would get the gate, we'll pull these rigs out."

Alf had no desire to cross the open area between the trucks and the gate. Cruz noticed Alf's hesitation and said, "I get the gate; you drive the truck."

With that, Alf crawled down from his perch, jumped in behind the wheel and followed Bob out. When they parked and got out of the trucks, it was more temptation than Bob could stand. "So, you're not from around here?"

"No, I'm from Bayonne, New . . ." he checked himself here. "How did you know?"

"Just a lucky guess. Listen you be careful with that bunch." Bob was warming up to his fun. "There are some right hooky bitches in that corral, and that little black bull is a genuine bad ass. Without a no shit, bull chewing, elephant dog to whip his ass once in a while, he will cause you trouble. Bob pronounced genuine with a long i affecting his best Festus Hagen accent. Alf was looking distinctly uncomfortable with this bit of knowledge, so Bob continued. "You're going to need your best hands to brand this bunch, no high schoolers flat assing calves for some townie arena ropers, no squeeze shoots nor calf tables neither. You're going to have to head and heel them." Bob knew that unless Indian Springs had some for sure hands hidden in the woods somewhere, their only chance to deal with the branding was with squeeze shoots and calf tables, but he was not trying to help; he was having fun.

All this was having the desired effect. So Bob kept at it. "Maybe you could ask Vince about having us come over and help with the branding."

Alf may not have been a cowboy, but he was no fool. If he had to try and hold a branding with his crew, the last thing he wanted was witnesses. The only cowboys they had were run off over a year ago when they didn't want to get with the program. The crew he had now had other skills. "We'll be fine, but I'll keep your offer in mind."

Alf led Bob and Cruz into the office where Vince and Jack were talking over coffee. The three late arrivals sat down, and Vince asked them, "Would you care for some coffee?"

Neither Cruz nor Bob wanted any so Jack caught the newcomers up on what had happened so far. He and Vince had agreed to stick with the original fence deal. It seemed Vince was unaware of the arrangement because it was agreed to by his previous manager. Once the fence deal was settled, Jack explained that by law the brand inspector, or livestock detective as Jack preferred to call him for Vince's benefit, could take possession of any stray cattle that were not claimed by Indian Springs immediately and sell them. He expected they would get a call from the brand inspector today. If the cows were still at Tres Cruces next Monday, Philly would be contacting them with official notice that they were in state possession and being sold by the state.

Vince spoke up now, "Tell you what Jack can I just pay you to have those cattle delivered to me here? That would save me a lot of time."

"No, we're starting our fall works next week, and I'm up to my butt in alligators at the moment. I don't have the time, and I can't spare anybody to spend a day hauling your cows. There's already better than two loads. By next Monday or Tuesday there may be more. What I can do is have somebody help your crew load them, but you'll have to give me a time when to expect you."

Vince looked at Alf, "You have somebody over there Monday morning. I want this off my plate as soon as possible."

"Yes, Boss, I'll get on it."

"Jack, as much as I appreciate your help and your men bringing our cattle back Wednesday, I must insist that your men not ride over to our side anymore."

"Are you serious? You do realize that was public land where they found your cows, and they rode over to bring them to you. Even that lot they penned them up in is public land. You have a special-use permit for that corral, well, and camp is all. You can't stop me or anybody else from riding across that land. All you control is the grazing rights."

Vince was not happy with this response. "I thought we could handle this like adults. I would prefer it if your men did not interfere with my operation, that's all."

"Don't worry. I'll put the word out that Tres Cruces cowboys are not to neighbor with Indian Springs. I expect to hear from you soon about picking up your cattle. Good day, sir." Jack was already standing by this time, and now he left with Cruz and Bob following behind.

When they got to the trucks, Jack told Cruz to go on back to Mountain Camp. Then he turned to Bob and said, "You drive. I want you to turn left up here and head for the highway. I need to see some folks." Bob didn't say anything. His uncle had the look of someone that did not want to be disturbed.

Vince's house had been impressive. Bob was struck by how out of place it seemed in these surroundings. From the little he had seen, it was furnished pretty much like houses back East or in the city. There was the occasional nod to cowboy or western décor, but it was tacky and fake.

Who are these people? Bob wondered. He detected no accent in Vince, but Alf was a sure enough big city easterner. Two things were for sure. None of them knew the first thing about cattle, and there was a real live marijuana patch up on the mountain.

After a while, Jack spoke. "The ranch is a cover for drugs. We know they're growing, but they might be smuggling as well. I don't like it. It's bad enough to have a bad neighbor, but this could be dangerous. Bob, I want you to be extra careful. Stay away from that bunch. Vince had heard about you and Cruz. He knew about you having words with his man. I got the impression he was unhappy with the outcome. He didn't like one of his men being backed down so easily."

"No problem, Uncle Jack. I didn't lose anything on that place."

They had taken the long way around on Highway 80 so Jack could talk to a couple of the ranchers that neighbored the east side of Indian Springs. He asked what they knew about the operation. They had no real information, just some suspicions and a desire to stay out of it.

After finishing Jack's business and grabbing a bite in Douglas, they were driving past the Cochise County Fairgrounds north of town when Jack asked, "Now that you've been back with us for almost a week, how do you feel about having Mountain Camp to yourself this winter?"

This caught Bob by surprise, and he was excited by the prospect. "I'd like that, but it's Cruz's camp; he's been there for years." Bob thought for a moment, "Is something wrong?"

"No, but he's getting a bit long in the tooth, I'm sure it would be easier on him and Isabel to be closer to town and have a house with power and a phone. I'll move them to Desert Flats where he can give me a hand down here and look after the first calf heifers. Besides, it was his idea, and I'm sure he will be finding his way up the mountain to join you from time to time. That old man has taken a real shine to you."

"Taken a shine to me," Bob said, shaking his head. "Go figure. I suppose he's just a bit short on good taste."

"I suppose."

"I like the idea. It will be a lot to learn, but I think I'm up to it."

"Cruz thinks you're ready. He said you'll need some help learning more about the cows; you know, things like how to spot and doctor the sick ones. He also said you need to get down your rope faster after tripping one of those bronco cows. You can't always find a convenient tree to jump behind. He wants to spend some time teaching you those things."

"That would be good."

"No one better to learn from. Maybe I should leave you up on the mountain with him until fall works. That would give you more time to learn what's going on."

"Whatever you think is best. I would like to help with the fall work, but I like working with Cruz, too."

"Let me think on it some. We will be working out of Headquarters the first week, then pulling the wagon out for the second and third weeks. I don't need so much help the first week or maybe even the second. I'll let you know by tomorrow."

"OK Uncle Jack."

CHAPTER EIGHT

"Here's to minor vices." Bob Hasett

Once they pulled into the yard, Jack said to Bob, "After you unhitch the trailer, be sure to catch up a horse for the morning. See you at supper."

Once again, Maria had outdone herself. The food was good, and there was lots of it. Afterwards, Jack and Bob were relaxing on the porch when Maria brought out the coffee pot and some cups. This was something that had confused him since he first started visiting the ranch several years ago. Bob decided he had to know. After Maria went back into the house he asked, "Uncle Jack, I thought Mormons didn't drink coffee. I understand you don't hold to the rules real strong, but Aunt Maria is pretty serious about these things."

"That's all true. I stray from time to time while Maria does hold pretty close to the rules, and the *Word of Wisdom* does indeed state, no hot drinks, but Maria figures a little coffee is a small price to pay for my piety in the big things. Besides she is Mexican, and those folks do like their coffee. She sneaks a cup once in a while herself."

"That's good to know. You can't trust folks that never give in to minor temptations. Before you know it, they'll be bona fide derelicts. Just look at Hitler."

"Hitler?" Jack asked? "What are you talking about now?"

"Hitler made a big show of not drinking or smoking or any of the normal vices, so instead he was a megalomaniacal mass murderer and sexual pervert."

Jack was looking at Bob with surprise written all over his face. "The world knows about his murderous side, but sexual pervert, you're pulling my leg, right?"

"Not at all, he was screwing his teenage niece, and when she got a little older and he started after Eva Braun, who was seventeen at the time, his niece killed herself. It has even been said that he was into some weird degrading shit."

"Go figure." then holding up his coffee cup in a toast, "Here's to minor vices."

"Minor vices," Bob joined in.

Just then Maria came out, "Jack, Cruz is on the CB. He said Suzie has a question for Bob."

"OK, Bob, go ahead and take it."

When Bob went into the house to take the radio call, Maria gave Jack a knowing look and sat down. "I think that Slaughter girl is sweet on him, Jack."

"There's far worse things to be a victim of than a pretty girl's affection. I should know." He said this with a wink at his wife.

"Oh, Jack, you are such a kidder, but thank you just the same."

"I'm no kidder. That's the truth. You were the prettiest girl in the entire state of Sonora, and now you're the prettiest woman in Cochise County. No, the prettiest in Arizona."

She reached over and gave his arm a squeeze before getting up and going back into the house.

Bob came out and said, "Uncle Jack, do you have anything for me tomorrow?"

"Your aunt wants us to go to the Sacrament Meeting in the morning. Other than that, there is nothing. I know you don't ascribe to the LDS faith, but it is important to her. Why do you ask?"

"Of course, I'll go. It's a small thing to do for her. I asked about tomorrow because Suzie wants me to come up tomorrow for Sunday dinner. She said something about taking Angelina for a horseback ride in the afternoon."

"That sounds like a good idea to me. We should be back here by ten thirty."

Standing back up and starting for the door, Bob said, "Good, I'll call back and let them know it's a go."

Jack smiled to himself and thought, oh, young man you're already lost. He could hear Bob inside on the CB, and as hard as he might be trying to hide his excitement, Bob was failing. Jack made the decision about the fall work. Bob would stay around Headquarters until Wednesday and help to get things ready, but as soon as Jack and the roundup crew trotted out for the first day of works, Bob would move to Mountain Camp. Jack would work out the details later.

When Bob came out, Jack explained all this to him. He also told Bob to take two of his horses up to Mountain Camp when he went up for the visit. He would still have two at Headquarters.

"Two?" asked Bob"

"Yes, two, I'm cutting Chango to your string. You're going to need five horses at least on that mountain this winter."

"Thanks, Uncle Jack. Who is Chango?"

"He's that little grulla. He's over in the rest-cavvy right now."

"I remember a grulla colt, but I don't remember his name being Chango. Is it the same horse?"

"Yep, it's the same horse. Come on; let's go out to the saddle house. I've got something out there I could use after dealing with that knucklehead today."

Once they entered the saddle house, Jack reached up behind some shelves and retrieved a mayonnaise jar full of clear liquid. Handing it to Bob, Jack said, "Here, have a snort of this."

Bob took a medium sip and felt the burning liquid slide down his throat. He handed the jar back to Jack and said, "That's some pretty stout stuff. What is it, moonshine?"

"Mexican moonshine, it's called Bacanora. It's made from a type of mescal plant."

"It tastes like tequila."

"It should. All those Mexican whiskeys are made from some type of mescal plant or another." Jack took a drink from the jar and screwed the lid back on. "Ah, that was good. I'm afraid I let that fella get to me today. I shouldn't have let that happen. I got hot and let my temper show."

"So, he deserved it."

"That may be but I showed him something I shouldn't have." Then looking at Bob closely he added, "You should keep your emotions in check when dealing with potential adversaries. It's like poker; don't reveal anything."

"So you're saying, be cold blooded."

"Yes, that's exactly what I'm saying. It's OK to get mad; we all do, but don't act on anger. Cool down before doing anything or at least act cool." Jack took another drink and handed the jar back to Bob. "Cruz gave me a blow-by-blow of your encounter with those two on Wednesday. He said you were cold as ice when you got in that man's face."

"I didn't feel cold as ice."

"You may have been hot, but you didn't show it."

"I guess. I don't know. I was half hoping he'd do something stupid." With that Bob took another bigger drink from the jar. "So, Uncle Jack, why name a horse Chango?"

"You remember that fella, Sam, that was working here a couple of years ago?"

"The one from the mountains of Tennessee?"

"That's the one. He was a pretty fair bronc twister, so I had him breaking some young horses that winter. The grulla was one of those horses. Sam couldn't quite get his tongue around the word grulla, what with that thick hillbilly accent; it came out more like grila, so he decided to call him gorilla or as he pronounced it, Go-Rilla. One day Cruz had come down to Headquarters and was watching Sam work Go-rilla. He asked what Sam had decided to name the horse. You remember the horse breaker names the horse, right?"

"Yes, Uncle Jack, I remember that."

"Good, well, Sam tells him it's Go-Rilla. Cruz, with his limited English has no idea what Go-Rilla is, so they get in a discussion where Sam is trying to explain to Cruz what a Go-Rilla is, and Cruz is not having any luck deciphering Sam's thick accent. It finally deteriorated to the point of Sam resorting to pantomime. He starts standing ape-like and scratching under his arms while going 'Ooo, Ooo, Ooo.' Cruz figures out that Sam is trying to tell him it's monkey, so he says, 'Oh, chango'. Sam then says, 'Does chango mean, go-rilla in Spanish?' 'Si.''Answers Cruz imitating a monkey with the scratching and ooo, oooing, ... chango.' Well, both of them were tickled by this so Sam decided the horse's name from now on was Chango. It was funny to watch. I suppose I could have helped, but that would have spoiled the fun; besides, we would not now have a horse named Chango."

"So, the name went from Grulla, to Grilla, to Go-Rilla, to Chango."

"That's right."

"It figures. I remember you telling me about how Nobody got his name."

Jack chuckled as he remembered that story, "Yeah, that's one of my favorites. Here's a little advice for you. Nobody is about next up in your string, is he not?"

"Yes, either him or Mumford."

"If I were you, I'd ride Nobody when you take that gal on the ride tomorrow. She's bound to ask how he got his name, and you can tell her. It's a good story and will make you look good to boot."

"OK, that sounds like good advice."

Jack offered the jar to Bob one more time. "Would you like a last sip before I put this up?"

"No, thanks, I'm fine," said Bob.

With that Jack put the jar back and told Bob, "Good night," before heading back to the house.

"Good night, Uncle Jack. I think I'll sit out here for a while." Bob sat on the step in the door of the saddle house looking out at the dark. It was quiet except for some coyotes off in the distance and some whippoorwills not far off.

Bob was feeling good about tomorrow. He had not had any kind of a relationship with a girl in a long time. His girlfriend from high school had sent him a Dear John letter shortly after he left for the Army, and except for the occasional blind date with somebody's visiting sister, there had not really been anything. Most girls were not interested in guys with short hair. There had been the girl in Australia, but that had ended badly due to Bob's foolishness, not hers.

So here he was, about to have dinner and a horse back outing with a truly pretty girl. He hoped he wouldn't screw it up like this morning when he first met her. As he sat trying to plan what he would say, the coyotes' singing got louder and more intense. A real coyote party, thought Bob. He wondered if he could talk Cruz into teaching him how to sing to the coyotes.

† † †

The service at the Mormon chapel was not too painful for Bob. He sat with his aunt and uncle and followed their lead. When it ended and folks were going through the usual obligatory greetings that seemed to follow all church services, Bob was introduced to lots of new folks. They all made a point of welcoming him. He felt they were genuine in their hospitality but wondered if they knew he was a gentile.

Jack was shaking hands and exchanging a few words with the man who had presided over the service. Bob assumed he was the bishop. He knew there was no love lost between these two, but they were being civil to one another at least in public. "Bob, I would like to introduce you to Brother Pratt."

Bob stuck out his hand and said, "How do you do, sir?"

The bishop took his hand in that iron grip that wasn't part of a contest or show but left no doubt about who was going to decide when the handshake was over. "How do you do, young man? I hear you're part of our community now." While he was saying this his left hand was gripping or rather feeling Bob's upper arm and then high on his back and shoulders.

This was more than Bob felt comfortable with and grip or no grip, he pulled his hand away and took a short step back. "Yes, sir, I suppose so."

The bishop, still smiling then turned towards Maria and engaged her in some small talk. Jack and Bob took advantage of this to excuse themselves and walked out to the yard where they waited under the cottonwood trees.

"Uncle Jack, what was that all about?" Bob was working to check his language, realizing where they were and not wanting to embarrass his uncle, but he couldn't keep all the incredulity out of his voice. Now he dropped his voice to a stage whisper, "That . . . that . . . SOB was squeezing and feeling all over my arm and back! If we had been in private, I believe he would have tried to feel me up."

Jack looked surprised then realized what had happened. He cracked a big smile. "Oh, Bob, it's not what you think. He was checking for your garments."

"My what?"

"Your garments, your temple garments." Jack could see that this meant nothing to Bob so he whispered, "Angel chaps or angel drawers."

The light went on in Bob's head, "Oh yeah I remember that's what Sam called them. So why was he checking me? I'm not LDS."

"He doesn't know that. Don't worry he's not queer just nosey."

"I suppose he'd really be tickled to know I go commando."

"What's commando?" asked Jack.

"Free balling, no drawers at all," Bob smiled.

Jack smiled again and slapped Bob on the back. "You are a piece of work."

It wasn't long before Maria had finished whatever business she had with some of the ladies of the ward, and she came out to join the two men. "That was nice. Thank you, Jack, for being polite to Brother Pratt."

"Oh, it's not me you need to thank; it's this nephew of ours. He had to stop himself from punching old Malachi Pratt in the nose."

Maria looked alarmed at this bit of intelligence. "Whatever for?" she asked.

"Good old Brother Pratt decided to check Bob for his garments. Bob had no idea what was going on and thought our bishop had gone light in the loafers and was making a pass at him."

"Oh, good grief, that's just ridiculous!"

Jack was enjoying his bit of fun. "The notion of old Malachi being queer may be ridiculous, but Bob thought it was true."

Maria looked at Bob and asked, "Did this old heathen," looking at Jack, "explain what Brother Pratt was really doing?"

"Yes, Aunt Maria, it's all OK."

Maria then threw a look at Jack that didn't portend well for his happiness the rest of the day. "Let's go home."

When they got in the Ford Bronco, which was Maria's car, Bob asked, "Can we stop at this little Catholic church up here? I told Cruz I would light a candle for Isabel."

"Sure, Bob, we can do that. It's OK, isn't it Maria?"

"Yes, of course, it can't hurt." Then quietly, almost under her breath, "Maybe the old saints can help her."

Once they got to the house, Bob changed into his work clothes. He was about to go jingle in the horses he was trailering up to Mountain Camp, when he heard a vehicle pull up in the yard. Stepping outside he saw it was a young cowboy in his mid to late twenties stepping out of an old pickup. Bob waved to him and asked if he was looking for Jack Barnes. The young man answered that he was, so Bob pointed to the house and said he was in there.

While Bob was saddling Pete, Jack brought the new man to the corral. "Bob this is Jim Burges. He's just signed on for the fall works." With that the two young men shook hands and exchanged greetings. "I need you to jingle in the horses at first light in the morning. I expect the rest of the crew to show up tomorrow. We can cut out their strings and give them Tuesday to tack on shoes.

"OK, Uncle Jack, first light it is." With that Bob swung up on Pete. "I better get to it, can't keep Cruz waiting."

Jack grinned at this. "Cruz is it? There wouldn't be any other reason for you to be in a hurry, nothing to do with long, dark hair and green eyes?"

"Of course not, Uncle Jack," Bob answered with a grin of his own, "adios."

"Adios," answered both Jack and Jim.

Bob had brought in the horses and was catching Crestnut and Nobody to take up to Mountain Camp. While he was doing this Jim came into the corral to have a look at the remuda.

"This bunch of horses looks pretty good. How are they really?"

"I'm not the right person to ask. Uncle Jack or Cruz Solano would be far better to ask than me. I'm pretty much a rookie."

"Jack thinks you've got it together. I never met him before, but his reputation is sound. I expect your opinion will be good enough."

"They're good stout ponies for sure; they're all home grown. Only the studs come from outside. Seems there is some Percheron blood in them from way back, and I know Uncle Jack likes to use a thoroughbred stud every ten years or so to keep some size on them. Other than that, they know a cow, are rock footed, and have lots of bottom, or so I'm told."

"That's what I heard back home. My Granddad bought some fillies from here some years back to use as brood mares. He has been pleased with the results. I've heard rumors of some thin skin."

"That's true enough. I've only had experience with about half a dozen of these horses, but I have to say only one has never bucked with me. I wouldn't call them broncs. Only one or two can really step with any authority, but the others are not averse to hunting a tree limb or waiting for you to lean over. They do have more than their share of buggers."

"Any suggestions on which I should pick for my string?"

"No, I'm afraid not. The ones I know are in my string or Uncle Jack's string. I would just trust Uncle Jack to do right by you. I never heard of him abusing a man with bad horses."

"That's good to know. I hear you're headed out for the afternoon."

"Yeah; that's right, dinner at Mountain Camp with Cruz and his family."

"Well, have a good time. Can I help you load these horses?"

"Sure, if you take that one, pointing to Crestnut, I'll take Nobody here. We'll just lead them out to the trailer."

CHAPTER NINE

"Isn't Nobody a strange name for a horse?" Angelina Slaughter

Angelina was dressing for her ride with Bob when she realized she had changed outfits three times. Suzie had told her to borrow whatever she needed, and she had done just that. As she looked at herself in the mirror, she paused and thought, "What am I doing?"

She sat down on the bed. For over a year she'd kept to herself, kept her thoughts and hopes deep down. But this Bob, after seeing him only one time, she was preening herself in front of the mirror like a thirteen-year-old. It was disconcerting. But, she decided, it was a welcome change. For too long there had been no hope, no joy. When her brother, Mark, died, she felt all that drain away. Her brother, her big brother, dead in Vietnam. His remains were returned, but the coffin had remained closed. She was never to see him again. She was too young to understand. Maybe she never would no matter how old she got. But this morning, for a short time, she was looking forward to something – a ride with Bob. Silly really, but silly was something she needed right now. She laughed, "Suzie was hoping for this when she set this up. Well, thank you, Suzie."

Taking extra care with her hair and makeup, she was finally ready when Suzie came back into the room. Suzie looked at her and smiled.

"OK, Suz, what's on your mind?"

"Look at you, sweetie, you're smiling AND wearing makeup"

Angelina laughed, "Am not, don't be crazy."

"Methinks thou dost protest too much. I think you've taken a liking to that young man."

Angelina was quiet then responded, "Well, what if I have. Mrs. Barnes says he's a good boy, and that's good enough for me."

"My mon and dad like him. Papa says he's derecho, you know upright, true."

"Derecho, I like it."

Bob rolled into the yard at Mountain Camp in the early afternoon. By the time he had unloaded his horses, Suzie and Angelina had come outside to see him. "Bob, dinner will be ready soon. We want to go riding after we eat. You're coming with us, aren't you?"

"Sure, if that's what you want."

Suzie couldn't resist teasing Bob a little. "It doesn't matter to us. It was Papa's idea. He's worried and thinks we need a man along. What do you want to do?"

Bob was a little unsure of this. He thought they wanted him to go, but it had been a long time since he had much to do with girls. With one short exception the last two years had been pretty much a purely male world. The only women a GI was likely to run across were offering friendship at a price. So here he was, caught up in the age-old game played by young men and women, and he was completely unprepared.

Angelina could see his discomfort, and she thought, his disappointment. She decided it was time to let him off the hook and take charge. "Oh, stop, Suzie." Then she took Bob by the arm and starting for the door, "Of course, we want you to go. Suzie is just teasing."

With Angelina holding his arm and leading him across the yard, Bob wasn't walking. He was hovering just above the ground. He had a truly beautiful girl on his arm, and he was grateful she had just saved him from further uncertainty. "Uh, thank you for getting me off the hook," he said.

She smiled up at him and answered, "Oh. That's OK. Suzie's just pulling your leg. Of course, we want you to come with us. It was our idea. When we told Mr. Solano, we wanted you to come along, he said it was a good idea, that's all."

"Oh, that's good." Bob answered clumsily then he thought, damn, that sounded dumb. He was worried that he was starting to act the fool again. He hadn't felt this awkward since his first date in high school, when he spent the entire evening at a dinner dance with a girl he had a terrible crush on and couldn't manage to say a single word to all night. Eventually, he had gotten over his shyness and had an active social life in school, but then came the Army, and he was out of the dating scene for two years and all the hard-learned lessons had gone down range.

He took a deep breath and stopped. Turning to face her, he said, "Angelina, I'm sorry I'm acting so awkward. It's just that I haven't been around girls very much in the last couple of years, and I am nervous." Saying that made him feel better and a bit more confident. He smiled now and added, "I'll try not to act like such an idiot from here on out."

Angelina just smiled and said, "Let's go in and have dinner."

Bob had tried not to be obvious, but he was in a hurry to start his afternoon out with this girl, and he wasted little time eating. This was not lost on Cruz or Isabel, who graciously pretended not to notice and hurried the meal a little. Isabel said something to Suzie who translated, "Mama will have sopapillas for desert after our ride." With that, the young folks excused themselves and went out to the corral.

"Suzie, what horses are you and Angelina going to ride" asked Bob.

"Papa said I should take Indio, and Angelina should ride Funion."

"Ok, I'll catch them. Go ahead and get the halters." With this Bob took the rope from his saddle and walked out into the corral. These horses could be caught with an easy approach or at worst a morrall with some grain, but that was not going to show off Bob's roping skills any. He shook out a big loop and twisted his wrist in a houlihan throw, dropping the loop over Indio's head. Indio just looked at Bob as if to say, "What's your problem. I'm right here."

Bob led him over to Suzie, who put the halter on him and draped a morrall on his muzzle. She gave Bob a knowing look and winked. "I guess these bronco horses are getting harder to catch."

Bob didn't answer. He went back to catch Funion who decided to make things easier and simply walked up to Bob, so he could just drape the loop over his head. Bob laughed a little, and as he walked Funion to the girls he said, "I guess they aren't even going to let me show off my roping." The girls laughed at this. They knew how boys were.

Bob had talked to Suzie about where she wanted to go, and she told him she wanted to go on the pack trail that led up to Camp Hill. "It's a nice view and not a long ride," she said.

Bob agreed and said, "If we go up the pack trail and then down the south side on that cow trail to the jeep road it should be about three miles. The sun sets around six. That gives us plenty of time."

"That sounds like a good idea," said Suzie as she stepped up on Indio as if she had been doing it all her life, which she had. "Bob, Angelina has not ridden much. You might help her up."

Bob had saddled Funion for Angelina and set the stirrups of Cruz's old saddle to a length that seemed about right. Then he handed her the reins and said, "Watch how I swing up. I'll help you, but it might help if you see it first."

Angelina thought that was silly. She had watched Suzie and besides, she had ridden a horse a few times. She thought, How difficult can it be? She started to say something but decided not to. Bob was trying hard; there was no point in sending him crashing back to earth in flames.

Bob explained how to swing up buckaroo fashion, which was much easier than the way one mounted a bronc. Then he swung up on Nobody's back, stepped back down again and dropped the mecate get down rope on the ground effectively ground reining the horse. Nobody, true to form, registered his displeasure by snorting and walking backwards a few steps to be sure his head wasn't tied. He was not happy with the on and off stuff, but he was satisfied that he was not tied hard and fast so he stopped.

Bob was oblivious to all this. He had other things on his mind. He held Funion and helped Angelina to swing up. "Now, wasn't that easy?"

Angelina was not sure she was real happy with her perch so high above the ground. Funion was a gentle, old horse, but he was big. Riding him was a bit like sitting astride a gasoline tanker, very tall and very wide. She looked down at Bob and smiled uncertainly, "Yes, it was not too bad. He is awfully big."

"Yeah, he's a big guy but gentle and very sure footed." Bob was about to say he was Cruz's babysitting horse for visiting dudes and kids but thought better of it. He gathered up his mecate get down rope and tucking it into his chaps, he swung up. Seeing everyone was ready, he opened the gate for the girls and said, "Well, let's go."

As the girls approached the gate Suzie reined her horse in and said. "Con permiso."

Bob smiled, tipped his hat and answered with a wave of his arm. "Pasale, por favor."

Bob and Angelina were riding up the canyon at a leisurely pace. Suzie had trotted ahead, and while Funion was a gentle horse, he did not have an easy trot. It was said of him, that in a trot, he beat the ground into submission. Angelina had let Funion speed up to a trot to keep up with Suzie and Indio, but after about a hundred yards, Bob had her rein him back in to a walk before she got tired of the beating she was taking.

Bob was riding beside her now, "Funion's pretty rough in a trot. I think we'll just walk. There's plenty of time."

"What about Suzie? Shouldn't we try to keep up?"

"She knows this country like the back of her hand. She should be fine, but if you want, I'll ask her to slow down."

Angelina thought about this for a minute and then said, "That's OK. I guess she knows what she's doing."

After a ride of just under two miles, the three had reached the top of Camp Hill and were taking a break sitting in the grass and enjoying the view. Suzie said, "We should have brought some beer up here."

"Oh, yeah, that would have gone over well with your father," Bob replied.

"What Papa doesn't know won't hurt him any."

"I guess, but if he found out, there would be hell to pay. Your old man trusts me; I don't think I could do that to him."

Suzie got a gleam in her eye, "Now if we met in town, we could just go across to Agua Prieta and have a drink, legally. That'd be different, wouldn't it."

"If your father thought I was taking you drinking anywhere he would be pissed. I'm supposed to treat you like a little sister."

Now Suzie had an idea, "You're not supposed to treat Angelina like a little sister. Maybe you could accidentally meet her in town and just take me along. I could be her dueña." Seeing Bob's look of confusion, she said. "You know, like the paseo in Agua Prieta on Sundays. Remember the girls walk one way around the plaza and the boys walk the other. All the single girls are accompanied by their dueñas, a married sister or an aunt ... a chaperone."

"Yes, I remember." All this was making Bob uneasy. He was trying to work up the courage to ask Angelina for a real date, but he was not counting on having Suzie tag along. "No, Suzie. Wait 'til your old enough."

"Oh, like you did I suppose. I know you and my brothers slipped off to Agua Prieta for a night on the town the last summer you stayed here. How old were you then?"

"Eighteen, but that was different."

"Oh, how so, because you're a guy, and I'm just a girl?"

Bob caught the expectant look on Angelina's face and knew this was dangerous country. He had better tread carefully. His mind was working at max speed to keep from screwing up his chances with her. "No, it's not because you're a girl. It's because your parents and brothers expect me to...to...." He was struggling here and forgot himself. "Shit! I don't know. If you want to go drinking, that's your business. The new amendment says you're old enough to vote. Just do me one favor, be careful. You're a pretty girl, and there are some real assholes out there."

Bob was on his feet now and feeling very frustrated. Why did Suzie do this in front of Angelina? He was trying his hardest to impress her, and now he'd lost it and gotten into a petty argument with Suzie. Bob was pretty sure he had just blown any chance he had for making a good impression. Dejectedly he walked over to the edge of the hill where it dropped off over a small cliff of thirty or forty feet. The view of the broad canyon bottom with the mountains on the far side was peaceful. Bob took a deep breath and was about to go back and suggest they continue their ride when Angelina came up beside him.

"Bob, don't mind her. She just likes to give you a hard time." Angelina looked back to Suzie then to Bob and continued in a voice that was both low and unsure, "I think she's a little jealous."

This caught Bob by surprise. "Jealous?" he asked. His mind was a little muddled here. Did Angelina mean Suzie was jealous of her? Did Angelina like him? He took another deep breath and steeled himself for the impending rejection that was sure to come next. "Does she have reason to be jealous?" He sounded much surer of himself than he felt.

With this Angelina answered a bit coquettishly, "Perhaps."

Something Bob's father had said to him came to mind just then. He had said that girls were much smarter about affairs of the heart than boys and much surer of themselves. Bob had to agree. If Angelina had not stepped up on this one, he would have foundered and the whole relationship would have ended on the rocks before it ever got started. Bob gave Angelina a grateful if tentative smile and said, "Perhaps, that's better than I expected." Then mustering his courage for the big question, he asked, "Would you like to go out sometime?" He could hear his pulse beating in his ears he was so nervous.

She smiled back and said, "Of course. I'd love to go out with you."

"OK, we are going to be real busy with the fall work starting soon. I'll be up here on the mountain with Cruz for a couple of weeks and then out on the wagon the last week or so. I doubt if I'll be able to get to town until it's over, unless we go before Wednesday."

"I can go before Wednesday if you can get away."

"OK, is Monday or Tuesday better for you?"

"Well, Suzie and I are going back to Douglas tomorrow morning. I don't have any classes until Tuesday afternoon, so I think my folks would let me go out tomorrow night."

"Good, I'll check with Jack when I get back to Headquarters tonight to see if I can get off early tomorrow afternoon. If it's not too late, I'll call up here on the radio and let you know when I can be there. If it is too late to call, then stop by Headquarters tomorrow on your way out, and Aunt Maria can tell you what's up."

"OK, that sounds good, I'm looking forward to it. Where are you taking me?"

"I have no idea. I don't know the first thing about Douglas. Whatever you want is fine with me. Where do I pick you up?"

"Do you have something to write with?"

"Yes," Bob said, pulling out his tally book and a pencil. Angelina gave him her folks address and phone number.

"There" said Angelina with a smile as she handed back his tally book. Then she asked, "What's out on the wagon mean?"

Bob warmed to this a little. "The wagon is the chuck wagon. When Uncle Jack goes out for the spring or fall works or roundups, he pulls a wagon out, and the crew camps. The camp moves every few days as the cattle are gathered."

"Is it a chuck wagon like in the movies?"

"Jack's looks more like a sheepherder's wagon, and he pulls it with a pickup, but it serves the same purpose. I hear some of the big outfits up in the great basin still pull theirs with horses or mules."

"So, when you get out on the wagon there won't be any trips to town?"

"No, I expect not, nor will there be any going to town when I'm on the mountain with Cruz. The fall works is a big deal. Everybody works straight through."

As they walked back to collect the horses and continue their ride, Angelina said, "Isn't Nobody a strange name for a horse? how did he get his name?" Bob smiled. Uncle Jack was a smart man.

CHAPTER TEN

Even the cows have their own cops.

Vince was standing at the window watching the two trucks from Tres Cruces drive away. Jack Barnes did not strike Vince as a man to be trifled with. That in itself did not worry Vince; he had dealt with worse, but he did not need anyone drawing attention to the operation. Shit, he thought. This could be a problem.

Mr. Vechio, the head of the Borgata or Family, sent him to Arizona to start a new operation. It was to be nice and quiet, under the radar, said Mr.V. Now this, another unexpected obstacle. He was frustrated. It'll be easy, they said. Mexico is right next door, they said. The cops are all hicks, they said. How hard can running a ranch be? The cows eat grass, have babies and hang out, they said.

Well, Mexico might be right next door and the cops may all be hicks, but nobody told him anything about this ranching crap. Like most big city boys, his experience with beef was limited to someone serving it to him on a plate. As for cows, he had thought he could just leave them to run around on their own. Who would know the difference? Who would care? "Damn." He said to himself. "Jack Barnes knows, and Jack Barnes cares."

Vince knew nothing about all this branding, spraying and fencing crap? And ... *mavericks* ... what the hell! Mavericks, really. He thought that was some kind of old B movie shit that went out with cowboys and Indians. On top of that there's a livestock detective? Christ, the cows have their own cops. How the hell do you grease a cow cop, gift him a new hat? He fumed to himself.

"Alf." He called out.

"Right here, skipper." Answered Alf, startling Vince who was unaware that he was still in the room.

"You are supposed to be the ranch foreman, right?" said Vince, sharply.

"Yes, skip."

"Then you need to start learning some ranch shit. I don't want any of these shitkickers having an excuse to question what we're doing here. You need to get a handle on this. You and Freddie both need to learn enough of this ranch shit to keep us from looking stupid. You might even try learning to ride a horse. We do still have the horses that came with the place when we bought it, don't we?"

Alf was caught off guard and it showed. "Yea, skipper, we have horses."

"Good, start learning to ride; start learning this job."

"But skipper, how do I do that?"

"How the hell do I know. Figure it out. One thing you can do is hire somebody to fix that fence. You know the one that Barnes is all pissed off about."

Alf was getting worried. He felt a little overwhelmed. This stuff was way outside any experience he had. His voice was betraying his approaching panic. "Where do I find fence fixers?"

It was Vince's turn to feel a little overwhelmed. He had given the job of ranch foreman to Alf because he was the simplest man in the crew, and he didn't trust him with anything complicated. In Jersey he was muscle, nothing more. That didn't require any brains, so Vince figured Alf could play cowboy and be backup muscle, if needed. It wasn't Alf's fault that Vince had made a bad choice, but it was now Alf's problem. "I don't know." He growled. "Isn't that what I pay you for, now get out."

Vince took in a deep breath letting it out in a sigh. The boss has dropped me at the edge of the world, he thought. It's a long way from New Jersey to this middle of nowhere shithole. A lot farther than the two thousand plus miles on the map; It's like stepping back in time. I'm as out of place as a whore in church.

Vince sat down at his desk and started taking stock. He was not happy with the situation. He needed to get things on track. He started cataloging what had happened over the past year.

He understood why he was here. Since the cops had cut off the French Connection there was no Turkish heroin coming into the ports back East. A new junk route had to be found. He knew it was a big opportunity. He just wished it had been found in a civilized part of the planet like Florida, or even Mickey Mouse Los Angeles. He couldn't even find a decent pizza out here.

It had been a year since Mr. V had bought the ranch. Vince had expected things to move quicker. He hoped he would have made some money by now, but all the money had been going out. He was spending money on things that were not a problem in the city. Things like building a decent house, buying a big generator, as there was no electric line out here, erecting storage buildings, building a new road and the airstrip had all cost a pretty penny.

That was now all under control. He felt good about that. Tomorrow would be the first shipment from Mexico. Artie and Anthony would drive it up to Phoenix and deliver it to Mr. V's contact who would get it back to New Jersey. If all went well it would just be a question of how much the Mexicans could deliver. Hopefully, the business end of things was now getting on track, and the money would start coming in.

That still left him with the problem of the ranch. When he came down here to start the operation there was a young cowboy on the place. He had worked for the old man that sold it to Mr. V. The plan was to have this cowboy take care of the cows and all the normal ranch stuff. If he fit in with the new operation that would be fine. Why wouldn't he? It would pay a lot more than he was used to. If he didn't fit, he would go. Vince hadn't counted on his pride. He didn't fit.

Artie had picked a fight with him right off the bat. Artie had badmouthed him the first day they met, talking shit and being the big man. The cowboy had not taken it for long and hit him. Anthony stepped in and got it settled down before it got to guns or knives. That had started things off badly.

Vince had managed to talk the cowboy into staying long enough to get most of the cows rounded up and the babies sold, but then he had quit. Vince had hired another cowboy after that, but he only stayed a week. He didn't even wait to be paid.

That ended Vince's attempts to be a cow man. He was not here to play John Wayne. He had a business to set up and run. Once things were up and running, he would readdress the ranch, or so he thought. Now he had to at least fake it. That meant first getting the cows that were over at Barnes' Ranch, and second getting the fence fixed. "Maybe I should just sell all these damned cows."

Well, he had the beginnings of a plan. He would work out the details and get Alf on it soon. He couldn't dwell on it any longer right now. He had work to do. There was a delivery due the next afternoon. This was to be the first delivery of Mexican heroin and it was the first delivery by air. In fact it was the first time the new airstrip was to be used.

Mr. V's connection in Mexico, some guy named Pérez, the Mexicans called him the Mountain Lion, was supplying the heroin which was grown in the mountains of Sinaloa. It was black tar heroin, a cruder form than the white powder they were used to getting before. At first this worried Vinc,e but Mr. V had dismissed his concerns with some comments about dumb junkies getting high on whatever they could get.

† † †

Vince was a little anxious about the day ahead. The plane was due this afternoon. Now he was waiting for Artie and Anthony to pick him up for the drive up to the airstrip. He wanted to be sure it was ready before the plane arrived. He had no idea what made an airstrip ready or not ready, but he had to do something; he was going nuts with the waiting.

Vince was wishing Artie was not part of his crew. He had tried to leave him behind, but he was stuck with him. Mr V was insistent on that point. Artie's father, Mr V's brother, had gone to prison for life when he was just a boy, and Mr. had just about raised Artie. Having no children of his own, he looked on Artie as a son. It was important to him that Artie have this chance to get it together. He wanted Vince to teach his nephew the business and maybe straighten him out some. A tall order, thought Vince.

Artie thought of himself as a tough guy and a lady's man. He was neither, but he seemed to be the only one who didn't know it. He was, however, a hothead and unpredictable. That made him dangerous, not only to himself and those he came across but to the organization. There was no telling what would set him off. His mouth, or rather his lack of judgement, was a big problem. More than once Anthony, his minder, or Vince had had to get him out of scrapes that were over his head. Of course, Artie thought he had handled the situation or at least had it under control and resented Anthony's and Vince's interference.

Mr. V had assigned Anthony the task of acting as Artie's body guard. Everyone else on the crew figured he was really Artie's babysitter. Anthony was one of Mr. V's enforcers and was the only member of the crew that Artie respected. Already Anthony had defused a couple of incidents that could have gotten out of hand. Now after Artie's confrontation with the two cowboys from Tres Cruces, the same two cowboys that came with Jack Barnes to bring the cows over, Artie had taken to packing a pistol. Vince had tried to talk him out of it, but Artie was having none of it.

Vince had done a little checking after Artie's run-in with the Tres Cruces cowboys. He didn't find out much, just that the old man was a Mexican cowboy that had been working for Jack Barnes for years. He was married and had raised three kids on the ranch. The young cowboy was Jack Barnes' nephew. He had just come back from Vietnam. Nobody seemed to know much about him. One thing Vince knew was that he had a pistol under his jacket when they met. He could see the bulge.

Vince did not consider these two cowboys a real threat to himself or someone like Anthony, but poor, dumb Artie could fuck up a wet dream, and he just might get hurt if he pressed these two. Thank God Anthony was shadowing Artie.

CHAPTER ELEVEN

"Salud, you old lobo." Bob Hasett

When Bob jingled in the horses early Wednesday morning, the crew were all in the corral. Jack had an old reata in his hands; he held a slight preference for the braided rawhide over the plant fiber maguey. He would not even consider one of the newfangled nylons. Each cowboy had a halter or under bridle in his hands waiting his turn to call out his horse for the day, which Jack would then catch. Bob had already sorted out the horses that he would be carrying up to Mountain Camp.

Before long all the cowboys had saddled their horses for the day and were ready to mount. They all watched Jack carefully for as soon as Jack's foot hit the stirrup, they would mount their horses. It was a serious breach of cowboy etiquette to mount before the boss, but you didn't want to be last up either. The one exception to this was whoever had drawn a bronc for the day. He would mount last surrounded by the others in case his horse broke in two. Sam, the young cowboy that had broken many of Jack's horses had drawn the rough string by choice, he waited on the others.

Jack grabbed his stirrup in his right hand and his saddle horn in his left. He raised his left leg and jammed his boot in all the way to the heel and swung up quite gracefully for such a big man. By the time his butt hit the saddle, all the rest were atop their mounts and getting settled in. Jack surveyed the crew and thought, it's good to be king. Soon they had formed a circle around Sam, who stepped up onto his horse slick as could be. Although his horse was as humpy as a camel, he decided not to put on a rodeo just yet.

Jack told Bob to see if Maria had any messages for Mountain Camp and then go ahead on up. "See you in a couple of weeks, Bob."

"Yes, sir, hasta la vista." Bob watched as they trotted out, a little regretful that he was not going along but glad at the same time to be spending so much time with Cruz before taking over Mountain Camp. Turning back towards the house he went to see if Aunt Maria had needed anything from him.

For the next two weeks Bob and Cruz had worked nonstop on housekeeping chores such as checking and mending fences, rebuilding water gaps, and making sure the waters were up and working. In a week or so Jack would be putting everything but the shipped weanlings, replacement heifers, bulls, and short age pairs into North Sabino Pasture; that would be something like a thousand head.

Now Bob was sitting outside the barn watching the moon come up over the mountains. It wasn't quite full, but it was impressive casting its silver light across the canyon. Bob was tired. It had been a long day, hell, it had been a long two weeks. Cruz had taught him a lot since he had come back up. Some was just cowboying in general while some was specific to Mountain Camp.

They had taken advantage of some of the Indian Springs strays they had gathered and used them as roping stock. It was not the way you would normally treat a neighbor's strays, but since Indian Springs had no problem letting their stock graze on Tres Cruces grass, Cruz and Bob had no problem using Indian Springs cattle for practice. Cruz taught Bob how to improve his roping skills, especially tripping, tying off, and getting down the rope faster, and even the best way to tie a cow to a tree without becoming part of the knot. Bob knew he had learned a lot, and he knew he had a lot more to learn. Cruz had promised to come up often and keep teaching him.

The coyotes started singing shortly after the moon made its appearance, and then Bob heard something in their singing that sounded different. It was deeper and somehow stronger, lacked the staccato yips and yelps that accompanied the coyotes' howls. It was eerie, it seemed to reach deep inside and touch some ancient nerve. What was that? thought Bob. It was quiet now; the coyotes had stopped. Then he heard the long, deep penetrating howl again. It raised goose bumps on Bob's arms.

Cruz came around the corner and offered Bob a beer. "You hear this thing?" he asked looking off towards the howl.

"Yes, what was it?"

Cruz was smiling now, "It is lobo. I not hear this thing for many years."

"Lobo, a Mexican Gray Wolf, right?

"Si, it is wolf in English, but I like lobo more better."

Bob took a deep pull on his beer, "I like lobo better too. I thought they were all gone."

"I think this too, maybe he coming up from the Sierra Madre. Still some lobos down there. Not good for the cows. They eat lotta much the babies and the big cows, too."

"Maybe he'll pass through and leave us alone."

"I hope he pass through quick. I not want to kill him, but if he stay no chance to leave him alone." Just then the wolf howled again; it was a long, baleful howl with no answer. "I think this wolf is alone. Wolves and coyotes no like to be alone. Maybe he is a little sad, need a girlfriend."

"Can you call to him?"

"Si, but not good to do this. If I call, maybe he come here looking. Better he go away."

The wolf gave a final howl, this one a little fainter. Bob raised his beer bottle, "Salud, you old lobo. Go back to the Sierra Madre and find a girlfriend. If you stay here Cruz will have your hide tacked to the wall."

"Salud," said Cruz in salute to the wolf, then he changed the subject. "Jack call, he want you leave one horse here and take rest to Headquarters in the morning. He want you there early, five hora. He say you bring..." Here Cruz searched for the right English word and failing in that, resorted to Spanish, "petate."

"Petate," Bob repeated searching his limited Spanish vocabulary. "Like bedroll?"

"Si, bedroll and other things, clothes and tools for shoeing, things for camp on the wagon. After do this thing come back here, and we go to Forest Service lookout in North Forest and start cows down to Big Bill Canyon. Jack want to meet us at Wild Cow Spring. I think you no have bedroll."

"I've got a sleeping bag and poncho."

"I have a very good bedroll and I not need. You take it, more better than sleeping bag."

Bob was about to protest but decided not to. It would be better to show up at the wagon with a bedroll. Besides if the weather got wet, a bedroll shed water a lot better than a sleeping bag. "OK, Cruz, thank you very much, muchas gracias."

"De nada, I like do this. Maybe better other cowboys see this."

Cruz went and got his beadroll and showed Bob how to pack his clothes and shoeing tools in it. The bedroll was a big affair with a thick foam pad and lots of blankets wrapped in heavy duty marine canvas and secured with a couple of leather straps. It was not made to be carried on one's back or behind a saddle. This was a bed intended for long stays outdoors.

After Cruz returned to the house Bob thought to himself, I'd like to hear that wolf again as he took another drink from his beer. He had had several this evening, hoping they would help him fall asleep. He was bone tired, but he had trouble falling asleep some nights and never seemed to be able to stay asleep. He would be sleeping soundly and then be bolt upright with his heart racing, and a sense that something was terribly wrong. On the worst occasions, he would be bathed in cold sweat. He never remembered dreams, but there must have been some. This was getting old. It had been going on since he returned from Vietnam.

As he sat with the chair leaned back against the wall, he dozed off waking when his chin bounced off his chest. That had been happening a lot lately, he thought. I never used to just nod off like that. Maybe I can sleep tonight. With that thought Bob went to his room in the barn and tried to sleep.

† † †

It was mid-morning when Bob and Cruz started up the mountain to the Forest Service lookout. There were a few cows in this high country that needed to be brought down. Jack and the crew had already gathered most of the high country in North Forest Pasture and pushed these cows into Big Bill Canyon. Cruz and Bob would get the few at the south end of North Forest and take them down to Wild Cow Spring.

It was a narrow trail so Bob was following behind Cruz, who was setting an easy pace for the sake of the horses. It was a long climb to the lookout, and Bob was not feeling up to a bunch of chitchat so he was glad of the quiet. It had been another rough night with little sleep and a serious night sweat that woke him up and kept him awake for a few hours. Now he was tired and wanted to sleep. He was grateful for the several cups of strong coffee Isabel had pushed on him this morning; that was probably all that was keeping him up.

His thoughts drifted back to his date with Angelina, as they often did. He counted the date as a success. He had met Angelina's parents and got along fine with them. Her father had put him through the normal grilling about where was he from, what his father did, and what he was doing these days. Bob answered his questions and explained that he had just returned from Vietnam. Mr. Slaughter seemed pleased by this and began to talk about his time in the Navy during WWII. While Mr. Slaughter was talking about his military experiences, Bob noticed the picture of a young Marine on the mantle. Angelina had told him of her brother's death, and Bob figured this must be him. Bob stood up and walked to the mantle. "Is this your son, Mark?"

"Yes," answered Mr. Slaughter. His voice sounded strained.

"Angelina told me about him." Bob turned to look at Mr. Slaughter, "I know this sounds trivial, but I am sorry for your loss. Everyone tells me Mark was a fine, young man. I wish I could have met him. I know Angelina misses him a lot."

"We all do."

Just then Angelina came into the living room ending the conversation and said, "I'm ready."

With that Bob walked up to Mr. Slaughter to say goodby. As they clasped hands, Mr. Slaughter put his free hand on Bob's shoulder and just held on for a few seconds as if he wanted to say something but couldn't. Finally, he smiled with his lips but not his eyes and shook his head and said. "Have a good time you two."

On the way out to the truck, Angelina asked, "What was that about?"

"We were talking about your brother."

"Oh, that explains it. It's been really hard on Dad. He misses Mark a lot."

"I'm sure. My aunt said nothing was worse than burying her son. Parents aren't supposed to outlive their kids."

They had dined at the Gadsden Hotel in Douglas and then caught a movie in town. The restaurant in the grand old hotel was nice. The dinner was good and the movie, "True Grit," was enjoyable, but the highlight of the evening was being with Angelina.

She had invited him to her parents' house for coffee, and they had sat on the couch talking while their coffee was forgotten and got cold. There was a lot of furtive touching of hands and the occasional leg brush, but it had all been quite tame until Bob said he had better go. With that Angelina had decided it was time to take matters into her own hands and planted a big kiss on Bob's lips.

When they separated and Bob got his breath back, he was trying to say something but had no idea what. Then Angelina said, "Bob, we are having a big dance at the college at the end of the month. It's the Fall Dance. Would you like to go with me?"

"Yes, sure, I'd like that."

Getting to her feet Angelina walked Bob to the door and said, "I'll get the details and mail them to the ranch since you might not be able to get into town before then."

"OK," Bob was pretty high above the clouds just now. "I'll look forward to getting your letter. As soon as I can, I'll get into town and give you a call. I hate to use Uncle Jack's phone for long distance. It's expensive."

"That's fine. It's a date," with that she opened the door and gave him a long, passionate, good night kiss, the kind that said a lot more than a few words.

† † †

All this was going through Bob's head when Cruz stopped and stepped down from his horse. "Bob, look at this thing," he said pointing to the ground.

Bob stepped down and walked over to Cruz. What he saw looked like a big dog or coyote track. "Is that the lobo?"

"Si, it is the lobo. He come through here this morning." Cruz continued to study the ground as he walked slowly up the trail following the wolf's tracks. "This is a very big wolf, but I think he is hurt; he has a bad leg. Cruz then showed Bob the irregular spacing of the tracks and the lighter indentation of the left rear paw. These were indications of a limp caused by an injured left hind leg.

Bob thought he could see the spacing, but in no way could he see that the left rear print was lighter than the others. Damn, he thought, this old man could track an ant across a rock. Bob continued to listen to Cruz and study what he was being shown.

Finally, Cruz stopped and pointed to where the wolf had split off onto a game trail. "He go that way. I not like this thing. He maybe go to Big Bill Canyon."

Bob could see that this bothered Cruz. The old cowboy had killed plenty of cats and coyotes in his day, but he didn't seem to want to have to kill this wolf. "I hope not."

"Si, I hope not, too." Cruz stood quietly for a while then turned to Bob, "I no mind kill some lions and coyotes. Sometimes they kill the cows, and I need to kill, but maybe this is last wolf. I not like to kill the last one. It is better to have some." He hoped Bob understood what he was trying to say, "Comprende?"

"Si, comprendo."

Cruz then muttered something under his breath in Spanish, but all Bob caught was lobo. "We go now." They swung up on their horses and continued up the mountain.

It was late afternoon when Cruz and Bob reached Wild Cow Spring with over fifty head. They had picked them up in the high country at the head of the canyon. Bob was thinking what a pleasure it was to move cattle that weren't always on the verge of a panic, just waiting for an excuse to run. These critters had moved easily. The few youngsters that got a bit trotty and started to run off had come back of their own accord when mom stayed with the bunch.

Jack and Scooter were waiting at the spring and helped them push the cattle into the water lot. Cruz filled Jack in on what he and Bob had seen during the day. Jack was satisfied that most if not all the cattle had been gathered from the upper canyon and that whatever might be left would come down with the cold weather. He told Cruz to go on back to Mountain Camp. He and Bob would take these cows on and put them through to Big Bill Pasture.

Cruz rode over to Bob to say goodbye. When Bob asked if it wasn't a long ride back, Cruz pointed to a low ridge to the south and told him, "No, Sabino Canyon is only two miles."

With this Bob realized that if Cruz went south two miles, he would be in the lower end of Sabino Canyon and only five or six more miles from Mountain Camp. "Adios, Señor, hasta luego."

"Hasta pronto, Bob."

Jack and Bob had walked the cattle the remaining mile and a half down the canyon and put them through the gate. Here Jack and Bob had held them once they had passed through giving them time to mother up. Mothers and calves were often separated when they were moved, and it was good policy to allow them time to find each other. Just ramming them through a gate was a good way to wind up with split pairs, lost calves and tight bagged cows. Once all the calves had found their mothers, they let the bunch walk off, but one cow stayed behind looking back up the trail from which she had just come. She had a calf somewhere as could be seen by her full udder.

"Bob, ease on up there and open that gate. This girl is bagged up and has a calf back there somewhere. We're going to let her back through. We'll get her later when we gather remnants."

"Yes, sir," answered Bob. He slumped in his saddle being careful not to look directly at the cow as he rode up casually to the gate. Even his horse seemed to be slouching and disinterested in the cow. She drifted down the fence a little, keeping an eye on Bob. Once he had the gate opened, he rode back to where he had been, turned his horse back around, stopped and sat up straight. The cow was still watching but had started back to the gate and walked on through.

"Bob, you did that well. A lot of young cowboys would have lined out in a hurry and had that poor girl running up the fence by the time they got to the gate."

"Thanks, Uncle Jack. Cruz and I have been dealing with a lot of trotty cattle from Indian Springs. He has taught me how to take an easy hold when we need them to calm down a bit. Of course, it doesn't always work. Some of those girls are just plain wild, but it sure helps on most of them.

"How's that working for you?"

"Pretty well when it comes to gates and working in the corral, but it appears nobody told the Indian Springs cows how it's supposed to work. They always run."

Jack laughed at this. "Those girls are entertaining. Let's get to camp and grab some supper before that bunch eats it all. Your horses and bedroll are already there."

At camp Bob turned his horse into the small corral at the water lot and tossed him some hay. He would keep him up for the night, since he was jingling the remuda in the morning.

As he was laying out his bedroll, Jack came up to him. "I have a letter for you, he said with a smile. I think somebody's sweet on you."

Bob took the letter and checked the return address. As he hoped, it was from Angelina. He smiled. "Thanks, Uncle Jack."

"Aren't you going to read it?"

"I'll read it in a minute."

"I guess you want some privacy," Jack said with a chuckle. "I'll get out of your hair in a minute. Tomorrow Jesse will wake you up at four o'clock. You need to get saddled quick and get the horses in. As soon as you've done that get some breakfast. I want to be out of here at first light. Check with Jim, he has been jingling up to now. He can tell you what the horse pasture's like."

"OK, Uncle Jack. I'll go talk to him as soon as I finish reading this."

"Good, oh, by the way, I'm sure Jesse will have some cake or pie in an hour or two. He's a fine cook."

"Thanks."

As Jack walked back over to the cook fire where everybody was sitting around, Bob savored the perfumed scent of his letter before opening it. It smelled like Angelina. He was anxious to read what she had to say. It was like mail call in the army. He had always been excited to get mail back then, especially if it was from his girlfriend. The Dear John she sent him managed to knock the stops out from under him for a while, but it didn't dampen his anticipation at mail call. It was always good to get something.

Angelina opened by saying how much she had enjoyed herself when they went out. She had told her friends all about Bob, and they wanted to meet him. Even her aunt said she wanted to meet him and be sure he was a good boy. Angelina gave Bob the particulars about the dance and said her folks had offered to let him stay the night at their house, so he wouldn't have to drive all the way back to the ranch late that night. Wow, thought Bob, that's a good deal.

There was more small talk and the usual questions about how things were going for Bob, but the end of the letter was back to how much she had enjoyed their date and how much she was looking forward to the dance. She signed off with "Yours, Angelina." It wasn't an "All my Love," but it was a damn sight better than "Sincerely" or "Your Pal." Bob was one happy cowboy. He kicked back and relaxed on his bedroll, rehashing the letter and glad he had the dance to look forward to, but his brief moment of reverie was soon over. It was now time to go over to the cook fire. He had to talk to Jim about jingling the horses and say hi to the other cowboys and the cook.

Bob walked up to the fire and made his greetings all around. Once he was done, Jack introduced him to the cook. "Bob, this is Jesse Arceneaux. He's the finest cook ever to work on a wagon." This was greeted with a chorus of approving comments by the cowboys.

Bob stuck out his hand, saying, "How do you do? It's nice to meet you."

Jesse was an old man with snow white hair, peeking out from under an old Brooklyn Dodgers baseball cap. "How do you do, young man? I've heard a lot about you. Oh, and by the way, that part about the best cook is all a lot of brown-nosing. They want more dessert this evening."

"I don't doubt this bunch would do a little butt kissing to get more sweets, but if Uncle Jack says you're the best, then you must be. I hope these folks haven't been too hard on me for screwing off in the mountains while they did most of the work."

Jesse laughed at this. "No, not too hard, but we are glad to have you with us. Your uncle is about to work these poor men to death."

"That doesn't sound very promising. I was hoping all the heavy lifting would be done by the time I got back from screwing off on the mountain."

All this was followed by some ribbing which Bob took in good stride. He would have to work hard to prove himself. These cowboys weren't interested in what he had been doing; they were interested to see if he could hold up his end on the wagon. Bob knew this and hoped he was up to the challenge.

After talking to Jim about jingling the horses in the morning, Bob was pouring himself a cup of lemonade when Jack motioned for him to follow him. Once they were away from the rest of the hands, Jack said, "Bob, these boys will be watching you close the next day or two. I don't want you to fret any. I know you have it in you to do just fine, and I also know that Cruz has been working the devil out of you and that you have learned a lot. He told me you were a good cowboy now. Not an average cowboy but a good one. You may have to take a little ribbing, but it won't last long."

"No sweat, Uncle Jack. I can handle a little ribbing as long as it's done with a smile."

Remembering Bob's reaction to the sheriff's deputy and the Indian Springs' man, Jack was not so sure that Bob was in the mood to put up with any foolishness. "Are you sure? I'd hate to see trouble over some foolishness."

"Uncle Jack, I'm not out of control. As long as none of these guys try to bully me, I'll be fine. I can handle good natured teasing as well as the next man, but I won't tolerate bullying."

"That's good enough. There are some damn fine cowboys in this bunch. Some are prone to practical jokes and funning each other a bit, but there are no bullies."

"Sounds good to me."

Bob walked back over to the fire and took a seat with the rest of the crew. Sandy Brimhall was working with a Mecate and being watched closely by the two young cowboys, while a couple of the older hands relaxed over coffee. Jesse was fiddling with the Dutch oven, and Jack tried to sneak a peak of Jesse's work only to get a sharp rap on the hand with a wooden spoon.

Bob was fascinated by how easily Sandy untied and retied the complicated fiador knot. Sandy Brimhall was an old school buckaroo from the great basin who had the reputation of being a fine hackamore man. Jack had known him for years; they had worked on the wagons together for one of the big outfits up north when they were both a lot younger. After Jack had bought Tres Cruses, Sandy would come down every year and help him with the spring and fall works. Bob had heard of Sandy from the home guard hands, but they'd never met before this fall. Watching this old buckaroo working with rawhide hackamores would be something new. Jack would say, "Watch, learn, and add it to your cowboyography."

While Sandy worked, he was explaining to the two young cowboys why he was tying his fiador with fewer turns. Tomorrow he would be riding a horse that took a light hand; therefore, he was using a thin pencil-thick hackamore and too large a fiador would cause it to hang wrong. Bob was thinking that was pretty amazing. Something no thicker than a pencil made of braided rawhide, bent in a loop and hanging on the great big muzzle of a horse could actually be used to control the animal.

Jesse came over and sat beside Bob handing him a big steak sandwich. "You need to eat, young fella. Dessert will be up in a half hour or so, but you need some protein in your system."

"Thanks, Jesse, you needn't have done that."

"Don't worry, next time I won't. You're on your own now, how you doing?"

"I'm good. "

Your uncle tells me you just got back from Vietnam."

"Yeah, about a month ago."

"Who were you with?"

"I was in the 73rd Surveillance Airplane Company; it was part of the 1st Aviation Brigade."

"That doesn't sound like choppers."

"No, we were an OV1 Mohawk unit. I flew right seat as a TO."

The conversation went on this way for a little while with Jesse asking questions and Bob explaining what he had done in Vietnam.

"Your uncle tells me you were recommended for the DSC."

"That's what my platoon sergeant said."

"So what's the deal?"

"I won't get it. I doubt if it will even be downgraded to an Army Commendation Medal. I expect it's in the circular file back at Brigade."

"Young man, I know a thing or two about soldiering and the Army. If you were put in for a DSC as an enlisted man you must have done something pretty special."

"I stayed alive is all." Bob looked at Jesse and recognized something in him. "You retired?"

"Yes, I retired back in sixty. I did the full burst of thirty and retired as First Sergeant."

Bob thought on this for a minute. "So you came in before integration."

"That's right; I was out here with the 25th Infantry Regiment for over ten years before the war. When the war broke out, we formed the nucleus and most of the cadre for the 93rd division that formed up here before going to the Pacific in forty-four."

"You must have seen some shit."

"Yeah, some; the Japs were tough, but I got to tell you, the jungles on Bougainville and New Guinea were really bad, and Morotai was no better. Sometimes I couldn't tell which was worse, the enemy or the jungle."

"I can relate to that. The jungle can be a bitch." Changing the subject, Bob said, "Whatever's in that Dutch oven smells good."

"It's a cobbler, should be done pretty quick. You finish that sandwich so you can have some."

† † †

The next week went about as Bob had figured it would. After he jingled the horses each morning, it was breakfast, and a day in the saddle from dawn until three or four in the afternoon. When they returned to camp for an early dinner, it was a big affair with lots of beef, potatoes, beans, and at least a nod to green vegetables such as green beans or peas. Later in the evening Jesse would have sandwich fixins and dessert before the crew bedded down, usually quite early.

On the first day they had gathered cattle off the foothills that had been brought down from North Pasture up in the high country and pushed them southwest onto the south flats. Then they had moved camp out to the flats setting up at Goat Well. This was a new experience for Bob. He had jingled horses from the horse pasture to Headquarters or a cow camp, but he had never moved horses from one camp to another. He was feeling pretty nervous about it when Jack came up and said Sandy was going to give him a hand moving the cavvy. "Sandy knows where we're going, and he can point the ramuda" said Jack.

"Thanks," answered Bob.

As Sandy and Bob moved the horses up to the new camp, Jesse loaded up his wagon, hitched it to the old pickup, and began making his way to the new location. While all this was going on, Jack decided to use the rest of the crew to throw one last circle and clean any remnants that may have been missed in the foothills. Everyone would meet at the new camp for dinner.

Working the flats was altogether different. Bob had almost always worked the mountains with Cruz on his summer visits and indeed had been doing the same since his return. The mountains were steep and had plenty of trees and big timber, but other than some ocotillo, prickly pear, and mescal plants, there weren't a lot of cacti on the mountain. Granted there was the occasional fish hook barrel and even a cholla from time to time but not like this. The flats had lots of cacti and even more mesquite, white thorn, and cat claw thrown in for good measure. Bob was really glad he was wearing heavy bat wing chaps. They had been worth their extra weight in the blood he had not lost due to cuts, scratches, and pokes. He had been scratched up some for sure, but it could have been much worse.

The one notable event of Bob's time on the flats came when he put the spurs to Mescal when an old, high-horned Braford cow had taken off crossing through a particularly thick mesquite bosque. They weren't far from the gate when she decided she didn't want to go that way and went crashing into the mesquite making a break for the open country on the other side. Bob was trying to stay ahead of where he thought she should be before he crossed the bosque himself. By the time he turned Mescal towards the mesquite where he hoped to find a way through, the horse had a full head of steam. It was then Bob regretted his mistake in letting Mescal run flat out because this horse was a bit short of whoa. In fact, he was near impossible to stop when going full speed. Bob realized he had no power to stop or turn this horse. All he could do was brace for the crash as they slammed into the bosque. By the time they came out the other side they were indeed in front of the cow, but Bob was surprised that he was still on the horse and even amazed that they had made it through at all. Mescal was fine now; once he saw the cow, he was all business. They quickly turned the cow back and put her with the bunch at the gate.

After putting the cows through and letting them mother up with their calves, Jack decided to have everyone step down and take a short break. As Bob was about to dismount, Pat Ochoa, one of the young cowboys, looked at him and started laughing. "What happened to you? You ain't naked, but you're close."

Bob knew he had taken a beating in the mesquite, but he had not had time to take stock. Now as he checked himself, he found his watch was missing, his heavy shirt was torn so badly he thought he would need a pitch fork to gather it up, the canteen and brush coat tied behind his cantle board were gone, and even the pocket on his leggings was torn half off and flapping like a broken screen door on a windy day. He was surprised to still have his hat. "Damn," he exclaimed. "I bet there's a hole in that old bosque that looks like this," holding his arms out to his sides with his mouth wide open and a scared look on his face, "and it's got all my gear hanging on the branches."

The other cowboys laughed at this. "That would make a good cartoon," said Sandy.

"Uncle Jack, I recon I better go back and police up my gear."

"OK, Bob, see you at camp."

† † †

A little over a week after Bob had arrived at the wagon camp, all the cattle had been gathered into the holding pasture, camp had been broken, and everyone was bunked up back at Headquarters for the last few days. The remainder of the works could be done from there.

Jack was going to hold a rodeo, pronounced roadear, sorting off the bulls, short age pairs and slicks. Bob had never worked a rodeo or roadear before, but Jack had filled him in on what to expect. He had told him they would gather all the cattle into the southeast corner of the holding pasture. The cowboys would hold the herd while Jack cut out the critters to be left behind. Once he was done sorting, the rest of the cattle would be walked to the corrals at Headquarters, a distance of only two miles.

 The next day would end the fall works. They would wean and ship the calves, ship the cull cows, and trailer the replacement heifers to Dessert Camp. After that, the wagon crew would be paid off. The rest of the work such as branding the slicks, moving the bulls, gathering remnants, and putting the cows back on their winter country would be dealt with by the home guard.

On that last day of fall works Bob had not saddled a horse since he was working footback. He was on one of the gates in the sorting pens. Jack who was horseback in the alley, would cut out a calf or calves and call out, "Ship" or "Keep" alerting the gate men to swing the correct gate sorting the calves into the right pen. The cows were mostly passed through to the holding pasture with the exception of a few old girls selected to be culled and shipped to the sale barn. Working the gate was simple but a bit hectic at times, trying to be sure to let the right critters in, keeping the wrong ones out, and not letting any of those already in the pen slip back out. At the end of the day, Bob was tired. They had weaned nearly a thousand head, and since Bob had the "ship" gate, the vast majority went to him. Only some undersized steers and the replacement heifers were put in the "keep" pen, no more than a hundred fifty. Bob had swung that big steel gate close to a thousand times. He would dream about the gate tonight.

Now that they were back at Headquarters, meals were a bit more regular than at camp. There was a big breakfast before sunup and a big dinner at midday with a decent supper in the early evening. Jesse was doing breakfast and supper, and Maria was doing the midday dinner which gave Jesse a bit of a break.

† † †

Bob called Angelina's house from Jack's phone as soon as they returned to Headquarters and left a message with her mother that he was sorry for the delay and did want to go with her to the Fall Formal. Mrs. Slaughter assured Bob she would pass on the message.

Angelina had been on Bob's mind to the point of distraction since inviting him to the Fall Formal at the college. He felt better now that he had called and confirmed his acceptance of her invitation to the dance, but he knew a letter was called for. She had, after all, taken the time to write him, and it was only proper that he write her back. The phone was fine for quick exchanges of information, but long distance was expensive, and it wasn't his phone. Besides, he wanted to write her a long letter, and he hoped she would write back.

He started by apologized for not writing sooner, explaining he had been busy with the fall works. He talked about rounding up the cattle, the camping on the wagon and told her about some of the cowboys, especially the older ones that he tried to learn from. He told her about Jesse as well, explaining about him being an old First Sergeant.

He tried to be humorous, telling her about his crashing through the Mesquite Basque, and having an argument with his horse, Nobody. An argument that Bob had lost. He was trying to be interesting and funny but was afraid he was failing.

Eventually, he got down to business and told her how much her letter meant to him, how it was the highlight of the past few weeks, only surpassed by his date with her when they went to the movies and dinner. He decided to risk a little by telling her she had been on his mind a lot. He said he was anxious to see her again and was looking forward to the dance.

Bob read what he had written and on thinking about it; he decided not to risk scaring her away by saying any more about his feelings for her. He did risk closing with Yours instead of Sincerely.

CHAPTER TWELVE

"It sounded like the goddamned world was coming to an end." Bob Hasett

One night after supper, Jesse hunted up Bob and asked if he could have a few words with him in private. Bob led him over to the saddle house, where he often went to be alone, and the two men sat on the step looking out into the darkness. The moon was not up yet, but there was a little afterglow left from the sun so they could see a little of the corral fence and the mountains.

"Young fella, tomorrow is my last day until spring works, and I'll be busy packing up tomorrow night, so I want to talk to you now about the Army."

"OK, that's fine by me."

"I know you're an Army brat raised on officer's row. Now that you've seen it from the other side, what do you think?"

"I don't quite know, Top. I have mixed feelings about it."

"Like what?"

"I like a lot of things about it, but some of it is pure crap."

"Yes, well, there certainly is a lot of chicken shit to deal with."

"That's part of it, but I'm more bothered by some of the assholes that abuse their power."

With this Jesse paused and thought about what to say. "Bob, there are assholes everywhere. A great many of them think being a prick and bullying is their right. Some use their authority to get over on others. They are not all in the Army. Hell, there are fewer in the Army than out."

"Now that's a sad statement."

"It is indeed, but it's true. In the military there are standards folks are supposed to live by. Leaders are supposed to be fair and put their mission and men before themselves. The military makes a formal study of leadership and takes pride in the notion of honor and integrity. A lot of time and effort are spent in developing training to teach leadership principals and in developing a sense of duty and sacrifice. Unfortunately, not everyone learns or holds to these standards, and there surely are some right ornery sons of bitches you run into on occasion, but by and large, they are weaned out. When you do run into a really no-good bastard who costs lives or abuses his troops, you know as well as I do that there are ways for GIs to fix things."

Bob looked hard at Jesse. It was pretty dark, but he could see enough. "Yes, there are."

"I'll tell you this; it is said that a good NCO loves his soldiers as much as he loves his wife and kids, some say even more."

"I believe that. I had two really fine NCOs and a couple of real good officers, but most were middle-of-the road, a few were a waste of oxygen, and one or two were just plain assholes."

"Well, let me tell you, out in the civilian world, there are a few good leaders and more than a few dirtbags, but what you called middle-of-the-road leaders in the Army are the average guys with no real natural ability, but they have training. Outside the military, they still have no natural ability, and they have no training so they don't even make middle-of-the-road. A half-assed Platoon Sergeant would make shop foreman of the year in a factory, assuming he wasn't a prick."

"So how do you rate Uncle Jack?"

Jesse chuckled at this. The boy was testing him. "Jack Barnes is an outstanding leader. You know how you can tell?"

"How?" asked Bob.

"You know he's good because everyone wants to work for him, and he operates his ranch in the black. His cowboys don't quit; they retire."

"So why's he good?"

"What do you know about his service in the war?"

"Not much, just that he was in the Pacific."

"Lord, son, he wasn't in the Pacific; he was all over the Pacific. He was in the 17th Infantry as a corporal when they landed in the Aleutians; he was a buck sergeant when they landed on Kwajalein; a Platoon Sergeant on Leyte where he got a battlefield commission; and he finished the war as a company commander in Okinawa. That's where he learned about leadership, not on some ranch. Your uncle is the kind they write books about. He has the natural talent, but the Army and the war honed it."

"I didn't know."

"No reason you would, he keeps it pretty close. Anyway, my point is that as bad as some of the assholes in the Army are, they may be better than you can expect in the civilian world."

Bob decided this was a lot to think about, and he wasn't sure he bought it lock, stock, and barrel; after all, Jesse was an old lifer.

"So tell me about that DSC."

Bob was looking down at his boots, "There ain't no DSC."

"Don't fuck with me, boy. I didn't just fall off the turnip truck. Tell me about it."

Bob heard the old First Sergeant in this and responded. Here was a man who had shown him some kindness and seemed to be genuinely interested in him. He also had that talent that good leaders possessed, the ability to make others want to follow his orders. "OK, Top, I'll tell you, but . . ."

"I know; I won't go blabbing it all over." Then with a smile, "That is unless it's a really good story, and then I'll just claim it was me."

As Bob stood up, he said, "Alright, but I need something to drink; how about you?"

"Sure," answered Jesse.

Bob had retrieved the jar of Bacanora from the shelf where Jack kept it and offered it to Jesse, who took a long pull and handed it back to Bob. "Jesus!" he exclaimed, "That tastes like pure rat piss. What is it?"

"Bacanora Mexican moonshine," Bob then took a long pull himself followed by a deep breath. It took him a while to gather his thoughts before he started.

† † †

"After I got back from R and R, I was sent up to Nui Ba Den to set up a ground station for receiving Infra-Red missions flown in Cambodia. Nui Ba Den was a big, old mountain that stuck up out of the relatively flat ground all around it, sort of like this country here with mountains popping up out of the desert."

"I thought you were air crew."

"I was, but one of our duties was operating these ground stations. We had never had one on that mountain before, and I got the honors to be the first. It was supposed to be for thirty days.

"Just getting that thing up there with the generators and antenna tower was a bitch. It took two sling-loads, and that was just the beginning of the fun." Bob took another drink from the jar and offered it to Jesse again, but he passed. "There were a dozen Air Force guys manning a radio relay station and a weather station and one other Army GI. He was a forward observer for Tay Ninh Arty, who had pissed someone off so he had been exiled to the Rock and given the call sign Rocky Top. He had an FM radio for calling missions, his personal weapon, and an 81mm mortar. Other than that, the only other good guys on that mountain top were thirty-five Regional Forces Militia or Ruff Puffs as we called them, not exactly elite troops but better than nothing.

"We were smack on top of that mountain inside a pretty small compound, and Charlie had the rest of the mountain. The only way in and out for us was choppers. There were plenty of VC on the slopes of that rock, but they left us alone for the most part. There was the occasional probe on the perimeter and a mortar round now and then but not much else. They had hit the place hard a few times in the past, but Tay Ninh Arty had defensive fires well registered. The Air Force was quick to get air support to protect their assets, so it was costly for Charlie to mess with us.

"Unfortunately, for us at any rate, there was an ambitious ARVN general at the bottom of that mountain with a division of pretty good troops."

With this Jesse stopped him and asked, "Isn't ARVN the South Vietnamese regular army?"

"Yes," answered Bob and he continued. "When this general decided it was time to kick Charlie off the mountain, our shit got weak. With him pushing up from the bottom and every piece of artillery within a dozen miles putting steel on the sides of that rock, things got pretty hairy for us."

"Nowhere for the bad guys to go except up, right into your laps, I guess." Jesse shook his head, "Did they give you any reinforcements?"

"No, but Rocky Top's NCOIC made sure we had plenty of ammo for our personal weapons and the mortar. Lots of frag grenades, some Willy Peter grenades, and lots of C rations. He knew we were in for a shit storm and did what he could for us whenever a resupply bird flew in. Tay Ninh Arty reregistered a lot of their defensive fires, and Rocky Top taught me how to work with them in case he was unable to. He also taught me how to fire the mortar."

"Was this your first time dealing with artillery?"

"No, I had dealt with it quite a bit from the aircraft but never on the ground. A lot of the procedures are the same, but things like visibility and the noise of close in stuff are a lot different."

"How about the Air Force and Vietnamese militia?"

"Oh, the zoomies were OK. Their highers made sure they had ammo and fuel for the generators along with some backup radios, all of which were needed. They kept those little Cessna O2 Forward Air Controllers, we called them FACs, busy hunting targets on the mountainside. They brought in a ground-based FAC to call in close air support, and that was a good thing. Their fast movers dropped lots of iron and napalm on the bad guys, and the C119 Shadow gunships expended beaucoup twenty millimeter cannon ammo on Charlie. If not for all that and our artillery support, we would have been overrun the first night Charlie hit us. The zoomies did fine being zoomies, but they aren't trained for ground combat; that was an issue when we were trying to establish fields of fire and maintain fire discipline. They were pretty nervous but willing, and as long as they had aircraft overhead keeping them busy and keeping their minds off things, they were fine.

"The Ruff Puffs knew it was going to be bad, and they wanted nothing to do with it. As things heated up down the mountain and the fight started getting closer, they began to disappear. Before long, they were down to about a dozen troops. It turned out that this dozen was hardcore. Some old regulars had been in the fight for years but were now in the regional forces due to age or injury, and they knew their shit."

"But no reinforcements. Was there an evacuation plan?"

"I don't know; that stuff was echelons above my pay grade."

Jesse shook his head, "Mm, mm, mm, sometimes you have to wonder about folks. Go on."

"Two or three days after the ARVN started up the mountain, Charlie decided we needed to go. At first, he hit us with a fair-sized probe followed by a pretty strong attack. We managed to hold them off with lots of close in arty and some air support. The Ruff Puffs lost one KIA, and one WIA who needed evacuation. There were a few more light wounds among them, and one of the Air Force weather guys, but that was all."

Jesse asked, "Did they use any preparatory fires?"

"You mean like mortars or rockets?"

"Yes, or artillery?"

"Not the first night, but that changed, and our casualties got worse. We were hit every night for four more nights. Each time they hit us with mortars and RPGs for a half-hour or more before the attack. Rocky Top would start calling in arty trying to put their mortars out of commission, but we had no counter battery radar and couldn't see where they were being fired from, so he had to guess. When we could see where the RPGs were coming from, we used our mortar on those positions.

"Once the ground attack started, I would start working that mortar as fast as I could adjust it, and Rocky Top would start working the arty like a mad man. This was when Rocky Top and the Air Force ground FAC earned their pay. Without them, we would have been history very early on."

Jesse was staring off into the night or maybe into the past, his memory jogged by this story, "All night attacks?"

"At first, but on the sixth or seventh day, they decided to hit us early in the morning. It caught us by surprise, and they were in the wire pretty quick. We had lost about half our Ruff Puffs by this time and one badly wounded zoomie. Most of the rest of us were sporting minor wounds of no consequence except Rocky Top, who was hurt worse than he let on. The biggest problem now was not enough people to effectively man the perimeter without having everybody on line. Only the FAC and Rocky Top were exempt. They were needed on their radios calling in arty and air support. All the rest of us were putting rounds down range or in my case lobbing mortar rounds until they got too close, and I had to switch to my M16.

"Finally, Rocky Top, with the Air Force FAC's approval, who was a captain and the senior rank left on the compound, decided to put the arty on top of our position. It was already danger close, and the only thing left was for us to go to ground while our own artillery pounded the shit out of us. It worked but at a heavy price."

"He called artillery on your own position?"

"Yes."

"I've heard of such things, but I never experienced it. It must have been bad."

"Jesse, it was worse than bad. The plan was for us to get under cover in the bunkers and for arty to use air bursts in a time on target delivery from three batteries. Since we had overhead cover, and Charlie was in the open, it would be worse for him than us, and it was, but it sucked just the same. There were sixteen guns in those three batteries. That T.O.T. was nearly a thousand pounds of explosives that hit within one or two seconds. The noise and concussion were incredible. It was so bad it made you feel nauseous. The arty guys continued to pound the shit out of us with 105 and 155 air bursts. This went on for about fifteen minutes. When it was over, we poked our heads out and began to clear the compound of any bad guys that were left. All we found were dead or dying Commies and some of our own dead."

Bob paused here and took another drink from his jar. "One of our dead was Rocky Top." Bob stopped for a few seconds to gather himself. He took a deep breath and continued. "After he called for the T.O.T. on our position and was waiting for it to impact, he stayed on top and continued to work a fourth battery to keep the pressure on Charlie. When that T.O.T impacted it sounded like the goddamn world was coming to an end, and we could still hear him adjusting fires on the radio. He stayed on top of the command bunker and kept working, calling for more fire, more tubes. then it just went dead. I don't know how he was killed. His body was in bad shape, but I know I owe him my life.

Bob looked at Jesse and said, "He knew what was going to happen to him. He called the mission; he knew that T.O.T. was going to hit while he was working that other line. That son of a bitch saved our asses. No, he did more than that, he saved our lives."

"Sounds like he went above and beyond."

"Yes, he did, not that anybody but us gave a shit."

Jesse sensed something here but decided to let it be for the time being. "What happened then? Did they get you out?"

"No, the fun was just beginning. We had lost another five Ruff Puffs, six Air Force, and Rocky Top, all either dead or badly wounded. We were down to fifteen warm bodies, all of whom were at least slightly wounded but ambulatory and able to handle weapons. We consolidated our position to just the command bunker and the fighting positions around it. It was like the Alamo.

"Captain Johnson, the Air Force ground FAC, called for medevac and requested that we be pulled out or reinforced. This man was no coward. He had worked his ass off exposing himself to enemy fire while directing air strikes, but he knew we were in deep shit and wanted us out of there. He took Rocky Top's loss real hard; they had become pretty close working arty and air together.

"They sent in two medevac birds, and we managed to get the wounded out but not the dead. Then the weather went to shit, and there were no more choppers that day. We moved our dead to a bunker and sealed it shut with sand bags and hunkered down waiting for Charlie. We still had plenty of small arms ammo, grenades, and two of the radios were still up, the FM for arty and the FACs radio, but the mortar was now out of commission. Our shit was as flaky as a box of Wheaties."

Bob took a short break here, lost in his own thoughts. Jesse then said, "Bob, you can finish later if you want."

"No, I'll finish now. I'll try and keep it short. They came back that night and due to shitty weather, we had no air support so it was all on me to call for arty support and whatever small arms fire we could put up. Our position was strong, but they were hammering the shit out of us with mortars and RPGs. They were close using our old fighting positions and bunkers so that artillery could not be brought directly on them without it being on us as well. We had no choice; we had lost about half our remaining folks when Captain Johnson told me to call the arty in on our position again.

"There was nothing fancy this time, no coordinated time on target of air bursts just a shit storm of 105 and 155 millimeter rounds slamming in all over us. Some were air bursts, and some were high-explosive rounds. When they lifted the fire, the compound looked like the moon. All the bad guys were dead, wounded, or gone.

"Some of our guys managed to get into the command bunker after the barrage started but not until everyone had been killed or wounded again either by Charlie or our own artillery. All of us were dead except two Ruff Puffs, one Air Force weather guy, Captain Johnson, who was hurt pretty bad, and me. One of the Ruff Puffs was bad hurt and died within ten or fifteen minutes; the other was not too bad.

"Captain Johnson told me to destroy the radios, CEOIs or code books, extra ammunition and the weapons. He told me to leave him and a rifle with enough ammo to make a short fight of it, and to get the other Air Force guy out of there. He also gave me an aircrew survival radio he had. I agreed to everything but leaving him. The Air Force guy, a young kid named Kocsis, patched up Johnson while the Ruff Puff and I gathered up what we could carry and stuck all the rest in the command bunker. After stacking all the weapons and radios on top of the small arms ammo, 81 millimeter mortar ammo, grenades, and the few claymores that were left, I burned the CEOIs. I had capped one of the claymores at the bottom of the pile hoping it would set off the rest of the heavy stuff.

"We gathered up what we could carry along with the Captain, who had a bad foot and needed a shoulder to lean on. When we reached the end of the claymore detonation wire, I had Kocsis and the Vietnamese guy take Captain Johnson to an old observation post outside the wire to wait for me. I hoped Charlie was not using it. Once they were gone, I found some cover and squeezed the firing device. It worked. That bunker went up with a big bang, and I hauled ass to the outpost where I found the others waiting. We then slipped out into the night. We needed a place to hide until the weather cleared enough for us to call for a chopper."

Jesse shook his head again, "Mm, mm, mm, just four of you made it out."

"Just four. The rest were dead or medevaced. The Ruff Puff had been on the mountain for quite a while and knew his way around. He took us to a spot where we could hide. It was a rock overhang behind some brush that looked like it might keep us hidden and was far enough from our old compound that we should be clear of any artillery or air strikes that friendlies might want to put on it.

"Kocsis, Tran the Vietnamese guy, and I took turns keeping watch while Captain Johnson worked the radio. He got somebody on guard pretty quick. They decided he should come up every two hours to monitor for messages or sooner if he had an emergency."

Bob looked at Jesse and grinned sardonically, "I guess we weren't quite ready to declare an emergency just yet."

Jesse chuckled, "Seems so."

"That was the longest night of my life. When it ended, the sky was still overcast and there was a light rain now and then, but nothing too bad. It looked like we were going to be stuck there for a while.

"Captain Johnson was starting to get feverish. He had several small shrapnel wounds in the arms and legs that were of no real concern and one in his foot that broke some bones, but the one in his abdomen seemed to be causing him the most trouble. The pain in his gut was getting worse."

Jesse said, "Abdominal wounds are bad. If the gut is perforated, the infection can be very painful and fatal."

"We decided to stay put; for all we knew the mountain was crawling with bad guys, and we seemed to be pretty safe where we were. One thing we did was push some rocks and dirt up in front of the opening to make a small berm for protection; it wasn't much, but it was better than nothing.

"The fight below us was getting louder. It seemed as if the ARVN might just make it to the top of the Rock and rescue us, but it did not happen that day. The next day Captain Johnson was in real bad shape, but he hung on and kept in touch on GUARD with our would-be rescuers. We did not know it at the time, but the ARVN really were trying to get to us. They were told about our GUARD transmissions and were trying to get through.

"It was now that Tran really earned his pay. He had already found us a good hiding place, and now he went out and scouted the area. While he was out, he also found some rice and dried fish and brought it back to us. He told us that the fight below was not getting any closer, so we knew we were stuck for a while longer.

"Kocsis and I took turns going out with Tran on his scouts. He was trying to get us familiar with the area and show us how not to be total klutzes in the boonies. He also improved our position making it stronger. He was a great help.

"We were just starting our third day hiding out when a VC carrying party stumbled on us. They were heavily loaded down with supplies and not well armed, but there were a dozen of them and only the four of us. The fire fight was quick but brutal. We went through over a dozen grenades and hundreds of rounds of ammo. When the smoke cleared, the VC had pulled out leaving half a dozen dead behind. We lost Tran, and Kocsis had been shot in the leg.

"We figured our time had about run out when Captain Johnson, who was just barely conscious, got excited talking on the radio. The weather had broken, and a chopper was on the way in to get us.

"The bird couldn't land so he had to extract us one at a time using a jungle penetrator. We sent up Captain Johnson first since he was the worst off. He argued, but we didn't listen; we just strapped him on and sent him up. Just as the penetrator was coming back down our VC buddies returned. Kocsis and I put as much fire on them as we could, and they pulled back. I got Kocsis on the penetrator, and when he started up Charlie started shooting at him. I went through a lot of rounds trying to keep their heads down, but Kocsis was in a bad position and so was the chopper. As soon as he cleared the tree canopy, the chopper flew off a little ways until he was aboard.

"While this was going on, Charlie started shooting towards me. I don't think they had me in sight, but they were shooting too close for comfort. I could hear them moving and talking as they got closer. Because of the terrain, there was only one way for them to approach so I waited, trying to decide whether to leave or wait for the chopper. All this took only a minute or so, but it seemed like forever.

"The chopper came back, and as soon as it started lowering the penetrator, Charlie opened up on it. That really pissed me off. That was my ride out, and these assholes were trying to run it off. I guess I went a little crazy. I had a bunch of frags left in a claymore bag, and I started throwing them as fast as I could pull the pins. I must have had three or four on the way by the time the first one went off. Then I charged, screaming my ass off and firing as fast as I could reload.

"I don't know what all happened, but it got quiet on their end, so I hauled ass back to the pickup point and got the hell out of there."

Jesse thought about this for a while, "That's quite a story. You should be proud."

"All I did was stay alive."

"Have it your way. Why don't you think you'll get the award?"

"When I got back, I tried to have Rocky Top put in for a Congressional Medal of Honor, but his chain of command nixed it. Seems he had really pissed off somebody back there before being sent up on the Rock, and he wasn't getting shit. So I tried for a DSC or Silver Star. I made a real pain in the ass out of myself until finally my own chain of command told me to let it go, but I didn't. When they told me he would get nothing, I told them to give him mine. He earned it more than I did.

"Finally, just before I came home, I was told Rocky Top was getting an Army Commendation Medal with V device. What a load of shit! I threw a fit, and I guess that was the end of my award. Fuck 'em if they can't take a joke."

"An ARCOM with V device? That's like a perfect attendance medal for Sunday School. People don't knowingly sacrifice their lives for others and get ARCOMs; they get Silver Stars or better."

"Who put you in for the DSC?"

"Captain Johnson submitted it from the hospital in Japan; he also endorsed Rocky Top's recommendation and added his write up."

"Does your uncle or your father know any of this?"

"My dad knows about Rocky Top and has tried to help, but I didn't tell him of the details about me, and all Uncle Jack knows is that I was put in for a DSC. I haven't told him anything."

"I bet you have a copy of the Captain's recommendation."

Bob looked at Jesse cautiously, "Yes."

"Can I see it?"

"What are you going to do with it?"

Jesse answered this as reassuringly as he could, "Just read it. I want to see what the Captain had to say. I'd like to see Rocky Top's, too. Is that OK?"

Bob took a deep breath. The war seemed to be yesterday one minute and ancient history the next. He wondered if it would ever end, but here he was sitting next to this old First Sergeant spilling his guts. Then he thought this old soldier put up with more shit in the segregated Army than I will ever know, and he still served his country for thirty years. He has earned the right to see whatever he wants. "Sure, it's in the bunk house. I'll get it for you."

"Just so you know, young man, I am going to tell your uncle about this. He knows the real deal and will understand. Besides he needs to know who he has on the mountain dealing with that bunch to the east."

Bob was resigned to the fact that his secret was out, "OK. That's fine."

CHAPTER THIRTEEN

"Hasta luego soldado." Carlos

Bob felt really good. The fall works were over, the wagon crew was gone, and he had a couple of days off. Best of all he was on his way to town to pick up Angelina for the big dance.

When Bob arrived at Angelina's home, her mother showed him to the guest room, so he could put up his things for the night. Then they went to the living room where Mr. Slaughter offered him a beer, and they made small talk waiting for Angelina. The conversation consisted mostly of the Slaughters asking Bob questions about the ranch work, but he managed to ask a few questions of his own about their lives. His mother had tried to teach him that folks want to learn about you, but they are usually flattered if you show an interest in their lives as well. He really wanted to impress these people. He was quite taken with their daughter and did not want them to disapprove of him.

When Angelina came into the room, she looked stunning. Bob thought wow she is a true beauty, and he thanked his lucky stars that she liked him. She was taller than most of the girls he had dated, about five feet six or seven inches, and she had what he figured was the perfect body slim waist, nice hips, and ample breast. All this was topped off with a face of classic beauty. Her high cheek bones were complemented by perfect skin, green eyes, and full lips, all framed with dark hair. What's more, she knew how to dress. She was wearing a simple black dress that showed off her assets to advantage. It was made of a fine material that was slightly clingy and had just enough of a plunge in the neckline to show a little cleavage but not so much that her father would be able to veto her choice.

Bob was breathless. "Angelina, you look great. I hope you're not embarrassed to be seen with a plain old waddie like me."

She smiled with confidence, "You're silly. I don't ask plain old waddies to accompany me to dances." Bob laughed nervously. They made their goodbyes to her parents and headed out to the truck.

Jack had loaned Bob the new ranch truck, and Bob had taken quite a bit of time to get it all cleaned up. Now he was wishing he had rented a car, something nice. "Sorry about the truck, I hope you don't mind too much."

"Don't worry, Bob, it's fine." Looking around she added, "This will be the nicest truck at the dance and the cleanest, too." She slid over next to him and gave him a peck on the cheek and took his hand. Bob was in heaven.

Angelina had made them reservations for dinner at the Gadsden Hotel, a fine old hotel that seemed out of place in this little border town. Her friends were going to reserve a big table for several couples and asked her to bring Bob and join them, but she wanted some time alone with Bob and had reserved a table for just the two of them. When they arrived, they were given a table in a secluded corner.

Soon after they were seated, a gentleman came up to the table and greeted Angelina. "Hi, Angelina, you're looking very nice this evening." Then looking towards Bob, "Is this the young man I've been hearing about?"

She stood up and gave him a hug, "Yes, this is Bob Hasett." Then to Bob, "Bob, this is my Uncle Gilbert Elias."

Bob stood up and took the hand Gilbert offered, "How do you do?"

"Very well, thank you," answered Gilbert. "How about you?"

"I'm doing well. Will you join us?"

"Just for a moment." Then Gilbert motioned a waiter over who had been standing by with a bottle of Champagne on ice. The waiter opened the bottle and poured each of them a glass. "My not-anymore-so-little niece deserves a toast on this night." Raising his glass he said, "To beauty and young love...Salud!"

Angelina blushed, and Bob looked at her a little self-consciously. Raising his glass he repeated, "Salud!"

They talked a bit, and Gilbert made some dinner suggestions which they accepted; then he excused himself, "I need to get back to work. Enjoy your evening." Looking at Bob, "Take good care of this young lady; she is special."

"I will."

Bob and Angelina enjoyed their meal, but neither was paying much attention to the food. They were absorbed in each other, talking, laughing, and gazing into each other's eyes. Bob had not felt this way about a girl since before the Army and maybe not even then.

After dinner, they stopped at the big table and had a quick chat with Suzie and a large bunch of Angelina's friends. Suzie teased them and said they looked like a couple of lovesick puppies. "It's just plain embarrassing," she said. "I could feel the heat from over here."

Bob blushed, and Angelina said, "Now Suzie...be nice."

Suzie smiled and said, "See you at the dance."
When they turned to leave, Bob was set back a little when he spotted three of the men, he had seen at Indian Springs Ranch. There were the two from the first day at the corral and Alf, the foreman. They were seated at a table that Bob and Angelina would have to pass on their way out, and they had already spotted Bob and Angelina.

Bob tried to ignore them, but he could tell they were watching and was afraid they would say something. Just as he and Angelina were about to pass the table where the three men sat, Alf got to his feet and stepped in front of Bob. "Hi, cowboy, I haven't seen you in a while." He had what Bob could only think of as a shit-eating grin on his face.

"I've been busy, Alf, how about you?" Bob was not going to be rude, but he wanted this over fast.

"We've been busy ourselves." Now he indicated the other two men. "I believe you've met my camp men."

Bob gave them a nod, "We've met. How're you doing?"

The one that had had the loud mouth at their first meeting stood up and cast an eye on Angelina, "Oh, we've been busy. You going to introduce us to this fine thing?" Then looking at Angelina he said, "Hi, I'm Arturo, my friends call me Artie. You don't want to hang out with this hayseed, beautiful. Join us, and you and I can have some real fun." Artie was determined to show up this hick. It wasn't about her, it was about stealing this cowboy's girl. He winked at her and stared at her breasts.

Bob felt his blood rise instantly. He stepped in front of Angelina and placed his left hand on Artie's shoulder pushing him back slightly, causing him to struggle for balance with the back of his legs pressed against his chair. When Artie tried to pull away, Bob squeezed harder, and leaned him back a little more causing him even more balance problems. Leaning over, Bob whispered in his ear, "Back the fuck off, shit bag."

Alf was getting a litttle excited and said, "OK, guys, let's stop all this. No need for trouble here tonight. Artie, you apologize to this nice, young lady for being such a jerk."

"OK, sorry, Sweet Thing."

"You can let him go, cowboy; he's not going to start nothin'."

When Bob released his grip and stepped back, Artie regained his balance and said, "We'll meet again, hayseed." Then craning his neck to look around Bob at Angelina, he added with a wink and a leering grin as he looked her over from top to bottom, pausing significantly at her breasts, "You, too, good looking. I look forward to getting to know you much better."

Bob felt his face flush, and before he knew it he had Artie against the wall gripping him by the Adam's apple. He was pulling his knife from his pocket, when he realized he was about to lose it; that's when he remembered what Uncle Jack had said about not losing control when dealing with an opponent. This was no time for emotion. This was a time for calm, cool thinking and if necessary, deadly action.

As the cold, empty look came into his eyes, pushing out the angry fire that had been there briefly, he stepped in closer to Artie, lifting him up to his tiptoes. This required Artie to use both hands to lift himself, holding Bob's wrist in order to keep from choking. Bob sank his fingertips a little deeper into Artie's throat and gave him a slight twitch, ensuring he had his full attention and softly said, "If you want to live, you'll stay clear of me and mine. I've killed far better men than you for far less. I won't hesitate to crush you like the meaningless, little bug that you are." Then he lowered Artie and let go of his throat. During all this he had kept one eye on the quiet man letting him know he was not forgotten. As Artie struggled for breath and Alf tried to help him, the quiet one gave Bob a nod towards the door that said, go, I won't interfere this time. Bob took Angelina's arm, guiding her out of the room, keeping between her and the Indian Springs men.

† † †

Angelina was concerned. She did not know these men but thought she may have seen them around town a time or two. They were unsavory for sure and doing a bad job of trying to pass as cowboys, but she had just thought they must be dudes or dude wranglers from some guest ranch. What she just saw told her something different.

She had seen something in Bob that surprised her. Every girl wants a man who's willing to defend her, but what was in his eyes when they left the Gadsden was different. It was cold, empty, and primitive. She really believed he would have killed those men and never given it a second thought. She shivered a little at this. She wondered who those men were, and who was this man beside her in the truck? Finally, she decided to break the silence. "Bob, what was all that? Who are they?"

Bob had sensed that Angelina was not comfortable. It must have been a trying experience for her. Artie's slimy behavior would have upset any woman. "They're from the Indian Springs Ranch east of Uncle Jack's place."

"They're not cowboys, who are they?"

Bob considered this for a moment and then decided to fill her in on all he knew. She may have to deal with these assholes in the future, and forewarned is forearmed. "They're Drug dealers, they're growing pot on the ranch up in the mountains and may be doing more. They're from back East, some place around New Jersey or New York. Uncle Jack has been having some problems with them. They're not tending to their cattle and fences so we're having to deal with that. One day Cruz and I had a run-in with that Artie and the quiet guy sitting next to him after taking a bunch of their cattle back to them."

Angelina thought about this for a little while. "Suzie said her father had warned her about some bad men. He wouldn't tell her much, just to stay away from anybody from Indian Springs. He said something about you two having a confrontation with some of them. Are they dangerous?"

Bob thought about this for a bit and answered in depth. "I can't answer for Alf, the one that first stopped us on the way out. He's the foreman. I've had very little to do with him, but he is the number two guy on the place. I imagine his boss didn't pick him for being a wimp."

"Artie thinks he is a badass, and I expect he tries to live up to that, but he's a bully. Like other bullies, I am sure he can be cruel but only when he has the advantage. He will back down from a direct confrontation with anybody he feels is not weak, but I would never turn my back on him."

"The quiet guy is the one I'd be worried about. He is all business no fuss: no brag, just serious business."

Bob and Angelina were at the college now. Bob pulled into a parking lot and was looking for a spot up close to the door, but Angelina asked him to park away from the building. He was about to get out when she said, "Don't get out just yet. I want to talk."

"OK, let's talk." Bob was getting nervous. Had he done something wrong? Had he said something to upset her? "Are you OK?"

Angelina wasn't really sure what she wanted to talk about, she was just sure she didn't want to deal with a bunch of people at the dance right now. The way that man had looked at her made her skin crawl. Like most pretty women, she was aware of having been mentally undressed by some uncouth would-be Lotharios, but this was different. This was scary. "Bob, he scared me. He made me feel dirty."

He looked at her and could see she was really bothered. He wanted to reach out to her and hold her, but he was afraid it might be the wrong thing to do. "Angelina, he won't hurt you. He's all smoke."

She sounded a little cross when she answered, "That's easy for you to say. You're not the one he just mentally raped!"

Bob was totally taken aback. He knew what a shit Artie was, and he knew Angelina was right about him, but he was surprised that she recognized what had happened so clearly. She had seen that he was really a threat. "Angelina, I'm sorry. I should have taken him out right there. I'm sorry."

She was really exasperated now, "Oh, Bob, shut up! Just hold me."

He was holding her close. She had her head buried in his chest, feeling the strength of his arms around her and beginning to feel better; yet she was troubled. There was something about this young man that was upsetting to her, maybe it was that cold emptiness she had seen at the Gadsden. She had sensed danger was very close at hand. She knew he posed no threat to her, and in fact, she knew he was protecting her, but this was not a schoolboy fight over a girl. There had been murder in the air, she had felt it, she had seen it in his face. She was a little unsure, maybe even a little afraid of him, and yet she felt she could trust him. "Bob, you were different back there. I've never seen that before."

He didn't answer at first. He was trying to figure out what she had seen that bothered her so. He knew he got cold when danger approached or he was really pissed. It was something he had picked up in Vietnam, probably on Nui Ba Din. But how had she picked up on it? "I wasn't different, just serious, I guess." He hoped this was enough of an answer. It wasn't.

"You said you'd killed better men for less. What was that about?"

"I meant in combat. I killed men I'd never met and had nothing against personally. I'm sure some of them were decent guys, which you can't say for our friend, Artie."

She accepted this answer. Whatever it was she had seen in him; Artie had seen it too, and it had backed him down. She was grateful for that. She decided she was safe here with Bob.

† † †

They sat out in the truck for quite a while before going into the dance. After touching up her makeup, they went in. Once inside, Suzie spotted them and came hurrying over with her date. "Wow, Bob, I don't know what those guys did to you at the Gadsden, but you sure stirred up a hornet's nest." Now she addressed Angelina, "Your Uncle Gilbert had words with them, and they left. I'm not sure what all he said, but we did hear him tell them not to come back."

Suzie's date was looking at Bob with something akin to wonder on his face. Sucking up his nerve, he said, "Man, you picked that guy up by the throat with one hand. I've seen him around, he's a real badass, and nobody has ever put him in his place before. Suzie said you were in the Army; what were you, some kind of green beret or something?"

All this annoyed Bob. He was pretty sure it would just upset Angelina, and he didn't want that. He had been looking forward to a nice evening with Angelina not all this damned drama. Suzie was prattling on excitedly about something to Angelina, but Bob wasn't paying any attention. He looked at Suzie's date and tried to be polite. "He's no badass, just a bully, and no, I wasn't Special Forces or any of that. I was just a plain, old doggie. Next time Artie tries to throw his weight around, just stand up to him. Watch out for his quiet sidekick though, he could be dangerous."

The young man just stood there looking stupid. Bob smiled and excused himself and asked Angelina if she would like to dance. She accepted gratefully.

It was a slow tune, the band was doing its best with one of the Righteous Brothers' belly grinders that all the guys liked, but they weren't the Righteous Brothers, and the wall of sound just wasn't there. What was there was a brief spell of privacy for Bob and Angelina. They didn't really dance; they just sort of swayed with the music. "I'm sorry for all this," he said.

"Don't be. It's part of living in a small town. By tomorrow it will be common knowledge."

"Great," Bob murmured.

"Let's just enjoy ourselves."

"Good idea, let's."

They stayed for about an hour dancing some and socializing some. Angelina introduced Bob to her friends and a couple of her cousins, all of whom were nice enough. Then as they were leaving, a young man approached them. Angelina introduced him as an old family friend named Carlos. Carlos was taking classes at the college but also was a cop in Douglas.

Carlos had something on his mind. He led Bob away from Angelina. "I want to talk to you about what happened this evening at the Gadsden."

Bob felt himself start to go cold as he pulled way back into his defensive shell, but when he looked into Carlos's eyes, he saw something he recognized. Looking for confirmation, he saw the jump wings tattooed on his forearm where he had rolled up his sleeve. "Airborne?" he asked.

"Yeah, 82nd from '66–'69. I deployed with the third brigade to Vietnam. You?"

"Army Aviation down south, Three Corps, Four Corps, and a lot of Cambodia."

"You bastards were crazy."

"That's what we said about you guys. What is it, you need to tell me, Carlos?" Bob was more relaxed now.

"That bunch you got tangled up with this evening is bad. I don't know you, but I know Angelina and her family. Her brother and I went to high school together. They're good people; they would never be mixed up with the likes of these guys. Are you involved with them in any way?"

Bob believed Carlos was genuinely worried about Angelina. "No, Cruz Solano and I had a run-in with two of them in the mountains when we were working cattle. Other than that we had to take some of their strays back to them, but that's all. We try to avoid them."

"Were they working cattle?" asked Carlos looking for a slip-up that might blow Bob's story.

Bob chuckled, "The only time these guys mess with a cow is after it's cooked. There isn't a one of them on that place that knows which end the feed goes in or the fertilizer comes out. Cows are not their business, just their cover."

"Carlos looked relieved. "Do you know what they're up to?"

Bob knew his uncle did not want him saying anything about his suspicions, but Bob was in a bad spot here. "I don't know anything for sure, but there is a lot of money on that place in buildings and vehicles and nothing being spent on the cattle operation. All I can say for sure is Cruz and I saw a field where somebody was growing pot on their forest allotment."

Carlos thanked Bob and took him back over to where Angelina was waiting patiently. "Angelina, be careful, if these guys from earlier ever give you any grief, you tell me pronto. By the way, your uncle thinks this guy here is some sort of hero. He told me how he stood up for you tonight."

"Tonight, he's *my* hero, and thank you, Carlos. We'll be fine."

Carlos took Bob by the hand and said, "Take care of this girl, she's special."

Bob smiled at Carlos and said quietly so no one else could hear. "Yes, she is. I won't let anything happen to her."

As they walked off, Carlos called after them, "Hasta luego soldado."

"Hasta pronto, amigo," answered Bob. This put a smile on Carlos's face.

CHAPTER FOURTEEN

"By the stacking swivel" Jack Barnes

It was Sunday afternoon; Bob was driving back to the ranch after spending a great weekend with Angelina. After the dance, they had stopped at the Dairy Queen for some ice cream and then gone on back to her house. She lived across the street from 8th Street Park, so they had gone over there and sat on a bench under the stars enjoying each other's company.

They had talked a lot. Each wanted to know about the other, and so lots of questions were asked about growing up and family. Angelina seemed genuinely interested in Bob's background. She had not known anybody who had lived all over the world and hung on Bob's descriptions of childhood in Alaska and Okinawa.

"Don't you miss not having a home town?" she had asked.

"No, I don't think so. Every Army post I go on is my home town. There is always reveille and the evening gun. These are the things I remember, and the cadence calls of troops in formation is a memory that goes back as far as I can remember. Even the sound of shooting on distant ranges is comforting."

"Do you miss it?"

"I'm not sure, maybe, but I sure like the quiet of the ranch. So, do you see yourself living anywhere but Douglas?" he asked.

"Yes, I think so. I plan to go to the University of Arizona in Tucson to finish my Bachelor's Degree. After that I think I might like to work in a big city like Tucson or Phoenix." Then she gave his hand a squeeze, "If I meet the right guy, I might live on top of a mountain or across the ocean."

This caused Bob's heart to miss a beat. He had been convinced since dinner that he had fallen in love with this woman, but he knew it was too soon, and he didn't dare to hope that she was beginning to feel the same way. They barely knew each other. They had only been out together three times, if you counted the horseback ride with Suzie.

He looked at her in the dim light of the crescent moon and saw that she was not making fun or talking in abstracts. She was serious. He couldn't think of a thing to say that wasn't stupid. He just looked at her and stammered until she leaned over and gave him a kiss, a long passionate kiss.

They had stayed out on the bench for a long time making out like a couple of high schoolers. The kissing and hugging were accompanied by furtive touches and caresses, all of which were well received. Finally, Angelina said, "We need to go inside. I'm sure Mrs. Gonzalez is already on the phone with Mom telling her we're making out in the park." She hesitated here and added, "Bob, I am head over heels stupid for you. I have never felt like this before."

It was his turn now. He held her close and whispered in her ear, "I love you, Angelina."

What a night that had been.

Before he knew it, he was pulling back into the ranch headquarters. All he wanted was to go back to town and spend more time with Angelina.

† † †

He put his AWOL bag in the bunk house and went to see Uncle Jack and Aunt Maria. Crossing the yard, he saw a few extra vehicles parked by the house. He recognized Cruz's truck and Suzie's car but not the Bronco. He thought nothing of it; Sunday company he supposed. Before he got to the door Jack stepped out on the porch and welcomed him. "Good afternoon, Bob, come in for some coffee and pie. You have a visitor."

"I do? Who would visit me?"

"Deputy Judson, remember him?"

Bob was at a loss then he remembered the sheriff's deputy he had saluted with the beer. "Sure, the fella that pulled us over."

"That's the one."

Bob stopped on the porch, "Is something wrong?" His defenses were starting to come up.

"No, he just wants to ask you some questions about the bunch over the mountain."

"Jeez, word travels fast around here. Is there anybody that hasn't heard about that mess at the Gadsden?"

"One or two, but they're on vacation," Jack chuckled at his own joke. "Bob, that confrontation happened in a public place. It involved some unsavory characters, one of the town's sweethearts, and a cowboy. On top of that Suzie was there, and she isn't exactly the quiet type."

"Uncle Jack, a cop from Douglas confronted me about it and asked about the Indian Springs bunch. I didn't offer anything, but I didn't lie. I told him what I knew.

"That's OK, Bob. I never wanted to hide what was happening, I just didn't want anyone going off and blabbing about it. You did fine, now let's go inside."

Suzie had filled everybody in on the run-in with the Indian Springs men and left nothing to the imagination. When Bob and Jack entered the living room, it got quiet. Bob said hello. Cruz stood up and walked over to him. Grasping his right hand and putting his other around Bob's shoulder, he gave him a big hug. "I told you only one thing, compadre; be careful."

"Gracias, Cruz, I will be careful."

Suzie came up to Bob and said, "I have to get back to the dorm and study for a test; I guess I'll see you next time you're in town. That shouldn't be long," she said with a wink, then gave him a quick hug and excused herself.

Maria brought Bob some coffee and a slice of apple pie then retired to the kitchen. This left Bob, Jack, Cruz, and Deputy Tommy Judson sitting in the living room.

Bob decided he was not going to open the conversation and took a bite of his pie.

Tommy then asked about the incident in the Gadsden. Bob told him about it but left out some of the details.

Jack butted in, "Bob, according to Suzie and other accounts we've been hearing, you lifted that bastard by the stacking swivel. She said she had never seen anybody as white as he was when you put him down."

"Suzie exaggerated; besides he is a pale son of a bitch on his best day."

Judson asked about Indian Springs. His questions were simple and to the point. Bob told him nothing he had not told Carlos the night before. Cruz corroborated Bob's story about the run in on the mountain, and Jack told what he knew and some of what he suspected. The deputy rose to leave and thanked them for their cooperation adding that he had better get home for dinner. His wife did not look kindly on him giving up family time for work.

Later that night Bob was lying on his bunk hoping for some sleep but hoping in vain. Thinking back he rehashed the conversation with the deputy. It all seemed like "much ado about nothing" to borrow a quote.

Jack had walked him back to the bunkhouse after everybody had gone and asked a few questions about his visit to town. Some were about the run-in, but many were just about his date with Angelina. Jack gave a sigh and said, "Young man, I believe you're smitten by this young woman."

Bob couldn't deny it, "Yes, I expect I am. Any advice?"

"No, it's too late now; you're done for. You might just as well try to push a limp rope as save yourself from your fate. If she has set her cap for you, you haven't got a chance. Just get ahold of the padre and get it over with."

"We just met. I think you're rushing things a bit."

"Did she say she liked you?"

"Yes."

"Did she say any more than that?"

"Yes."

"What?"

"She said something about following the right guy anywhere."

"And are you that guy?"

"She said so."

With this Jack Barnes let out a belly laugh. "It's a good thing you have the mountain camp. You're going to need the room for all the kids you two will be populating the countryside with." He slapped Bob on the knee. "Good on you, Bob. She is a fine young woman and comes from two of the finest families on either side of this border."

Bob was a little embarrassed by all this, but he was glad to share his good feelings with his uncle. He had some reservations, however: "Will her family accept me? I'm an outsider and a Protestant."

"You're no outsider; you're my nephew, and as far as religion goes her father is Catholic for convenience, and I don't know that her mother would object. You are, after all, something of a catch."

"I'm no catch; hell, I'm damaged goods."

"Oh, you're wrong. There's two things that make you a catch. One, you're a genuine war hero, and now that you stood down those ruffians, you're a local hero, as well. Two, you're my nephew. Tres Cruses is the largest ranch in the area, and Maria and I have no heirs. Considering that, you start looking pretty good."

"Oh, Uncle Jack, I'm not going to inherit this outfit. You have other kin, and I figured Aunt Maria would want it to go to the church, if nothing else."

"One never knows."

CHAPTER FIFTEEN

"Men are such idiots." Angelina Slaughter

Bob had been at Mountain Camp on his own for a couple of months. He was very busy with all he had to do: prowling the cattle to check for problems, looking after the waters, pulling the occasional cow out of a dirt tank when she got bogged in the mud, and keeping mineral and salt out. He was also busy pushing cows up the mountains and ridge tops so they could utilize that feed before any snow might push them back down to the canyon floor.

In spite of his busy schedule, he was still managing to see Angelina once or twice a week. Jack had said it was OK as long as the work got done, and he was letting Bob take the old ranch truck that stayed at Mountain Camp as long as he put some gas in it from time to time. At first Jack was a little concerned that Bob was in town too much, but all the work was getting done, so he had no complaints. The only thing he wondered about was when did Bob sleep?

Bob was sitting on Mumford watching a bunch of cows graze a ridge top. He had spent the better part of the morning pushing them up to this spot where there was lots of unused feed. They seemed content, and he and Mumford were parked on the only trail that led back down unless the cows wanted to walk a few miles, and that didn't seem to be in their thoughts.

He stepped down and loosened the cinch on his saddle then raised the rear of it off Mumford's back to give him a little break. Mumford was not the brightest horse on the ranch. In fact, he was just plain dumb, but he was honest. Aside from the habit of trying to bite whoever was drawing his cinch tight or ringing your spur rowels with his back feet if he thought you were taking him through too much thorny brush, he was OK. He covered ground pretty fast at a walk or low trot, and he didn't buck. Jack said it was because he was too dumb to buck, and that if he tried, he'd just get tangled up in those long legs and fall over.

While standing next to Mumford and propping the saddle up to cool his back, Bob watched the cows as his mind wandered to Angelina, as it often did. They had been seeing each other for a few months now, and things had gotten pretty serious since the big dance. Neither of them had spoken directly about getting married, but it was certainly there. He wondered if he should go ahead and pop the question. It seemed a bit redundant since they seemed to be taking it for granted that a wedding was in their future, and it was really sappy, but he had learned that Angelina seemed to like sappy. He had also learned that doing those little sappy things paid big dividends. He smiled, remembering.

"Oh, Mumford, here we are on top of this mountain watching a bunch of cows chew their cud. I guess it's better than watching grass grow, but it sure doesn't hold a candle to what I could be doing with Angelina right now." Bob and Angelina had not had sex, at least not intercourse, but there had been a lot of kissing, heavy petting, and groping, but it always stopped just short of the real thing. "You may be lucky they cut your nuts off, at least you don't have to deal with blue balls. Don't misunderstand me, you old caballo, I don't want to trade places with you, but I sure hate going to that empty house at night. It was easier being alone before I met her." Bob looked at his horse who was busy chewing some grass. "You haven't been listening to a word I said." Mumford turned and looked at Bob as if to say, nope. Bob laughed.

After holding the cattle in place for another hour, Bob headed back down to Mountain Camp. Since he was making dinner for Angelina tonight, he needed to be sure the house was neat and everything was just right. She was coming out to visit him for a change. He was pretty excited about this.

Getting the house ready was no big deal as he kept it pretty straight anyway. Living in army barracks for two years had reinforced what his mother had taught him about picking up after himself. It was easier to keep it straightened out than to have to clean up a week's worth of mess.

Dinner, on the other hand, was a bit trickier. He was marinating some beef cuts that he hoped weren't too tough. The old cow that was killed for the ranch beef last time around had seen better days; even the good cuts were pretty chewy. He hoped the marinade would serve its purpose and tenderize the meat a little.

He was going to do some baked potatoes and green beans on the side. He had salad fixings if she wanted any, but he had opted out of pie for dessert. He knew that would be a disaster, so he had ice cream instead. When he had done all he could to prepare, he took a quick shower and put on clean clothes.

Angelina showed up right on time at five o'clock. Bob met her with a big smile and was rewarded with a big kiss. He led her into the house pulling out a chair at the kitchen table for her. "Would you like a glass of wine?"

"Yes."

"I hope it's OK; I'm not much of a wine connoisseur," he said as he poured her a glass of rosé. "I know a red is called for with beef, but I thought you might like this better. It's a bit lighter." Bob was having trouble keeping the nervousness out of his voice. They had seen a lot of each other, but this was new. They were alone, and there was no one around to interrupt. They had the evening all to themselves.

"I'm sure it's fine."

"They clinked glasses and drank a silent toast."

Bob had put the potatoes in the oven and got the mesquite going on the grill for the steaks. Angelina had come outside and sat on the porch watching the sunset behind the mountains that bordered the canyon on the west sipping on her wine while Bob tended the fire.

When he figured he had monkeyed with the fire long enough Bob came over and sat beside Angelina. It would be a little while before the mesquite had burned down to coals, and he took the opportunity to relax. "Nice sunset tonight."

"Yes, it is. I love these sunsets. I wonder, do they have sunsets like this in other places?"

"I have lived from Germany to the Far East. I have seen some pretty nice sunsets but not like here. Here they're not just now and then, they're so common we almost take them for granted." Looking to the west, he added, "It's like the sky's on fire. Here the colors are brighter, more intense, alive. It's as if the sunsets are trying to impress."

"Who are they trying to impress?"

"I don't know . . . God maybe." Bob said this with some trepidation, not sure how Angelina would react to him bringing God into the discussion.

"My aunt said they are God's masterpiece."

"I like that."

"I'd like to travel like you have someday."

Bob swallowed hard and braced himself. "Angelina, I can take you to those places."

"How?" she asked.

"I could go to college and get a commission through ROTC, and then we could travel the world." His heart was pounding so hard he could feel it in his temples.

She sat quietly for a moment and then looking a little amused asked, "Are you asking me to marry you, or am I to be a kept woman?"

Now he was really in a mess. Taking a deep breath to calm his nerves he said, "Yes, I mean no." Now he was in a real jackpot. "I mean I'd never ask you to be a kept woman."

This was followed by a long, pregnant silence. Bob was sure he had just screwed the pooch on this one; this was worse than being surrounded by a bunch of bad guys trying to kill you. Angelina was wondering, are all men this dumb? Her aunt said they were.

Bob decided something had to be done, so he took the risk of making even a bigger mess of things. "Angelina, will you marry me?" Bob was terrified. They had known each other for less than four months. She might say anything but yes, and he was sure he was about to go down in flames.

She took his hand with a soft smile and said, "Yes, of course. I thought you'd never ask."

The tension dropped like a lead weight off his shoulders. He was giddy with relief. "I never thought you'd say yes."

"Men are such idiots. I love you Bob Hasett, even if you are a bit slow."

Later that night they were lying in bed. Angelina had decided earlier that if Bob asked her to marry him that she would not stop at making out. Her parents were out of town, and she had told her aunt that she was staying with Suzie and her folks for the weekend. She wanted it to be like this, not in the back seat of a car or the front seat of the old ranch truck.

She was looking at him lying next to her as the moonlight cast a dim glow through the window. The only other light was from the propane fire in the wall heater. She could sense that Bob was awake, "Bob?" Passing her fingers over some raised scars on his belly, "What are these?"

"Wounds."

"Do they hurt?"

"Not anymore."

She rolled over to him and pulled him close. "My poor baby, I'll keep you safe."

† † †

The weekend had gone way too quickly. Before they realized it, it was time for Angelina to go back home. Her parents were due in from Las Vegas late that night, and she needed to be there when they arrived.

They made plans to go to Tucson the coming Saturday to get a ring. Once it was on her finger, they would make the announcement.

"Bob, are you going home for Christmas?"

"Yeah, I already have my ticket. I want to stay here with you, but Mom really wants me home this year. I missed last Christmas."

"I wish you could stay, too."

"I know, why don't you come out with me?"

"I can't do that. Mom and Dad expect me to be here. Christmas is hard on them since my brother's gone."

Bob thought about this for a minute, "I get it. You need to stay." Bob paused here and then said, "I've got an idea, why don't you come out for a few days around New Years. We can fly back together. I'd like you to meet my folks."

"That's a lot of money. I doubt I can afford the ticket."

"I can. I have money saved. I didn't spend much in Vietnam. I can buy your ticket."

"I'm not sure I want you to buy my ticket. It doesn't seem right. I have some pride."

"Since we're getting married, I think it's probably OK. It's not like I am giving you something. We are a couple now, right?"

She warmed to the idea and said, "OK, I'll tell my folks after we get the ring and make the engagement formal. Are you sure it'll be OK with your parents?"

Bob was smiling from ear to ear. "It better be, you're their future daughter-in-law."

CHAPTER SIXTEEN

"This ain't the middle of nowhere, this is home." Jack Barnes

It was April and what passed for winter in southeast Arizona was about over. Most of the snow was off the high country. The days were warming up nicely, although the nights were still cold enough for a bit of frost at Mountain Camp. The cows were in good shape, and there were lots of calves on the ground. The spring works would begin in less than a month, and only a few weeks after that Bob and Angelina would be married. The wedding was set for early June.

Bob was laying in this morning. It was Sunday, and he had very little to do in the way of work today. He had not been to town to see Angelina since Friday night. Her wedding shower was Saturday afternoon, and some of her girlfriends were having a sleep over that night. It was one of very few Saturday nights they had not spent together since getting engaged.

She had had a late period scare after her weekend at Mountain Camp, which had caused her to be more cautious where sex was concerned. Bob was not real fond of this, but they would be married soon.

In spite of her mother's wishes, Angelina planned to go on birth control pills. This was a source of tension between Angelina and her mom, so she was holding off starting until a month before the wedding. She figured there was no reason to aggravate her mother for any longer than necessary. She doubted she could take them without her mother knowing since she lived at home with her folks, and her mother had never been overly worried about Angelina's privacy.

The end result of all this was that as far as pure sexual satisfaction went, Bob had the memory of their weekend together but not much else. As he lay there he gazed at the place on the bed where she had lain and imagined her there. In his mind's eye, he could see her sleeping next to him with her beautiful face and perfect body, her dark hair contrasting with her ivory skin further accentuating her beauty and adding to her sensuality. It was a vision to hold on to forever.

Well, I better get up, Bob thought. This is going nowhere. As he stretched, he smiled and said out loud, "On top of her good looks and drop-dead gorgeous body, I really do enjoy her company; she's lots of fun. Lucky me."

† † †

Preparing for spring works Bob spent most days gathering the cattle that had moved back in the more remote canyons as they followed the snow melt up the mountains. He was putting them through to South Sabino Pasture, saving the high country for the summer. The bulk of the cattle in North Sabino Pasture had already been put through, and only some remnants in the remote areas were left.

The spring works would go pretty quickly as they would have the cattle in the relatively easy country of South Sabino when they went to gather them for the branding. South Sabino was also a good place to put the bulls on the cows after their winter off. Being a fairly small pasture of easy country, the bulls would be exposed to the maximum number of cows in the shortest period of time, which should result in a lot of pregnant cows in short order.

Cruz had been coming up to help every few days as had Bob's Uncle Jack. Jack told Bob they would be bringing the bulls up in two days, and he would need Bob to come down to Headquarters and help. It wasn't that Jack, Cruz, and Scott, the West Camp man, couldn't handle ninety head of cattle by themselves, but ninety fairly young bulls that had been taking it easy on good ground with lots of feed and some protein supplement to boot, would be a handful. Fresh bulls had a habit of being full of themselves, and a band of them could test a cowboy's patience. They weren't mean or aggressive towards the cowboys as a rule, but they spent a lot of time testing each other, leading to slowdowns, stoppages, and the occasional small wreck.

✝ ✝ ✝

Chango was up the day they moved the bulls. That was OK with Bob. Chango had made a decent horse. He had lots of bottom, was very quick, and didn't seem to have too many buggers, but true to his grulla color he could be a hard head. When they arrived at Headquarters to start the day of moving bulls, Bob unloaded Chango and put him in the corral before heading to the house.

"Oh, good morning, Sobrinito," Maria greeted Bob with a hug. "We don't see enough of you these days. Every day you don't work, you are in town. You need to stop by and see us more often."

"Aunt Maria, I see Uncle Jack every few days."

"That doesn't count; that's work. You need to come by for dinner. You are not eating very well. Look at you, so skinny. Come sit down. I'll fix you some breakfast."

She had already handed him a cup of coffee when Jack came in. "Good morning, Bob, it's a good thing you're early this morning. Maria was going to feed you no matter what I said, even if it meant starting late."

"Good morning, Uncle Jack. I'm glad I came early, too. This way I can enjoy my breakfast and not have to wolf it down and chew it later."

"Scott and Cruz are supposed to be here in about an hour so take your time. How about a little coffee for me, old woman?" Jack said with a grin.

"Old woman! Get it yourself, Viejo." Then a bit softer, "You want chorizo with your eggs this morning?"

"Yes, Maria, that sounds good," answered Jack as he poured his coffee.

They had gathered up the bulls and walked them a little less than four miles to South Sabino Pasture. True to form the bulls had not been a big problem, but gathering and moving them had taken half a day just due to their orneriness. After putting the bulls through the gate, Jack called Bob over. "Bob, I'm going to ride back to Mountain Camp with you. Cruz will bring the camp truck back up, and you can give us a ride back to Headquarters."

"OK, Uncle Jack, is something wrong?"

"No, not really, we just haven't had a chance to talk in private, and I wanted to tell you about some things and ask about some things as well."

"OK," answered Bob. He stepped down and closed the wire gate after Cruz and Scott started back for Headquarters.

On the ride back to Mountain Camp Jack updated Bob on what he had learned about the Indian Springs bunch. It was all unsubstantiated, but from what Judson had been able to find out, the new owner, Vince Turturro, was a Capo or Captain in a crime family back in New Jersey. While he had a rap sheet, there were no outstanding warrants for him, so he was legal. The foreman, Alf Giunta, was a soldier in the same family and also had a rap sheet but no current warrants.

The names he had for the others did not appear with criminal records, but he suspected they were using aliases. When the deputy had spoken to a detective back East on the phone, the general reaction was surprise. "What the hell is Vince Turturro doing out in the middle of nowhere?" asked the detective.

Jack gave a bit of a sneer when he repeated this. "This ain't the middle of nowhere, this is home. What a bunch of gunzels."

He continued to tell Bob that the detective had also said he suspected Vince was involved in heroin trafficking. That had been part of his business back East. There were rumors of a new connection from Mexico.

The detective couldn't place the other two by the names they were using, but he thought he knew who they really were. Based on the descriptions, the detective thought they were probably Arturo Vechio, the nephew of the family boss and his babysitter, Anthony DeLuca. DeLuca was a made man, a man with some status in the mob.

He said if they were who they sounded like, it made sense that they were with Vince since they had been part of his crew back East. It looked like the old man was trying to get Artie out of sight for a while hoping he would grow up a little.

The detective had explained about Artie's family and relation to old man Vechio. He also told them what they already knew about Artie's being a hothead with a reputation of getting out of control. They had no case against him but suspected him of some gruesome murders. He was considered his own worst enemy, impetuous and not too bright. The other one, Anthony or Tony, was a for real badass. He was the one to keep in front of you.

Judson said the detective had finally wrapped up the call with a warning. "You guys aren't used to these kinds. I know you have your own brand of crooks out there, but these Mafiosi are different. Be careful; if you need some advice, or if you get some solid information, call me."

"That all sounds interesting, so I guess the reason they are still running around and not in jail is that nobody has enough to convict them, is that right?"

"That's about the size of it. Bob, I want that trash out of here. We have enough to deal with without them. Smuggling has been a way of life around here for generations but not the way these guys are playing it. If some old contrabandista brings a burro train through with tropical birds or duty-free merchandise, we don't lose any sleep over that. I expect once in a while they even bring in a bit of that funny weed the young folks are smoking these days. All that is minor, and these old smugglers have some sort of code they live by, but now it's changing."

"How's it changing, Uncle Jack?"

Jack took a minute to think on this then answered. "Like I said, smuggling has a long history around here. They don't bother us, and we don't bother them. They always leave the gates the way they find them. They don't camp on the waters, and sometimes they even leave a little something behind, like a jug of Bacanora or a bolt of cloth from way down south or maybe some ironwood carvings done by the Seri Indians, but there is no trouble.

"Now we are beginning to see some changes. There is more and more dope being smuggled in. The old contrabanistas seem to be disappearing. A new crowd is moving in, and they are not playing by the rules. We haven't seen it on the Tres Cruses yet, but just south of us and over to the east the ranchers are finding a lot of abandoned campsites at the waters. The gates are left open, and the fences are even being let down. Vern Redfield told me his camp man was shot at by a bunch he surprised up in the Peloncillos. I think this bunch at Indian Springs is a part of this, and I want them out of here."

Bob looked at Jack not quite sure where this was going. "Are you asking me to get rid of them?"

"No, no, not at all," Jack was taken aback by this. "I want to get proof of what they are up to so the law can get rid of them. Maybe you can help with that."

Bob was getting interested in this. It might be fun to put it to that bunch. He sure didn't want them around. "I expect you have a plan already."

Jack smiled at this. "Why, yes, I do. Can you talk to some of your Army buddies and get them to fly over Indian Springs country and get pictures of the dope patches?"

"I can try. Why doesn't the Sheriff talk to the Army and make a formal request?"

"He can't ask the Army for assistance in civil matters. There is the little matter of Posse Comitatus." Jack could see that this did not register with Bob. "It forbids the Army from getting involved in civil law enforcement without a declaration of martial law."

"So this needs to be done under the radar."

"Yes, what do you think?"

Bob was quiet for a while thinking of possibilities. "I can talk to Danny. He's an instructor, and I know he gets in some flight time. Maybe they can do a training mission over this way or a maintenance test flight."

"Can they find that stuff with a plane?"

"Yea."

"When can you talk to your friend at the fort?"

"I don't know. I'll have to call him and see when we can meet."

"OK, when you drive us back to Headquarters, you can use the phone then. Have you seen any sign of those guys?" indicating the Indian Springs Ranch by pointing east.

"Nothing more than we talked about before. The fence crew I ran into before the snows came, but nothing more."

"Tell me again about them."

"They know how to build a fence. That fence is straight, tight and the water gaps are well done. I think they were camped on the mountain, but I'm not sure. I tried to talk to them a little, but they were suddenly struck dumb."

"Is there any sign of them now? Have they come back?"

"No."

"Any sign of Indian Springs stock?"

"Yes, I have seen fresh sign on the Northeast Pasture side of the fence near Red Rock Springs, but nothing in Sabino Pasture?"

For the rest of the ride to Mountain Camp, Bob's mind was working on the problem of finding the dope patches. He knew where one was, but there could be more. He would have to find out more about the country to let Danny know where to look. He smiled and said to himself, "This could be fun."

Uncle Jack interrupted his thoughts, "Now Bob, I don't want you doing anything foolish."

"No sweat, Uncle Jack, I won't."

CHAPTER SEVENTEEN

"... don't queer the deal. It's not just about you" Danny Mohan

Bob was on his way over to Tombstone to meet Danny Mohan. They were going to grab a bite at the Lucky Cuss and go over some maps to see what they could come up with. He hadn't been to Tombstone since he had left for Vietnam. It would be nice to see the place again. He wondered if old Marshal Brownsey was still walking up and down the sidewalk saying, "Howdy, boys" or "Howdy, ma'am" to all the out-of-towners as he passed. He looked quite the part in his big silver belly hat. With the town Marshal's star pinned on the left breast of his long, brown, sports coat which he wore over his Colt revolver carried in a carved leather holster hanging on a matching gun belt all finished off with a pair of cowboy boots. Bob had always assumed he was the real deal, but now he wondered if it was just show.

Bob parked the truck on Allen Street about a block from the Lucky Cuss. The town was full of tourists, as it usually was in the cooler months, all ambling down the sidewalks and stopping without warning to gawk at the trinkets in the shop windows. Bob didn't do tourists well. A trait he'd picked up while going to high school in the Washington, DC, area.

As he walked to the Lucky Cuss, Bob had to negotiate a clot of tourists who were all standing around old Nino, taking turns paying to have their picture taken with this old Indian, who professed to be the grandson of Cochise. Bob wondered if he really was or was just an old man trying to get by. This was after all "Tombstone, The Town Too Tough to Die." With the OK Corral and Marshal Brownsey how could anyone question Nino's authenticity as grandson of Cochise. Bob smiled.

Danny was waiting for him. He had two beers on the table already. He stood up and stuck out his hand, "Hi, Hasett, how the hell are you?"

"I'm fine, Danny; how's it hanging with you?"

Mohan looked deep in thought for a second, shoved his hand deep into his pants pocket then responded with a grin, "A little to the left."

"That kind of shit is why the girls at the steam and cream called you dinky dau Danny."

"It's good to be remembered."

While they were going through the menus, Danny asked. "What can I do for you, Bob?"

"I need a favor. Can you fly a mission over by the ranch and get some photo coverage?"

"Probably, what gives?"

Bob looked around; there was no one seated near them, and there was enough noise so their voices would be masked. He lowered his voice and said, "We have a drug outfit to the east of Tres Cruces. We need to find out where their pot fields are, so we can tell the Sheriff."

"You know the Army can't do that, right?"

"Yeah, I know; posse come and get us or some such as that."

Danny laughed, "Posse Comitatus, you idiot. Are you sure you didn't take a big bump on the head up on that rock?"

Bob smiled, "I might have. I know it can't be official, but I was wondering if you could work it into a training flight or a test flight or something."

"I think it's doable. What do you have for location?" With this Danny pushed a map across the table to Bob.

Opening the map, Bob saw that it was 1:250,000 scale Joint Operations Graphic of southeast Arizona. He pointed at the area he was interested in and said, "This is the general area. I can give you more specific coordinates of a spot I know of, but I will need a 1:50,000 scale map to take with me. I can also narrow down the other possible locations and give you a manageable search area."

"OK, take this with you. I have some one-to-fifties in the car. We'll see if they are what you need when we leave. Do you remember the Round Ranger?" Asked Danny.

"Yes, he was one of my IPs."

"He's back again, and I am sure he would like to do something like this as long as it stays quiet."

"That's good. I remember him as a good guy." Said Bob.

"Danny nodded, "He is."

"My plan is to get as much info as I can to help you plan the mission. Once you get the photos, we can sanitize them so they can't be attributed to the Army, just in case. Any areas on the imagery that look good, I will check in person and record on hand held photos to confirm what I see. That's what I'll take to the cops . . . the hand helds. They'll never see or hear of any aerial photos."

"OK, Hasett, get me that information, and I'll get it set up."

They enjoyed their meal and shot the bull for quite a while drinking a few beers and relaxing. After a while, Danny said, "Bob, somebody's been making noise about your award. I don't know who, but I got interviewed by some investigator who wanted to know about the whole mess." He paused for a minute, "Not the citation or the action, but what you did to cause it to get shelved."

"Wonder-fucking-full. That's all I need, some jerkoff crawling up my ass to investigate. If they come back, tell them I said to leave it be, and I don't want to talk to anybody." Bob sat and steamed for a minute. "Fuck that, tell them where to find me, I'll tell them to put that goddamned citation where the sun don't shine."

Danny sat quietly, a rarity for him and then got serious, another rarity. "Fuck you, Hasett. There's a lot of folks that want you to have that DSC. Don't be such a selfish shit. Big Sarge stuck his neck way out for you by continuing to push that snowball up hill. He got his ass in a wringer over you. Don't throw that back in his face. He's earned better. He pulled your fat out of the fire more than once."

This caught Bob off guard. He had a bit of a surprised look on his face and with a note of contriteness he said. "I had no idea. Big Sarge is a good guy. There is no BS with that man. I know I owe him a lot. If it's important to him, then I won't cause any trouble. Of course, you know it's not going to happen."

"We'll see. Somebody has sure stirred it up. It seems the shit has hit the fan, and no telling who is going to get hit by flying fecal matter." Danny looked seriously at Bob and said, "Do you know what sound shit makes when it hits the fan?"

"No."

"Hassssseeettt!"

"Fuck you, Danny."

"OK, here?" Danny was grinning. He got serious again and said. 'No shit, ass hole, I hope you get it. You know, it is a big deal. how often does a puke like us get the DSC? I'll tell you, not often. Some colonel gets one for flying over a fucking fire fight in a Huey and directing his troops, but you hold off the whole damn North Vietnamese Army and don't get shit. Did they at least give you Charlie's Bolo Badge for getting shot?"

"Yea, I got a purple heart — and it wasn't the whole NVA. I wasn't alone either."

"Bullshit, details, you earned it, and all us pukes want to see you get it . . . get it for us, especially for us TOs. We flew our asses off over there. We flew every fucking night, not two or three times a week like a lot of the pilots, but, every goddamned night and sometimes twice a night, and what did we get? I'll tell you what we got. We got half or more of our flight time given to some REMFS so they could draw flight pay and get our air medals. Then they gave us the Green Weeney . . . the goddamned ARCOM, and the officers got Bronze Stars and Distinguished Flying Crosses." Danny was getting hot, having to fight to keep his voice down and not succeeding.

Bob thought hard about this. He had heard about the flight hours and knew he'd only received credit for thirty-two and a half hours a month. Thirty-two and a half hours a month was crap. His platoon maintained a flight time board, and all the TOs were logging 60 to 100 hours a month. "I hear you, Danny, but Rocky Top should get his shit before I do."

"One fucking battle at a time, GI. Make Rocky Top's CMH your life's work if you want, but get that DSC for us pukes. Let folks help out and don't queer the deal. It's not just about you."

CHAPTER EIGHTEEN

Angelina knew this was the dress.

Angelina had a fitting appointment at the bridal shop for her wedding dress. Her mother and her aunt were with her. This was a big deal. It was important that her mom and her dueña be there with her. As they approached the shop, she could see through the window that it looked crowded inside. Her mother smiled and said. "Looks like the word got out and all your girlfriends are here."

Before they got through the door Suzie rushed out and threw her arms around Angelina. "We're all here for you." She said gesturing towards toward the crowd in the shop.

Angelina was taken aback as she realized that all her female friends and relatives were here to see the dress and enjoy this moment with her. This was not what she expected. She had hoped for a quiet session with her mom and aunt but, that was not to be. Angelina took in a deep breath, smiled, and thanked everybody for the wonderful surprise. Her mom and aunt looked at her knowingly while Suzie smiled from ear to ear, pleased that her idea was such a success. In spite of herself Angelina was touched. She gave Suzie a big hug and whispered, "Thank You."

Pilar, the shop owner and distant cousin to Angelina on her mom's side welcomed them to the shop. Ushering the two older women to the seats closest to the dressing room and assuring they were comfortable, she then asked everyone else to have a seat. Taking Angelina's hand, she led her into the dressing room.

Angelina was a bit excited but apprehensive. She had shown a picture of a dress from the cover of "Brides" Magazine to Pilar, and even though Pilar said she had found a close match, Angelina was worried it would not look good on her. What if it didn't fit? What then? Sensing her unease, Pilar assured her it would be fine … even better than fine.

When Pilar brought the dress in Angelina's fears were allayed. The dress was beautiful, and it fit her like a glove. Looking in the mirror she could see that it flattered her figure.

When she walked out to model the dress for her friends and family, they were all impressed. There was a lot of smiling, chatter, and compliments, but Angelina was not paying attention; she didn't hear any of it. She was staring at the window. The smile was gone from her face as was the color. Leering back at her was Artie. She spun on her heel and hurried back into the dressing room.

Angelina was beside herself. How did he know where she was? Had he followed her here? This could not be a coincidence. She shivered at the memory of his look. He made her skin crawl and worse he scared her.

She sat and began to cry softly. Pilar had seen the way Artie was leering and making obscene gestures at Angelina through the window. "Don't worry, I'll get rid of him." With this she left Angelina in the dressing room.

"What now?" she asked herself. "I can't wear this dress. Bob was supposed to be the first man to see it on me, not that animal. I can't get married in this dress. I'll have to get another ... there isn't enough time. I'll never be able to get as nice a dress so soon. Artie has ruined everything. He made me feel dirty."

Pilar returned to the dressing room. Angelina had removed the dress and said she needed another. She explained why and her explanation was accepted. After discussing it for a while, they agreed not to say anything to the others about Artie.

Pilar brought out another dress for Angelina. It was more expensive, but Pilar had decided to cover the difference herself. After all Angelina was family. It was a stunningly beautiful dress. It was even better than the one before. Angelina was very pleased but worried about the price. "I love it but can't afford it."

"Oh." Said Pilar. "It's the same price as the first one." She lied. "It looks great on you. It's time to show the others. I'm going out to be sure nobody's at the window. I'll let you know when to come out."

When Angelina entered the room to show the dress to her friends and family, there was silence. Everyone just starred. She looked beautiful. Even more importantly Angelina knew this was the dress, and Bob would be the first man to see her in it.

CHAPTER NINETEEN

"Prior Planning Should be done in Advance." Anonymous

It was May; spring works were over, and there wasn't much for Bob to do. He had cleaned the few remnants off his country, mostly Sabino Pasture, branded the few calves and kicked the lot onto the desert country. Now all he had to do was check on the waters and mend fences. Jack would be moving some cattle up to Bob's high country in a month or two. He took this opportunity to start scouting the Indian Springs country.

His uncle didn't want him going over there, but Bob knew that asking Danny to bore holes through the sky over a large search area was asking too much. It was not outside the Mohawk's capabilities, but it was a favor he was asking for, not a mission he was tasking. The fact that what they were doing was against official policy and might even be illegal had a bearing on what he was willing to ask of Danny. So, he would scout the area to narrow down the search area.

Bob had made arrangements with Cruz to come up and prowl the Sabino country for him for a few days. His excuse for being away from camp was the need to search the high country checking the waters and fences. This was standard practice before moving cattle in. Fences needed to be mended, water gaps may need repair after the spring runoff, and the waters needed to be in working order. All this had been cleared with Jack. Bob suspected Jack was not fooled by the ruse, but he had not objected.

It was first light when Bob swung up on Crestnut's back and started east leading Chango and Mescal, both of whom were carrying packsaddles and light loads. They would be fresh enough to act as remounts for the next two or three days.

He planned to make his way over to Indian Springs and start locating pot fields along with stashes that he could confirm, and other potential areas of interest for Danny to fly. He was also going to avoid the area near the known pot field and the headquarters. At best, he would locate some more drug related sites, at worst, he could eliminate areas that did not need to be over flown.

One complication was that fence crew had returned. He would have to avoid them, but that should not be a big deal as they were camping near the fence. That should keep them pretty far west of the areas he would be prowling. He just needed to be sure not to leave tracks where they might find them and not to skyline his silhouette where they might see him. He would avoid the trail where he crossed into Indian Springs country and keep to the military crest on the east side of ridges and peaks.

Bob followed the same path he and Cruz had used to take the Indian Springs cattle back several months before, being careful to stay off the trail itself. He continued east until he picked up an old cow path and followed it to the north. This was unknown country to Bob, well within Indian Springs country.

He had a one to fifty thousand scale tactical map of the area, and Danny had brought some gross scale vertical photographs used for mapping and a stereoscope. The photography along with the stereoscope allowed him to get a feel for the topography. Of course, the map had the contours, but good stereo gave a real feel for the country.

What Bob had learned from the imagery and map was that he was headed into rough country with high peaks, steep-sided ridges, and deep canyons. Nothing new there, but he could also see that there were some nice flat areas on top of some ridges and hills that were like mesas. Some of the canyons had fairly broad bottoms. These were the areas he was most interested in. He only had today, tomorrow, and part of the day after before he had to be back at Mountain Camp.

At midday Bob stopped for lunch. He had covered a fair bit of ground. This was country he had looked over from the mountains in Northeast Pasture, but from there it just looked like row after row of mountains and ridges. Now he could see the detail. Bob unsaddled the horses and after hobbling them, let them graze. He was on a fairly open ridge with good grass and an unobstructed view of the country to his north and east.

For lunch he had brought an apple and a couple of tortilla sandwiches. He couldn't really call them tacos or burritos. They were just tortillas with mayonnaise rolled up around bologna. They did the trick.

After he ate he took out a pair of binoculars and started looking over the country below. He was looking for anything out of the ordinary. The map showed no roads up here so that was the first thing he looked for. He could see some of the old burro or wagon trails that side hilled up to some old mine workings, but that was not what he was interested in. He figured what he wanted would be down in the bottoms or on the flat-topped mesas and ridges.

As he glassed he saw one spot through a break in the trees in a canyon bottom that might have been a road, but he could not be sure. As he looked at it trying to decide if it was a road or not, he heard a plane's engine. It was a light plane not unlike an Army Bird Dog. Looking up ahead of the sound, he spotted a small plane that appeared to be dropping in altitude. It was headed towards one of the flat-topped ridges.

This ridge was a few miles to the northeast, and while its top was below him, it sloped downwards a little to the east masking his view of most of the area on top. As he continued to watch the plane, it began to look like it was making an approach to land on the top of the mesa. Bob got pretty excited about this, and steadying his binoculars on a rock, he settled down to see what transpired.

To Bob's surprise, the plane continued to descend and did in fact land on the mesa top. He couldn't see it, but there was the unmistakable sound of the chopped throttle as the plane flared before settling in and disappearing from Bob's sight and sound. As he watched he thought he caught a little movement from time to time but could not be sure. Whatever was going on was masked from his view.

After about a half hour, Bob heard the sound of the plane's engine revving up, and soon he heard it go to full power. Then there it was rising from the ridge top and turning back in the direction from which it had come, south.

Bob continued to watch the mesa but could see nothing. He would have to go there to see what was going on. He looked over the map carefully and even took out the aerial photos and stereoscope from his saddle bag and looked hard for the best way to approach the mesa. Once he had a plan, he gathered up his horses and headed off the ridge to the canyon below.

What he had seen on the map and the images was a road on the east side of the ridge that headed back towards the Indian Springs Headquarters, but he had to remain cautious as he neared the bottom of the canyon because he was still not sure if there was a road there or not. The maps showed nothing; neither did the photos, but they were a few years old.

When he reached a low spur just near the bottom of the canyon, he could see a road, more of a jeep trail really, running next to the small stream on the canyon floor. As he looked at this for a minute and was gathering his thoughts, he heard the faint sounds of what might be an engine. Looking up to his north, he saw dust and heard what was now the unmistakable sound of a vehicle coming down the trail.

Bob stepped down and led his horses behind a small bunch of pinyon pine, which masked him from the road. Peering through the small vantage point he had between some of the branches, he saw a familiar sight. It was the same two men he had met on that day with Cruz at the corrals, Artie and Anthony. Now Bob knew he had to get a look up on that ridge top.

He couldn't use the trail in the canyon bottom as there was too big a risk of being seen or leaving sign, so he found a rocky stretch of the trail where it forded the stream and crossed there so as to leave little in the way of tracks. He then worked his way side hilling up to the north end of ridge.

Here he found a small flat of a couple of acres surrounded by decent-sized pinyon and juniper trees. The small park would provide some cover and a good camp site with grazing for the night. It was fifty feet or so below the top and maybe a quarter mile distant, which Bob hoped, was far enough. He would continue on foot.

When he reached the top of the mesa, he kept under cover and scouted around until he was sure he was alone. Then he explored the top. What he found was a revelation. There was a strip of mashed grass and dirt about maybe four or five hundred meters long, along with fifty-five-gallon fuel drums, a hand pump, hose and nozzle, and a locked shed. This was quite an operation. There was even a windsock. Bob figured the field must be clandestine since it didn't show up on the Joint Operation's Graphic, which should show all registered strips. This operation was looking like a big deal. He pulled out his compass and shot an azimuth of the airstip's heading; it was 210 degrees magnetic.

After scouting the rest of the ridge top, Bob returned to the small park where he had left his horses and decided it was time to make camp for the night. The sun would be setting soon, and he did not want to have a fire or use any white light at night as long as he was prowling around in Indian Springs country.

He had watered the horses when crossing the stream below so that was taken care of, and they were grazing happily on a good supply of blue grama and side oats. So after making sure the horses hobbles' were not too tight, Bob set up his bedroll and broke out a box of C-rations.

Tonight would be beanie weenies, his favorite. He had some heat tabs, which gave him the luxury of a hot meal and some hot chocolate. After eating the main course, he took his time with the cheese and crackers that came in the B-2 unit of his C-rations and watched the sun set over the mountains to his west. He never tired of this scene. He decided to save the John Wayne bar for later. The John Wayne bar was so named because it was said it could knock the shit out of John Wayne. Bob thought a little constipation may not be a bad thing right now, thus the John Wayne bar would have to wait.

† † †

The night was crisp and Bob slept well. He awoke with the first hint of light. After emptying his bladder and checking on the horses, he made a cup of hot coffee with a heat tab and the C-ration coffee mix. It was not anything to write home about, but it was hot and it was coffee. He breakfasted on a couple of boiled eggs, some tortillas, and a can of peaches he had packed.

After putting morrals on the horses with a little grain, he brushed his teeth and shaved, habits he had had drilled into him in the Army. "If personal hygiene is important in garrison, it is ten times more important in the field," was what he used to hear, and he believed it. Besides one must maintain his dignity. It was OK to be dirty from working hard, but being a slob was unacceptable.

He saddled up his horse for the day and packed his camp on the other two then started out to see what he could find to the north and east of the ridge. He wanted to check the area just north of the mesa for any more jeep trails, and if there were none, he would work his way around to the east and then south. If nothing diverted him from this, he could pass south of where he and Cruz had found the dope patch and do a quick check of that area before getting back to mountain camp.

He avoided using the road that ran to the base of the mesa by sticking to some old cow trails and bushwhacking when necessary. He wanted neither to meet anyone nor leave any sign on the road. Somebody had gone to a great deal of effort to maintain what was a pretty substantial road. It was much more than just a jeep trail like the one that split off from it and circled around to the west side of the mesa, the one he had seen the Jeep on yesterday. It turned out that this road swung east then south. Bob suspected it ran to Indian Springs Headquarters, something he would check out if he had time.

After looking around, one thing was sure, there were no jeep trails or roads heading north, just an old pack trail that showed no sign of recent use. Bob thought that figured as he had no faith in this bunches' ability to pack anything on a horse, mule, or burro. Anything they were involved in would involve vehicles, and as it turned out aircraft.

As the morning wore on, Bob had worked up a ridge to the east of the road and glassed the country around. To his south, he could see dust. It was the dust of a vehicle moving on a dirt surface. As he watched, it continued heading to the northeast up a large canyon that eventually ran below his position. He could see no road or trail directly below him, but that didn't mean there wasn't one masked on the other side of the cottonwood and sycamore that grew along the creek bed.

As he continued to watch, the dust stopped about a mile to his southeast. It did not reappear. The vehicle had stopped, and Bob wanted to know why. Did it stop at another dope patch or stash? He decided against eyeballing it, but marked the location on his map for Danny. It was a potential surveillance target. After an hour or so the dust reappeared, this time heading back in the direction which it had come from.

Bob tightened up his cinch and checked the pack horses to be sure everything was secure. Then he mounted and started heading to the south. He would stay high as much as possible to give himself the advantage of being able to spot someone before he could be spotted.

For several miles Bob saw nothing out of the ordinary unless you didn't count unbranded yearlings and two-year olds. There were plenty of these running wild along with some older branded stock. They were trotty and wild as deer. This just confirmed what Bob already knew. There was no cattle ranching taking place on Indian Springs. He was curious about what the land management agencies like the state land office and forest service's take was on all this. Surely, they had noticed something was odd. He would have to ask his uncle about that.

After lunch Bob was working his way south of the ranch headquarters in the rolling country to the east of the mountains being careful not to expose himself or kick up too much dust. He had just crossed over the main drive that led from the forest road to the Indian Springs corrals when he heard a vehicle coming down the drive. He pulled up into a small copse of trees and waited. It was not one vehicle but several. There were a couple of sedans, a pickup, a van, and one rental truck. Bob decided to wait a few minutes and then try to get to some high ground that would allow him to see where they were going.

They passed by the ranch headquarters and continued on to the north. They could be going to the airfield or the spot where the other vehicle had stopped in the morning. If no plane showed up, it was probably the latter. Bob decided he had all he needed and was anxious to get back up in the mountains. He would get at least past the dope patch and then make camp for the night. He could then take his time getting back to Mountain Camp the next day and see if there was anything of interest in the area above the dope patch.

CHAPTER TWENTY

"He's fucking dead. Whatever he did, he more than paid for." Bob
Hasett

Danny was sitting at Jack Barnes' kitchen table, spreading out a map
and some aerial photos as Maria poured him a cup of coffee and set
down a plate of pastries. Bob and Jack were waiting anxiously to see
what he had to show them.

Danny had called a couple of days earlier and said he had the
information Bob had asked him to collect. He told Jack that there was
some interesting stuff on the photos, and he could come over on
Saturday if that was OK. Of course, that was OK with Jack; he wanted
to know what was going on.

"Danny, that didn't take too long. I only passed you the locations last
month," said Bob with a wink.

Danny smiled, "No sweat, GI, the timing was tough. There was no
opportunity until Round Ranger had a couple of test flights
scheduled. We didn't want to make something up. Best of all, one was
for an IR set so we not only got daytime photos, but we flew IR, too.

"Now what you have here is pretty interesting. That airstrip you told
me about is right here," pointing to the map and one of the photos.
"It measured 1700 feet long and at an elevation of 5900 feet. It should
be able to handle something on the order of a Cessna 185 if it's not
too heavily loaded and if the pilot knows his shit. The D.A. could make
it iffy in the summer."

Bob saw that Jack was not familiar with the term D.A. "Uncle Jack,
D.A. is Density Altitude. It is measure of apparent altitude. If the D.A.
is high you will need more runway to takeoff."

"OK." Answered Jack.

Danny continued, "I could find nothing more to the north.

The other side of the ridge to the east of the airstrip is a different story; there is a nice road with two clusters of small buildings tucked up under the trees, and the day we flew this, there were several vehicles parked at one of these areas. None of this is on the map." Danny looked up and pushed the photos of the buildings across the table.

After Bob and Jack had time to look the photos over, Danny went on. "We checked out the dope patch you told me about and found two more in the same area," he was pushing more photos across the table and pointing on the map to their location. "That was all we found except that the IR picked up a lot of activity around the buildings late at night. It seemed out of place at zero two hundred in the morning."

"What buildings?" asked Jack.

"These up here," he said, pointing at the building clusters in the canyon, "and these," he added, pointing to the ranch headquarters.

Bob was looking hard at the photos and the map. "All three of the dope patches are on trails that aren't on the map, or at least they aren't shown as jeep trails, just pack trails. When you add the airstrip, the road with the building sites, and these trail improvements, it seems these guys have put a lot of time and money into infrastructure."

"Lots more than running cows require or can pay for," said Jack. "This is what I've been needing. Thanks, Danny."

"No sweat, Mr. Barnes." Danny then turned to Bob and held out an envelope for him. "Here, this is for you."

Bob looked at the face of the envelope which bore his name and rank. Then looking at the return address, he saw the familiar Department of the Army return address for Commander Fort Huachuca with an attention line to a Lieutenant Colonel he did not know and an unfamiliar office symbol. "What's this?" he asked looking at Danny.

"Something the IG told me to get to you."

The room was quiet now. Maria was not sure what was going on, but Jack had some notion of the function of the Inspector General. Bob hesitated.

"Open it, Bob," said Jack.

Bob was nervous about this, but he opened it anyway. It said the IG wanted to interview him regarding events in the Republic of Vietnam. Specifically, he was interested in the events that took place at the fire base on top of Nui Ba Din and the actions of all those involved. Bob looked up at Danny and Jack, "I guess I better go see the IG. Danny, are you the POC on this? Can you get me a time and location?"

"Yes, how is Monday at 1500?"

Bob looked at Jack, "Is that OK with you?"

"Yes, that works well with what I need to do Monday. Be here at seven for breakfast. You can keep me company while I take care of some chores in Wilcox, and then I'll run you over to the fort."

† † †

Bob and Jack were sitting in a corner booth in a small diner in Willcox along with Deputy Tommy Judson. Jack had completed some business at the sale barn and arranged to meet Tommy before taking Bob to Fort Huachuca. This was a bit out of the way, but it was better to meet here than in Douglas or Bisbee. Less chance of their being noticed.

Jack started, "Tommy, about that bunch to my east. Bob here did a little reconnaissance on the Forest Service country over there and found some interesting stuff. Bob, tell him about it."

Bob told the deputy about the airfield, the hidden buildings, the new road, and the pot fields. No mention was made of the Mohawk flight. When Tommy had asked how he came about this information, he said he became suspicious while returning some stray cattle to Indian Springs and did a little checking on his own after that.

At this point, Jack took up the case and pointed out that there was a lot of night activity taking place over there and emphasized the importance of the airfield and the small plane that made regular visits. All of this, of course, was embellished a little to make the point.

After reflecting on all this for a while, Tommy asked if they had any physical evidence. "What do you need?" Jack asked.

"Photographs would be nice."

With that, Bob pulled out some photos he had taken on his ride. He had some handhelds of the airfield, the new road, and one of a dope patch, but nothing of the building clusters. He hadn't gotten close enough that day to get any.

Again, Tommy took his time considering the photos and then asked, "Do you have locations for all these?"

"Yes," answered Bob, turning over the photos and showing Tommy the six digit UTM coordinates written on the back of each photo.

With this, Tommy smiled, "Good work. Do you have the locations of the buildings as well?"

"Yes," answered Bob, pulling his tally book out of his pocket and showing Tommy the page with the two sets of coordinates, "here."

After copying the locations, he put them and the photos in his pocket. "You've done a good job here, Jack. I will get with the boss and fill him in."

"Is it enough to get rid of them?"

"I think it's enough for us to have a look at their operation."

"Good," said Jack Barnes. "I want that scum out of here."

A couple of hours later after signing in at the main gate of Fort Huachuca, Jack was driving Bob to the old part of post where the post headquarters and the IG's office were. Bob had not seen much of the old post when he was a student. It was not a place for a private to hang out being the site of the generals' and colonels' quarters and presumably generals' and colonels' daughters. The MPs weren't going to tolerate any lowly private hanging around this august ground. Besides as long as they were vigilant in keeping the riffraff out, it meant less competition, and one never knew, a strac MP might just get lucky with some colonel's daughter. Bob was not a big fan of MPs.

The old part of post was interesting. The barracks were two-story affairs with full-length covered porches on each floor. They were obviously designed to take maximum advantage of air circulation and shade in the summer. To the west of them were the old stables, one of which was now the post commissary. To the east of the barracks, across the parade ground was officers' row, the senior officers' quarters. The post headquarters and various other offices were on the cross streets. These buildings had all been built in the late 1800's during the Indian Wars. It was a picturesque old post, set back in the oaks of Huachuca Canyon with the cottonwood lined stream running next to the old stables.

They found the IG's office, and Bob went in for his interview, leaving Jack fretting in the outer office. "Would you like a cup of coffee?" asked the NCO sitting behind the desk looking at Jack.

A little startled, Jack looked up and realized the sergeant was talking to him. "Oh, sure, that would be nice." Watching the sergeant pouring two cups of coffee Jack thought, some things never change; it's nearly supper time and this old NCO is still drinking coffee. It reminded him of the old regulars he served with in the war. Whenever time permitted, they would have coffee or booze, sometimes both together.

The sergeant brought him his coffee, offering the cream and sugar which Jack accepted. "He'll be fine," reassured the NCO.

Jack looked at him and saw a knowing smile. "You're sure?"

"Yes, sir. They just want to ask him about an action he was in."

"Do they think he did something wrong?"

With this, the sergeant looked a little surprised and shook his head. "Oh, no, they think he did something pretty extraordinary. I can't say anymore. I just don't want you to worry." The sergeant paused and then said, "He called you 'Uncle'; are you really his uncle?"

"Yes, on his mother's side. He's working on my ranch as a cowboy."

"I worked for his father a few years ago. I was his operations NCO in Vietnam. If this boy is anything like his old man, the Army has lost a fine man, and you have gained one."

"Yes, I have, thank you."

With that the sergeant went back to his desk and continued to shuffle whatever papers are required for the continued running of the Army.

In the IG's office, Bob was being reassured that there was nothing wrong; the IG was simply looking into the action at the fire base on top of Nui Ba Dinh. There was the matter of some decorations that had been submitted but not awarded. After listening to what the IG had to say, and his request for a detailed description of the action as well as anything he knew about award recommendations, Bob decided to get it all off his chest, if this Lieutenant Colonel had the time, he would pull the chocks and tell him everything. "Sir, just how much time do you have? It's a long story."

"I have all the time you need. If it goes late, I'll have Sergeant Stevens pick up some dinner. Now go ahead and take your time. I am going to record your comments." With that he pushed the record button on a small cassette recorder.

After three hours, several cassette changes, and a break for burgers and fries courtesy of Sergeant Stevens, Bob was done. He had told the IG about the action, about his recommending that Rocky Top get the Medal of Honor for knowingly sacrificing his life. He told the IG about getting in a pissing contest with Rocky Top's chain of command about the award recommendation and how he had continued to push for the award recommendation to be put forward but to no avail.

It seemed Rocky Top had made enemies pretty high up his chain of command, and they weren't of the forgiving type, even for a dead hero. Bob's continued pushing had the opposite effect of what he wanted. Instead of getting the Congressional Medal of Honor (CMH) for his comrade, it resulted in a campaign of silence about the action. Not only did Rocky Top not get the CMH, neither did Captain Johnson get his Air Force Cross, and Bob's DSC recommendation, which had been put forward by Captain Johnson was probably buried in some circular file or was ashes in a burn barrel.

The IG turned off the recorder and sat back, "Are you bitter?"

"I don't know. I was raised in this army on officers' row, and I expected better. I think I'm disappointed but not bitter." Bob took a deep breath, "Sir, he gave his life for us. He didn't get fucked up by some random accident of war like a booby trap or errant arty round, which is bad enough but still random bad luck. He chose to stay out in the open and call arty down on his own head while we all hunkered down below in bunkers. He knew he wasn't going to make it." Bob paused again a for brief moment. "Fuck those bastards in his chain."

"You don't think there could be something he did that was bad enough to warrant them withholding the recommendation?"

Bob shot a sharp look at the IG. "He's fucking dead. Whatever he did he more than paid for."

The IG was quiet for a while, thinking hard of what to say. Bob's story had touched him. "I will complete my investigation and send it forward. I'll inform you of the final disposition of this case. Thank you for taking so much of your time to talk to me." Now he looked Bob straight in the eye, "We hear so much from the press about troops refusing orders and avoiding fights. I am proud to meet one that fought so well and wish I had a battalion of Rocky Tops. Thank you for renewing my faith."

"Yes, sir, thank you, sir." Then he added, "The press is full of shit."

When Bob stepped into the outer office, he was greeted by not only his uncle but also Danny and Big Sarge. Bob was pleased to see his old platoon sergeant and stuck his hand out. "Goddamn, Sarge, I thought you were at Fort Hood. What are you doing here?"

Sergeant First Class Pahoa took Bob's hand and pumped vigorously. He was a big man, as solid as a tree trunk, with black hair and an olive complexion. He carried himself with that easy confidence and dignity of someone perfectly comfortable with himself. "I could ask you the same thing. You are a civilian now, but I have to say finding you in the IG's office is no big surprise," he said with a grin. "To answer your question, I'm here for the D model transition course. The Army is doing away with all the B and C models, so us old Mohawkers have to get brought up to date."

Danny had already introduced Bob's uncle to Big Sarge, and as they left the building Bob was struck by how similar they seemed. Other than superficial physical differences, it was as if they were cut from the same cloth.

As they walked out of the building, Danny suggested they head to the NCO club for a beer. Jack said that would be all right, but he and Bob could not stay long. It was a long drive back to the ranch.

They stayed longer than expected, and it was midnight before they got back to the ranch headquarters, but both felt it was worth it. Jack had talked at length with Sergeant Pahoa, and Bob always enjoyed Pahoa's company; he considered him to be the finest NCO he knew.

Jack learned a lot about his nephew from his former platoon sergeant. This included many of the details of the fight on Nui Ba Dinh, and the "shit storm" Bob had caused over Rocky Top's award. Now he understood a little more about the young man's makeup. Pahoa had said that Bob was the kind of troop you wanted in a tight spot but he didn't suffer fools well. When he thought something was not fair, he was a stubborn pain in the ass. That's when his mouth could be a problem. He could be led and was loyal to a fault if he trusted you, but trying to push him was a mistake.

CHAPTER TWENTY-ONE

Thank you, Tom Jones.

Bob and Angelina were married in early June as planned and had gone on their honeymoon to Las Vegas. Angelina had often talked of how much her mother and aunt enjoyed going to Vegas and catching Tom Jones's act. She thought it would be fun to go herself. Bob's parents decided to give them the trip as a gift.

Bob had enjoyed Vegas, but then he would have enjoyed any place that put him in bed with Angelina. Enjoying the frantic lovemaking of a young couple that had mostly refrained from intimacy beyond the normal courtship rituals of kissing and petting, they had nearly missed the Tom Jones show, and would have if it had been up to Bob. Angelina, however, was not going to be denied, besides her mother and aunt expected a full report on their favorite singer's performance and would be disappointed without it. She had put Bob off, and they had gone to the show. After they returned to the room, Bob was glad they had gone. Old Tom had a way of heating up the women in his audience, and it worked to Bob's advantage.

On returning to the ranch, they set up housekeeping at Mountain Camp. Angelina's mother and Aunt Maria had spent some time sprucing things up a bit. Maria had insisted that Angelina should return to a nice home with some feminine touches and family reminders, not a bachelor's cow camp no matter how clean and tidy it was.

"Oh, Bob," said Angelina "it is just wonderful." She was looking at some of her personal possessions and a family portrait that had hung in her parents' house now hanging in the living room of her new home. "How did you know what to bring? When did you get these things here?"

Bob was surprised. He had worked hard to make sure the little house was clean and neat, but he had never been much for knickknacks and decorations that is other than a well-placed gun rack, a mountain lion pelt, and a beer mirror. Now he walked into a house that had the unmistakable civilizing effect of a woman's touch. He was speechless. After a while, he recovered from his surprise and smiled at Angelina, "I would like to take credit for being this smart, but my guess is Aunt Maria and your mom are behind this. Did they do a good job"?

"Yes," she said tearing up a little. "It is starting to feel like home already."

† † †

Angelina dove right into her new role as the wife of a cowboy. While normally they were alone, and she often helped Bob prowl the cows or check the waters, she also cooked for the crew on those rare occasions when they would have a big job on the mountain.

She had spent enough time horseback that her legs had strengthened, and she was comfortable moving at a trot, something that only people who earned their living horseback or at least spent several hours a day in the saddle accomplished. Cowboys habitually put their horses into a trot as the most efficient way to cover long distances. It was the best gait for the horse but was hard on people that were not conditioned to it.

When Bob and Angelina had started riding together quite a bit, Bob had not spent a lot of time trotting but had held his horse to a walk for Angelina's sake. He encouraged her to practice trotting but didn't push it. She was aware of Bob's taking it easy on her and made up her mind to master at least this one aspect of cowboying.

On their rides Bob often made sure to show Angelina something interesting. There were the old Indian sites, some soldier graffiti from the late 1800s, and the ruins of the old Army camp in the canyon, a relic of the Indian wars.

The Indian sites were several hundred years old. They had been lived in by a people that farmed as well as hunted. There were pottery shards, the occasional stone tool or point, and the sets of grinding stones called metates and manos. The metates were the large, flat stones often with worn, concave tops that formed the bottom or anvil of the grinding set, and the manos were the hand stones used to grind corn or mesquite beans or whatever was on the menu. The action of grinding a mano against the metate is what resulted in the concave top.

One day they came across a site with a large metate and when they dismounted to look closer, they found some pottery shards and some stone flakes, which were the residue of tool making. Angelina had looked these artifacts over closely paying special attention to the metate and said, "Bob, these people must have eaten a lot of ground-up rock with their food. Look at the wear on this metate."

"I never thought about that before. I expect you're right."

"Were these Apaches?"

"No, these people were earlier. I don't know who they were, but they weren't Apaches."

These mountains had been home to the Apaches, but they were relative latecomers having only been in the area for maybe two hundred years. Late though they were, it was the Apaches that the area was associated with and the ones that left a lasting mark, if not on the landscape, then at least in the names, history, and lore of southeast Arizona. The Chiricahua Mountains share their name with that branch of the Apache family that ranged from north of the Gila Mountains of New Mexico, south all the way into the Sierra Madre of Mexico.

Bob said, "The Chiricahua Apache were here after these others; maybe they drove them out. I don't know. The Chiricahua were the last Indians to be subdued by the U.S. government. According to some of the old-timers, they were as tough as this country. Do you remember me talking about old Bill Reed over in Double Adobe?"

"Yes, you said he was an old friend of your uncle's. You met him when you started coming out here."

"Yeah, I did. He used to tell me stories about when he was a youngster out here. He said Al Sieber, a scout for the Army back in the 1800s, told him the Apache moved through these mountains as easily as we walk down the street, and that they could cross more desert on foot in a day than most whites could cross horseback. He said the only reason we ever caught them was because we used other Apaches to track and fight them. He didn't believe we would ever have caught them otherwise."

While Angelina looked around the site some more, inspecting a bit of pottery here or maybe a stone tool there, Bob gazed at the canyon and mountains surrounding him. It was as if one could feel the ghosts of those that had been here before. They lived here for hundreds if not thousands of years. Maybe there was something left of them besides some old artifacts. Well, they're gone now, Bob thought. We're here now.

CHAPTER TWENTY-TWO

There was one last long howl from the wolf that trailed off to silence.

It was getting to be late in the summer, and Bob had worked hard to get ready for the fall. Now he had a little breathing room, so he and Angelina were taking some time off. They were riding up to a spot high in the mountains that had a nice spring at the edge of a small park where they were going camping for a few days. Angelina had never been up this high in the mountains, and Bob wanted to show her some of the beauty that was up there.

It was a warm day in the high country of the Chiricahua Mountains. The sky was a brilliant blue, and there were a few puffy, white clouds drifting overhead. Bob looked up at the clouds and thought they might build as the day went on resulting in a summer monsoon storm. He would have to keep his eye on them.

Angelina had grown up in Douglas and was used to the semi-arid grasslands and Chihuahua desert that made up the broad expanses of the flats that covered so much of the southeast corner of Arizona. Since meeting Bob, she had become familiar with the Madrean Woodland of the mountains and canyons around her new home where she often rode with Bob. The juniper and evergreen oak that made up so much of her surroundings were augmented by some half dozen species of pine trees and a few Douglas firs. There was also a healthy population of cottonwood, sycamore, ash, and walnut along the creek, but her favorite trees were the large Arizona cypress with their corrugated bark that seemed to spiral up the trunk and resembled twisted rope to her.

Now they were climbing up a pack trail that would take them to the top of the mountain range. As they climbed, the oak disappeared and the number of pine, especially ponderosa pine increased. The juniper soon thinned out, and where the various pines were only a part of the woodland below, they now dominated along with Douglas fir.

After several miles, Bob stopped. "Angelina, we should take a break for a while and give the horses a chance to rest."

"We could have lunch now if you want," said Angelina.

"That would be good." Bob answered as he stepped down, hobbled his horse, and pulled the saddle off. He then went over to the pack horses and hobbled them. "I'm not going to unpack them until we get to camp," he told Angelina.

They were sitting on a log enjoying the cool breeze and each other's company after finishing lunch. Bob looked up at the clouds building overhead. He guessed they had a few hours before the storm. "We should get going so we can have camp ready in case those clouds build into a storm."

"Do you think they will?" asked Angelina.

"I think there is a pretty good chance of it. We may get lucky, but it's best not to take a chance." Bob rose and caught up the horses while Angelina packed up the lunch leftovers.

They reached the camp site well before the rain started. Bob set up the canvas tepee they would be sleeping in and rolled out his bedroll, which would be big enough for both of them. It was a tight fit, but for a couple of newlyweds that was fine. Angelina helped him set up a picket line for the horses and then led them to the springs, so they could water while he dug a shallow fire pit and set up the grill and tripod.

By the time the rain came, they were all set up. While many of the monsoon rains were actually violent thunder storms, this one was quite mild. There was a little lightning and thunder but not much, and the wind was not strong. The rain itself only lasted for a quarter of an hour or so and wasn't heavy. Bob had set up a tarp as an awning, stretching it between some aspen trees. They sat under it out of the weather and watched the rain.

The small park where they were camped was high. The trees that surrounded it were mostly aspen with some Engelmann spruce and white fir coming up through the aspen stand. The ground fell away to the north and west allowing a view over the treetops of the mountain ranges that rolled on one after another as far as the eye could see.

The rain stopped, and the clouds broke up letting the sun shine on the mountain. "It's beautiful up here," said Angelina.

"Yes, I like it. Cruz brought me up here for the first time when I was a kid, and I've been coming back every year or two since then. Here we sit nice and cool in the aspen with the smell of spruce and fir in the air." Then, pointing to the desert valley below them to the west, he said, "Hard to believe we are only a few miles away from desert brush, cactus, and one hundred-degree temperatures."

"Yeh, hard to believe." Angelina stood up giving Bob a playful punch on the shoulder and asked. "What's for supper?"

"Steak." He answered jumping up and grabbing her before she could run away.

She knew she couldn't pull away using her strength, but she knew her husband was extremely ticklish, so she used that bit of knowledge to escape. They horse played like this on the mountain top for a few minutes before ending up in the tepee where things got more personal.

The next day Bob had taken Angelina to the northeast where they had a picnic overlooking Cave Creek Canyon. The ride over was along the crest of the mountains which was pretty easy going on the whole, but you didn't have to look far to the sides of the trail to see some pretty dramatic changes in terrain. There were steep sided canyons that fell away sharply into heavily wooded forests, there were sharp rock outcrops protruding from the sides of the canyons, there were bare rock ridges and spurs that often had vertical or near vertical cliffs. On the last part of the ride to the picnic site, they were working along a narrow spur that had a steep drop on one side and a sheer cliff of hundreds of feet on the other.

The site Bob picked for lunch had a spectacular view of tall cliffs, red rock formations, and huge vistas with the mist rising from Winn Falls as a bonus. The weather had been perfect, and as they were relaxing and taking in the view, a circling red-tailed hawk had entertained them with its call. As the shrill call echoed off the cliffs, Bob squeezed Angelina's hand, "It doesn't get any better than this."

After supper on their third and last night in camp, Angelina asked, "Why do we eat steak every night up here?"

"Because steak is easy to cook, no pots and pans, just the fire and grill."

"Hamburgers can be cooked the same way." She answered.

"Yes, but you get your hands all greasy patting together the patties. If you want to keep it easy, pack steaks, some potatoes, and a few cans of veggies or beans. You grill the steaks, wrap the potatoes in foil and put them in the coals to cook, and the veggies can cook in their cans on the fire. You can even use the folded back lids of the cans as handles if you don't want to wash dishes. No pots and no pans, just a coffee cup, maybe a dish, and knife and fork to clean."

"You use a frying pan for breakfast to cook the bacon and eggs, and we haven't been eating veggies out of the cans."

Bob smiled at her, "That's because I love you and didn't think you would want to have a slice of bologna rolled in a tortilla for breakfast and lunch, and I figured you'd prefer your supper on a plate rather than out of a can."

"Really, you did that for me?"

"Well, yes," he answered. "And I know what a wild woman you are and thought a descent breakfast might give me needed strength."

"Me! I'm not the horn dog up here, you are."

"Is that a problem?" Bob was smiling.

She smiled back, gave his hand a squeeze, and said, "Of course not, I wouldn't have it any other way."

The sun went down with one of those unbelievable fiery displays of roiling clouds and burning sky that is an Arizona sunset during monsoon. Now they were lying out in the open looking up at the stars and enjoying some hot chocolate that Bob had brewed up on the camp fire. The sky was clear and dark, and the Milky Way was stretched across the sky from horizon to horizon. There was a slight breeze rustling the aspen leaves, and the big dipper was looking huge.

"Look, a shooting star!" said Angelina pointing up at a brilliant light streaking across the sky.

Bob just grunted in reply. He was enjoying the majesty of the clear, night sky that only these desert mountains could afford with no city lights nearby to interfere and very little atmosphere at this altitude to attenuate the starlight. He was also thinking that they would have to return to the ranch the next day, and he would miss the time he and Angelina had spent together on the mountain. It was like a little honeymoon away from the cares and worries of life.

Then he heard it, the unmistakable howl of the wolf. It was the first time he had heard it since that night at Mountain Camp with Cruz nearly a year ago.

Angelina stiffened up beside him and squeezed his hand, "What was that?" she asked.

"It's a wolf, a Mexican gray wolf, a lobo."

Then the wolf howled again. It was long and sounded mournful. It made the hair stand up on the back of Bob's neck. He sat up, and then stood facing in the direction the howl came from and listened. Angelina stood beside him holding his arm tight. They listened for a time then, there was one last long howl from the wolf that trailed off to silence. It was farther away now.

He's heading back to the south, Bob thought. "I wish I had seen him just once." Bob raised his cup of hot chocolate in salute towards the wolf, "Salud, you old lobo. Stay safe."

"What was all that?" asked Angelina.

"I think it's the same old wolf that came through the Sabino Pasture country when I first got back here. Cruz and I heard him then and saw his tracks. Cruz said he's an old male with a bad leg. There aren't any around anymore, at least not in the U.S."

"Are we safe?"

"Yes."

† † †

It was chilly in the morning at a bit more than 9000 feet above sea level. Bob and Angelina were enjoying a last cup of coffee before breaking camp and packing up for the ride back to Mountain Camp. She put her arm through his and pulled close to his side. "I am really glad you brought me up here. It is lovely. It is wild for sure and a little scary but beautiful all the same."

"Scary, do you mean the bears and lions or the old lobo?"

She hesitated a little then answered. "That's part of it. The bears, lions, and wolves are part of this place, but it is more than that. It's the wildness of these mountains. There is something powerful and hidden, something mysterious, almost as if the mountains are alive. It's like they are watching to see if you are allowed here...no, that's not quite it. It's more like they are watching to see if you are worthy of this place. Should they let you stay or should you be run off? Worse yet, should you be destroyed for defiling them? There is no doubt in my mind that these mountains can be dangerous." She looked at Bob then continued. "Something like you, maybe that's why you love them so much, and why they have accepted you."

With this Bob laughed, "I'm not dangerous. You tamed me, remember?"

"Yeah, so you say."

Bob was taking a different trail back to Mountain Camp. It was a little to the east of the trail they had ascended. It was a bit shorter but steeper, which was why he had not used it on the way up. In spots, this trail side hilled along some pretty steep terrain, which had lots of rock outcrops and cliffs.

The clouds were moving in early this day, and when they got to the point where the trail started to descend from the crest, they were looking down on the tops of the clouds that filled the canyons and valleys. Only the tops of the peaks and ridges showed above the clouds.

"It looks like a sea of clouds with islands rising above it ... no not just islands but sky islands. It's like heaven or at least the wilder side of heaven," said Angelina.

"Yeah, it's pretty special."

As they worked their way down through the clouds, it was as if they were in a fog bank. Bob was not comfortable bringing Angelina down such a steep trail with its damp conditions and reduced visibility, but there was no real choice at this point.

They passed shadowy cliffs and spires that seemed to emerge from the white wall of fog as if they were alive. It was a bit spooky, Angelina thought.

When they passed below the clouds where their view was better, they could see that the cliffs were made up of huge spires soaring high into the clouds. These spires were so tightly packed that they formed near solid rock walls only broken by the regularly spaced vertical cracks between them. The wispy white mist that descended from the bottom of the clouds acted as a thin shroud adding a sense of eeriness to the entire scene. These spires looked like a military formation of giants standing hundreds of feet high, marching right out of the mountainside. Giants that were cloaked in thin, white shrouds as if dead. Some of these giants stood out ahead of the formation as if surveying their surroundings. They seemed to be searching, looking over these mountains and canyons as they had done for tens of thousands of years. Bob thought they resembled individual sentinels or maybe warriors advancing ahead of the formation seeking individual combat in the old way. Pointing at the spires Bob said, "These are hoodoos."

"It looks almost as if the cliff is giving birth to them, and they are marching away," said Angelina.

Bob looked at the hoodoos and said, "Yeah, I guess they do, but I have to say they march pretty slowly."

"I have never seen anything like this before." She said looking up at tall spires on either side of the trail as it wound its way through the hoodoos.

"So I take it, you haven't been to the Chiricahua National Monument."

"No, I haven't."

"Well, we'll have to go. It has forests of these hoodoos, and they are even taller."

"I'd like that. Let's go soon."

By the time they reached Mountain Camp a serious thunderstorm was threatening. Angelina went into the house to start supper, and Bob took care of the horses. He got through just as the storm struck with an explosion of thunder and lightning. He ran to the house but was soaked by the time he got under the porch roof. Here he stood and looked out watching the fury of the storm as it lashed out with wind, rain, lightning, and thunder. The thunder was so frequent that the gaps between the closer loud claps were filled by the rumble of distant thunder. It was continuous with no let up.

It reminded Bob of the noise he had heard on Nui Ba Den when the sound of everyone firing small arms, mortars, and grenade launchers was punctuated by the explosions of claymore mines, satchel charges, and rocket propelled grenades all to the accompaniment of a heavy artillery barrage. His mind started to drift back to that fight. He could hear the gunfire and feel the panic that had to be controlled. He shook his head and returned to the present. It had been the shits, and he had no idea why he was alive when so many others were dead. It was as random as getting hit by a bolt of lightning. It was just plain, dumb luck, nothing more, nothing less. "Fuck it, don't mean nothin'."

Well, he was alive, and he was one lucky son of a bitch to be loved by this fine woman and to be cowboying for his uncle. He couldn't bring Rocky Top back, but he would never forget that Rocky Top was the only reason anyone had survived that fight, the only reason he had this life to live.

CHAPTER TWENTY-THREE

". . . they are a bunch of hayseeds but they're local hayseeds and this is their country." Vince

Vince hung up the phone and sat back in his chair. He was frustrated, he was exasperated, he was mad. How had he let this happen? He knew the answer. It was Artie and his god damned foolishness, his stupid pot fields and his tough guy arrogance.

The call had been from his contact in the Cochise County District Attorney's Office. Someone had tipped off the sheriff about their operation. They were planning on conducting a search of the ranch as soon as the judge approved the warrant. His bought man assured him that he would delay the warrant request as long as he could. He was confident he could gum up the works long enough to delay it by a month, but any more would look suspicious. "That was money well spent." Vince said out loud. "If he wasn't in my pocket, we would be truly screwed." Vince called for Alf. When he came into the room Vince told him to go find Artie, Anthony and Freddie. He needed to see all them now.

The pot fields had been a bone of contention between Vince and Artie from the start. They were Artie's little sideline. He figured he would become the pot king of the West. When Vince had told him no, Artie had gone to his uncle and convinced him to let him have a shot at it. It would be his business enterprise and would make money for the family. Mr. V had agreed to placate his nephew. "What can it hurt?" Mr. V had asked. Vince had answered there was no reason to grow anything. All the product they needed was brought up from down south. There was no reason to run the risk. Now it was an excuse for the cops get involved, just what Vince had been trying to avoid.

Vince looked over the men seated in the room. What a crew! Anthony was the only one with a brain, Freddie wasn't too bad but untested, Alf wasn't the sharpest knife in the drawer, and Artie was a constant pain in the ass. "OK, we have a problem. The sheriff is going to come out here with a bunch of deputies and search the ranch." Looking at Artie he said without mirth, "That's cops to you."

"So — they ain't going to find shit."

"They are going to find your pot fields. They have their locations. They also know where the airstrip and the storage buildings on the east spur road are. We can't do much about the airstrip, but we need to be sure the storage buildings are clean, and we have to get rid of the pot in the fields."

Artie jumped to his feet and shouted. "Bull shit, you're not trashing my pot. I worked hard on it. It's producing." His face was red and he was losing control of his temper. "I don't believe this crap. You are making this up as an excuse to get rid of my pot. You never wanted me to have it. Fuck you!"

Vince was fighting to keep control of his temper. He would not have taken this from any other soldier in the family. "Sit down and shut up." He took a deep breath and continued. "This is not just a scare. My man in the DA's office gave me the warning. It's real."

Artie continued to protest, getting louder and more belligerent. Finally, Vince lost it. "I said sit down and shut up! Be glad I'm not having you whacked right now. If you weren't Mr. V's nephew, they'd be hunting your bones in the desert. Your damned pot and your fucking mouth are the reason we are in this fix."

"What are you talking about, my mouth?"

"You pissed off that bunch over the mountain trying to be the tough guy. To you they're a bunch of hayseeds. Well they are a bunch of hayseeds but, they're local hayseeds and this is their country. Our best chance for success is to be quiet and keep to ourselves, but no, you have to be the smart assed, tough guy. It started with you talking trash to those cowboys when they brought the cows back. That might have been forgotten and everything would've been fine, but no, it wasn't enough for your dumb ass. You had to insult that cowboy's girl in town. He nearly choked you to death then. You're lucky Anthony and Alf were there to calm things down. All you did was draw attention to yourself and the rest of us. That's bad for business. What do you want to bet that cowboy has been sneaking around over here and is the one that passed the information to the sheriff about our operation?"

Vince laid out the plan for getting things cleaned up. Vince wanted a buffer. He said they had three weeks to get it done. He and Alf would take care of the storage buildings and checking the airstrip. Artie, Anthony and Freddie would deal with getting rid of the pot fields. As soon as the cleanup was done, Artie and Anthony were to go to Phoenix and stay there until Vince sent for them. He did not want Artie anywhere near the sheriff.

He was comfortable with being able to clean up any evidence in the storage buildings. The airstrip should not be any problem either. The pot fields on the other hand could be a problem. He knew they could not get rid of all the traces of the pot plants, but he would argue that it was forest service land and anyone could have planted the stuff. It was a weak argument that no one would believe, but it would have to do.

CHAPTER TWENTY-FOUR

He had picked a winner.

The morning air was chilled. Even though it was October and the days could still be pretty warm, the promise of cooler weather was unmistakable. Nights were always cool in this part of Arizona, especially in the mountains, but the chill in this morning's air was different. Fall was coming. Soon the cottonwood and sycamore would turn along with the big tooth maple and the aspen up high. There had already been some frost on the valley floor.

Bob looked over at the woman next to him and admired her beauty. She was sleeping soundly, and he had no intention of waking her. They had been married for a little over four months, and while they had had some adjusting to do like all couples, Bob could not be happier. She had adapted to living in a fairly remote cow camp with no regular source of electricity, and no phone, both of which she grew up with in town. He was impressed by her stamina and attitude. He had picked a winner.

He eased out of bed and padded into the kitchen to make a pot of coffee. Aware of the fact that the cold was raising goose bumps on his flesh, he thought it might be wise to put on something. He had stayed in the habit of sleeping nude after marrying Angelina, a habit of which she approved. Bob smiled to himself. One fine woman he thought.

Being Sunday, Bob had no real work to do, just see to the horses when they came in for water. Other than that, all that was on the agenda was a dinner at Headquarters and maybe a church run if Angelina wanted to go to Mass.

Aunt Maria was having Angelina's folks out to join them for dinner. Fall works had just ended, and it had been a few weeks since Jack and Bob had been available for any family socializing. She also thought it would be a good thing to celebrate the end of a successful business year. They had had a fine calf crop, and the sale prices were good.

Angelina came into the kitchen wrapped in a robe against the cold and gave Bob a big hug. "Good morning, my naked stud," she said with a grin. "Aren't you cold?"

"Good morning to you, too. You're bundled up like an Eskimo in winter. I'm a little chilly, but I hate to disappoint you first thing in the morning. You are a pervert."

She hit him on the shoulder saying, "I am not; I just like the view."

"Well, I like a view too; what about me?"

"Sorry, it's too cold," she answered, pouring herself a cup of coffee, "besides it's Sunday."

Cold he understood but Sunday? This line of thinking always confused Bob. Didn't God and the church encourage marriage and all its attendant activities? No matter. "Other than dinner at Uncle Jack's and Aunt Maria's, what have you got planned for the day?"

"I would like to go to Mass. Saint Francis in Elfrida will be fine. I don't want to drive all the way to Douglas."

"Do you want me to drive you?"

"What, and have you wait in the truck? No, I'll be fine. You stay here and prepare for your time in purgatory." She smiled at the last.

"OK, I'll work on my fanning."

With that they took their coffee to the bedroom.

† † †

Angelina was feeling pretty good about life. Taking Communion always helped her outlook, and the morning had started off with a bang. She smiled at herself and felt a little naughty thinking of her Sunday morning tumble with Bob.

As she turned off Highway 666 and headed east, there was a Jeep pickup on the side of the road at the intersection. As soon as she passed, it pulled out behind her and stayed close. She could see two men in the cab, and she thought she recognized them as being from Indian Springs.

On one long, straight stretch the Jeep accelerated and pulled out as if to pass. Angelina worked to keep her cool, keeping her eyes straight ahead. When the Jeep pulled up beside her, it slowed to match her speed and began blowing its horn. When Angelina looked over, she saw Artie in the passenger seat grinning at her and motioning her to pull over.

She had no intention of pulling over. She was scared now and knew she was in a bad situation. One she had to get out of. She mashed the accelerator to the floor of the pickup. The Jeep was no match for the Ford big block V8, and she quickly got back out front and stayed in the center of the road to block any attempts by the Jeep to get around her.

Then she remembered the gun Bob kept in a rack behind the seat. She reached over the back of the bench seat and found it easy to reach in the hooks. She pulled it out and put it on the seat beside her a short-barreled Browning saddle carbine chambered in 243 Winchester. If it came to it, she would shoot these two men to defend herself. Bob had spent a fair bit of time teaching her, to shoot this gun and the others at the house, and she felt comfortable with her ability. There was no question in her mind; if pressed, she would shoot. She was suffering no doubts at this time. She was in survival mode.

She kept her speed faster than she was comfortable with, but she had no choice. As soon as she reached the drive to the ranch headquarters, she turned in rather than continue up to Mountain Camp. The Jeep stopped on the road apparently unsure as to what to do next, but when she began blowing the pickup's horn as she sped up the drive, they left.

Bob had hurried down to Headquarters as soon as he got the radio call. Maria was comforting Angelina, and Jack was on the phone with the sheriff. He had spoken to the sheriff's office and was not satisfied with the response he got there so he called the sheriff at home. Bob could not hear all of what was being said, but he could tell that Jack was being respectful but forceful. Things like, "I've known you for years," and "I have backed you in every election," popped out from time to time along with "What do you intend to do about this bunch of riffraff?" or "I want them out of here, how is it that they are still here?"

The sheriff was explaining to Jack that the raid had gone badly, not enough evidence was found to do any good. This was the first Jack had heard of a raid. "When did this raid take place? I heard nothing."

"Three weeks ago."

"What! Three weeks ago. Didn't anybody think to tell me?"

"There was nothing to tell. We found a little pot in the fields, and it was obvious that someone had recently pulled up all the plants. As it was on public land, the ranch manager argued it was not theirs. We can't do anything with that. I contacted the Forest Service, and they made note of it, but they can't really do anything either without catching them red-handed."

"And you found nothing more. Dammit, Jimmy! You have a leak," Jack bellowed. "Somebody tipped them off." Now he regained control so as not to upset the household. "I guess that means they will be after me and mine now, which explains what happened today. What are you going to do about this?"

"There is no reason to believe you have been linked to the raid."

"That's total and complete bull crap, Jimmy, and you know it. If they knew you were coming, then whoever told them knew it was because of what you learned from me. There is no way your leak kept that tidbit under wraps, and oh, by the way, it's not your family in the cross hairs here; it's mine."

Bob wanted to continue eavesdropping on his uncle but needed to be with Angelina. After being sure his uncle knew he was there, Bob left him to his phone call and went into the living room where he sat with Angelina. His Aunt Maria left and went into the kitchen giving him a significant look as she left.

"Baby, how are you?" he asked. He was sitting on the couch with her, holding her hand.

"I'll be all right, Bob. It was that guy from the Gadsden, the one you threatened." She shuddered a bit. "They followed me, and when they pulled up beside me, he just leered at me and wanted me to pull over. I was really scared." She was crying softly.

Bob held her tightly and just whispered, "I love you, Baby. It will be OK. He can't hurt you now."

She pulled back and looked at him hard. "Maybe not right now, but what about later? He's evil, and I'm scared."

What Bob saw in her eyes was genuine terror, the kind that comes from knowing you're not safe, knowing that someone wants to hurt you and is willing and able to do just that, and knowing that you are powerless to stop them. "I'll take care of him."

"No, you won't. That's just what I need, a husband in jail for going after a gangster, or worse yet, a dead husband. I won't have it, DO YOU HEAR!" She was frantic now.

"Yes, I hear." He pulled her close and held her tight while rocking her back and forth. She began to feel safe in his arms. Relaxing a bit, she said, "Next time you can drive me to Mass."

"Of course, I'd be glad to drive you. Did you remember the gun behind the seat?"

"Yes, I pulled it out and had it on the seat, in case I needed it."

"Good, you did good." Bob made a mental note here. He would have to spend some more time getting her comfortable with firearms. Maybe he could pick up something with a bit more firepower than a lever action saddle gun. It wasn't that he thought it was underpowered or inaccurate. It was not. He was just concerned that five rounds may run out too quickly if she found herself in a tight spot. Maybe he could find a civilian version of an M16. He knew they had them at Interarms in Alexandria, Virginia, but that didn't do him any good here. He would have to check on that soon.

By the time Angelina's folks showed up, things had settled down. Angelina did not want to upset them, so she had asked that nothing be said about the confrontation earlier in the day.

That evening on the way back to Mountain Camp, Bob followed Angelina. She was driving his new truck, and he had the old camp truck. He was disturbed by what had happened. He knew Artie was capable of anything, and he figured the whole Indian Springs crowd was up in arms after the Sheriff's raid.

The bad news was that very little had been found on the raid. The dope patches were cut way back, and being on public land, no real case could be made against Indian Springs as there was no sign of them being involved. The two building clusters were on patented ground belonging to Indian Springs but they had been cleaned out, and while they were suspicious, no dope was found, so no arrests were made. It was obvious Indian Springs had been warned and probably knew the source of the tip that led to the raid.

Bob sighed deeply. It was not the worst situation he had found himself in. He knew he could deal with these assholes, but he was really worried about his wife. She was an easy target for them, and he believed they had just demonstrated their willingness to use her to get at him. He was going to have to get her out of here and then deal with Artie and company.

They talked long into the night about what to do. She agreed she should go away for a time. She wanted to go to Douglas and stay with her folks, but Bob said that would not do. He wanted her to go back East and stay with his folks. She finally agreed, and they went to bed. First thing in the morning he would take her to Headquarters and work on getting her back to his folks for a while. He didn't want her staying at camp by herself. Something he had neglected to mention to her was the fact that he had been seeing tire tracks around Sabino Canyon the last several days. The tracks weren't from the ranch truck, he had checked that. They may have been from Artie's Jeep pickup; he wasn't sure, but it was disconcerting. "It's on," he said beneath his breath.

"What?" Angelina asked.

"Nothing, I was just mumbling to myself."

"Are we going to be all right?"

"Yes, these guys are all noise," he lied. "Besides your heading to Maryland soon to hang out at Fort Meade where you'll be safe."

† † †

Bob had his 45 on the night stand and a shotgun in the corner next to the bed. He didn't believe he would need them, but it seemed to be the prudent thing to do.

He didn't know how long he had been asleep but not long. He looked at the clock and saw it was a little after two a.m. Something wasn't right. Bob slipped out of bed and eased over to the window with the shotgun in hand. Just as he was pulling aside the curtain with the barrel of the shotgun, all hell broke loose.

Bullets were pouring in through the window along with shattered glass and wood splinters from the window sill. Bob dropped to the floor and shouted for Angelina to get down on the floor. "Hit the dirt, get down, get down."

During a brief lull in the shooting, he rose up and spotted a muzzle flash not far away and cut loose with a load of 00 buck shot. The cry was unmistakable; he had hit his mark. The gunfire increased again in response, and he could make out at least two more shooters from their muzzle flashes. He fired at the muzzle flashes which drove the attackers to cover stopping the incoming fire, but when he squatted down to reload, another burst of fire from an automatic weapon ripped through the bedroom. It was during this fusillade that he heard the sickening sound of a bullet thumping into flesh and the soft whimper of his wife.

He dove to a prone position and started low crawling back across the floor. He found her on the floor near the closet with the saddle gun next to her. Instead of getting down and taking cover, she had gone to the closet for the gun. He looked for and found the wound. It was high on the right side of her chest just below her clavicle. He couldn't see color in the dark, but he could feel the sticky warmth of her blood and heard the sound of a sucking chest wound. She tried to talk but couldn't.

The shooting had stopped, and Bob heard the sound of vehicles driving away in a hurry. He turned on the battery-powered lantern Angelina kept next to the bed and began working feverishly to save his wife. He ripped a plastic bag off a dress in the closet and managed to stop the air from leaking out of her chest by pressing it against the wound and sealing the hole. She was coughing up some blood but not too much. The wound in her back also needed tending, so he rolled her gently on to her side and found the wound. It was in the middle of her back and bleeding profusely. It wasn't arterial spurting, just lots of blood leaking out. Bob did the only thing he could think of, pressing hard to try and stop the bleeding.

While all this was going on Bob was talking soothingly to his bride, reassuring her. He tried to make her comfortable while keeping pressure on her wounds. "It's not too bad. I have dressed wounds like this before. You'll be fine." She knew he was lying.

Then he heard Jack on the radio trying to raise him. He couldn't leave Angelina; her color was going, and her breath was getting shallow. Bob had seen this before. She was bleeding out, and there was nothing he could do. If he left her, she may be gone when he got back. Now her breathing was almost imperceptible, and a rattle had started. She was losing consciousness, and in spite of all he hoped and prayed for, he knew she was going. He removed his hand from the chest wound, reached up onto her nightstand and got her rosary, and placed it in her hand. She knew the feel, and a faint smile crossed her lips. Then she was gone.

In the distance as if from another world, Bob could hear his Uncle's voice crackling over the radio. "I can't raise you, so I'm sending in the blind. Maria has called the Sheriff, and I am on my way up. Hang in there."

Bob just sat on the floor in a pool of his wife's blood holding her lifeless body in his arms, rocking back and forth.

CHAPTER TWENTY-FIVE

"My home is a little place in the mountains." Bob Hasett

Bob stood at the graveside long after everyone else had left. The gravediggers wanted to get on with filling in the hole, but they knew better than to pester this young man right now. "I sure do miss you, Baby. I don't know what I'm going to do without you. The only thing I know for sure is I'm going to take care of that son of a bitch and all his friends. I know you don't want me to get hurt, but if they get me, I'll be with you. If they don't get me, I'll get them. I love you, Baby. Why didn't you tell me you were pregnant?" With that, Bob put his hat on and walked away.

Bob's parents had returned to the ranch with Jack and Maria. When Bob finally returned from the cemetery, they told Bob they would stay longer or fly him back home to Fort Meade. He said he would be OK. He needed some time alone, besides his home was a little place in the mountains.

Before going to Tucson to catch their flight, Bob's father asked to speak to him in private. "Now son, I know this has to be hard on you. I know you want to settle the score. Please, don't, your mother and I can't handle another funeral. We got you back after Vietnam; it would be wrong to lose you now."

"I've dealt with more dangerous challenges than a bunch of city dudes in my mountains, as have you. These punks are out of their element."

"It's not them I'm worried about, it's you. If you go and blow them all to hell, I won't care, in fact I would welcome it, but the cops will care."

"I know." Bob answered, but other than that he was non-committal.

His father looked sad when he left. He squeezed him in a hug and said softly. "Be careful, son . . . please."

There was a little small talk around the supper table but not much of substance. Finally, Bob said, "Uncle Jack, I need a little time. Can I take some time off and just get lost for a while?"

"Of course, take whatever you need. Remember, you need to take care of some details this week. It would be good to clear all that off your plate first, and Jimmy and his boys may want to talk to you."

"Jimmy and his boys can go to hell. They have done nothing but screw this up from the get go. Angelina's dead because of that bunch of corrupt, incompetent idiots." Bob realized he was starting to raise his voice and managed to get it under control so he added sarcastically. "Well, I guess if I want to get a message to the mob boys at Indian Springs, I could just tell the Sheriff. That communications link seems to be operating loud and clear."

"Now, Bob," said his aunt. "That's not fair."

"No, Angelina dead is not fair. Calling that sheriff and his band of Keystone Cops incompetent and corrupt is fair."

This was followed by a long silence. Maria decided it had gone on long enough. "There were lots of people at the service. Angelina was very well loved by all the people in Douglas and Agua Prieta."

Jack added, "The church was overflowing. There were people standing outside. I've never seen that many people at a funeral before." Then looking at Bob, "You didn't have her long enough, but you had her for a while. She was special, maybe too special for this vail of tears. Try and take some comfort in what time you had together. I know it's hard but remember the good; don't dwell on what might have been."

This was not too well received by Bob, and Jack feared he had said too much. All Bob said was, "Sounds like good advice, I'll try. I'm sorry Aunt Maria, but I'm not hungry. I think I'll go home and try to get some sleep."

"Oh, Sobrinito, you can stay here. It might be too lonely at the camp. I worry about you."

"I'll be OK, Aunt Maria." Bob's voice was starting to betray him, and he needed to get going. He gave his aunt a hug and headed out the door with Jack close behind.

"Bob, I wasn't going to say anything in front of your aunt, but what do you have in mind? I hope you aren't fixing to do something rash?"

Bob continued to walk to his truck. This was a conversation he didn't want to have.

"Bob, please at least join me in the saddle house for a drink, and let me try and talk some sense into you."

"I don't need or want any sense right now."

"OK, then let me give you some pointers."

With that, Bob stopped resisting and went with his uncle. They sat in the door like that first night over a year ago and passed the jar back and forth a few times. "Bob, I know what you have in mind. If it was me, I'd feel the same way." Bob said nothing. "You know they will be waiting for you if they haven't already left the country." Bob nodded. "You know that if you are successful, the law will have you as the number one suspect." Bob nodded again. "So what do you have to say about all that?"

"I never said I was going after them."

"True but you are; I know that."

"You never heard it from me. You have deniability as long as I say nothing."

Jack was a little perturbed and injured by this. "I'm not so sure about that, but let me tell you this." He had raised his voice a bit, and there was an edge to it. "I don't need your goddamned deniability. I am your uncle; I'm family, and you ride for me. That is more than enough to seal my lips."

Bob was taken aback by his uncle's tone. He did not mean to insult this man. "I'm sorry, Uncle Jack. I didn't mean to imply that you would ever say anything, only that I didn't want to put you in a difficult position."

"My loss is nothing compared to yours, but Angelina was part of this family . . . she was part of this ranch. Her murder puts us all, to use your words, in a difficult position," he paused here looking hard at Bob. "Now let's talk serious."

CHAPTER TWENTY-SIX

"A deal is a deal." Bob Hasett

A couple of weeks after the funeral, Bob was riding Crestnut and leading Chango and Mescal who were packed with light loads. He didn't have three horses because he was packing a lot but because he figured he might be out a while and would need the extra horses as mounts. He had chosen the three horses he was bringing because of their endurance; all three had deep bottoms which he expected he'd need.

His camp was made up of a good cowboy bedroll capable of shedding water and snow if need be, fire-making tools, canned and dehydrated food, coffee, binoculars, small shovel, ax, and just in case an extensive first aid kit and firearms. For firearms he was carrying his M1911 45, and he had a 12-gauge, auto loader shotgun with a cut-down barrel in the saddle scabbard for close work, but his go to weapon was the old sporterized Swede 6.5mm bolt action rifle he had slung across his back. The old Swede was one he had bought as a teenager. He had a pretty nice piece of glass on it mounted high enough so he could use the iron sights, if necessary. He was very comfortable with this rifle out to 600 meters.

Bob was going to set up where he could monitor the Indian Springs country and see what was going on. He had to locate Artie, Alf, and Anthony. These were his main targets, and while he knew they had left, he hoped they would be back before long. Anybody else that got in the way or interfered with him achieving his goal would be taken out as well. As far as he was concerned, there were no innocents at Indian Springs.

He set up under a rock overhang Jack had told him about. It sat on the east facing outcrop of a ridge a half mile west of the Indian Springs Headquarters. While the ridge sloped steeply to the east, its west slope descended gently to a small park or clearing with a spring only fifty meters from the overhang. There were some old pictographs on the rock ceiling of the overhang, nothing fancy, just hands and round swirly things that the Indians had painted long ago.

Bob settled in and began watching the ranch headquarters and the roads leading in and out. Jack had told him the Sheriff had no leads. They found blood at Mountain Camp where Bob had shot one of the attackers, but nobody had reported treating a gunshot wound, and no bodies had turned up. When the Sheriff had gone to Indian Springs, he was told Vince was on a business trip, and Artie and Anthony were on vacation. Jimmy was told all three had been gone for over a week. The sheriff had checked their alibies, and of course, they were confirmed.

The Sheriff's people were not able to come up with much in the way of evidence. The tire tracks at the scene were indistinct, and the brass they had picked up was 45 and 30-06 brass. Based on the amount of brass and Bob's description of the gunfire, it seemed there had been at least one submachine gun, and one machine gun or automatic rifle, such as a BAR. The FBI was supposed to check the brass and some recovered bullets and see if they could determine the model of guns used. The bullet that had killed Angelina was not recovered or at least had not been identified but was probably from the 30-06. If Bob wound up in a fire fight, he would have his hands full, but that was not his intention. This was a hunt not a duel.

Nothing happened for three days. Not one vehicle came or left the ranch headquarters day or night. Then on the fourth night, lights appeared on the drive leading up to the house. There were two vehicles. They continued past the house, headed north in the direction of the airfield and the building clusters. Bob could not tell more than that, but the lights reappeared after a couple of hours. One set of lights pulled into the ranch yard, and the other appeared to pull into the garage.

Bob could not tell what vehicles they were or their occupants. He stayed awake and kept watch until sunrise. Once the sun had risen a bit, and the glare was out of his binoculars, as he was looking just south of east, he saw the vehicle parked in the yard. It was the Jeep pickup.

Bob's heart raced a little as he began to believe maybe he would get his chance. Keeping a watch on the house, he ate a cold breakfast and only used a heat tab to warm some water for instant coffee. A poor substitute even for cowboy camp coffee, but it was hot and it had caffeine. Nothing happened until late morning, and Bob was having a great deal of trouble keeping his eyes open when he saw movement at the headquarters. Looking through his binoculars, he could see four men in the drive. He thought he recognized Vince and Anthony, but he knew he recognized Artie; the fourth man might be Alf. He was leaning on a cane.

A car was brought out of the garage, and the four men got in with a driver and left. An older man had come out of the house to see them off, but then somebody, a younger man, came out of the house with a suitcase and the two of them got in the Jeep pickup and headed north. That was the direction of the buildings and the airstrip.

Bob tried to follow their progress by the dust kicked up on the road, but before long they were being masked by higher terrain. It didn't matter though, for in a half hour Bob heard the unmistakable sound of a plane. Scanning the sky, he saw a light plane heading towards the airfield and descending. Soon it dropped out of sight, and within fifteen minutes he saw it ascending and turning south.

Before long the Jeep returned, and the old man was not in it. Bob could only speculate as to what was going on and who the old man was, but that didn't bother him. The younger guy had come back. Bob would get what he needed from him. Now it was time for some sleep. He would be busy this evening.

Bob's horses were content to be grazing in the small meadow just west of the ridge where he was camped. He had hobbled them where they had plenty of good grass and spring water. He would not need them tonight.

† † †

Just before sunset Bob walked down to the ranch headquarters where he found cover and watched. He saw no sign of anyone until the same man he had seen drive the Jeep earlier in the day came out the back door of the main house. Bob watched as he wandered about a little and smoked a cigarette. It looked like he was just bored.

It was almost full dark now, and there was only a quarter moon high overhead. Bob eased out of his hide and crept up to the house. He worked his way to the back and closed the distance between himself and his quarry. When he was no more than a step away, the man sensed his presence and spun around while reaching under his jacket. It didn't matter; Bob gave him a solid vertical butt stroke with his rifle. As the man stumbled back Bob stepped towards him and putting all his weight behind the blow rammed his rifle butt into the man's face. He went down like a sack of potatoes. Bob looked at the unconscious body on the ground and thought, that time on the bayonet range came in handy after all.

Bob felt around and found the man's pistol. He tucked it into his belt. He tied the man's hands behind his back with a pigging string and gagged him. Then he began slapping him to bring him back around. Once he was conscious, Bob helped him to his feet, none too gently and shoved him away from the house to the east. Once they had moved east for a few hundred meters, Bob turned north and circled around the ranch headquarters eventually leading his prisoner to the back side of the ridge where he was camped.

Just as dawn was breaking, he sat the man down next to the spring seep, pulled another pigging string out of his small pack and tied the man's feet.

Removing the gag Bob asked, "Who are you?" There was no answer. "Who are you?" he asked again, again no answer. With that, Bob pulled out his 45 and shot the man in his knee.

The man shrieked in pain and disbelief. "You shot me, you son of a bitch; you just shot me."

"Who are you?" The man was looking at Bob in disbelief when Bob pointed the pistol at his other knee.

"Freddie, I'm Freddie Buono. For God's sake, don't shoot me again."

Bob shook his head in frustration, "Freddie Buono, who is Freddie Buono? Are you going to tell me Cher is your sister-in-law?"

"What — no. I'm nobody, just Freddie Buono, that's all," he muttered through clenched teeth.

"It is now time for you to stop fucking with me. I really don't give a rat's ass what your name is. I want to know who you are, why you're here, what you're doing, and where the others are? A bullet in your knee will be the highlight of your day if you don't start telling me what I need to know."

Freddie hesitated, and Bob calmly shot him in the other knee. Freddie cried out again, sucked in several deep breaths and then began to lose consciousness. Bob reached into his pocket and pulled out an ammonia ampule, smashed it between his fingers, and waved it under Freddie's nose. It worked. Freddie remained conscious.

Bob reached down and untied Freddie's legs. "You don't need this anymore."

"You're crazy! You're fucking crazy. What do you want out of me? What did I ever do to you?"

"I don't think you ever did anything to me, but you have information I want."

"Who are you?" Freddie groaned. He was in a great deal of pain, but now he was beginning to understand that the pain he was suffering may be nothing to what he was going to endure. He looked in disbelief at this crazy man sitting near him. When he looked into his face, he saw nothing. He had known some mean sons of bitches in his time, but this guy was different. "Why?" He asked.

Bob thought, fuck this bastard I owe him nothing. I don't need to say shit — but if it gets him to talk. "Your friends shot up my house and killed my wife. I want them. You are nothing to me. You can live or die; it is nothing to me either way, but them, that's another story. Now you can tell me what I want to know, and I'll be done with you, or you can make me work for it, and that will go hard on you. Either way you will tell me in the end."

"Oh, man, it wasn't me. I was in Jersey when all that went down. It was that crazy Artie. He's out of his mind. He did it."

"Who was with him?"

"Alf and Anthony."

"Where are they now?"

"I don't know."

With that, Bob grabbed Freddie's foot and gave it a twist. He screamed and passed out. Bob revived him with the ammonia ampule and asked again, "Where are they?"

"Vegas, they went to Las Vegas."

"When?"

"They left right after the shooting."

"Why were they here yesterday?"

"I don't know; they don't tell me shit. I'm just a soldier; I got no clout."

Bob reached for his leg again. "OK, OK," Freddie blurted, "Mr. Vechio wanted to be sure all the papers and cash was hid real good."

"Mr. Vechio, is he Artie's uncle?"

"Yes."

"He's the big boss, right?"

"Yes."

"He's the old man that you took to the plane yesterday?"

Freddie was looking at Bob with real fear in his eyes. "How do you know all this?"

"Never mind. Was that him?"

"Yes."

"Where is he now?"

Again, Freddie hesitated and Bob reached for his leg. "No," Freddie cried, "I'll tell you. He flew down to Mexico."

"When is he coming back?"

"You know I can't tell you that. My life won't be worth shit if I tell you that."

Bob laughed, "Your life isn't worth shit now." Then leaning forward to within inches of Freddie's face and for the first time since the interrogation had begun, Bob looked menacing. "When is he coming back?"

"Why should I tell you if you're going to kill me anyway?"

"Because you'll die much harder if you don't, and nobody will know what a stud you were. You won't make it into the Mafia Hall of Fame."

"I'll make a deal. I'll tell you everything if you just stop hurting me and get me to a doctor instead of killing me."

"If you tell me everything, I will stop fucking with you and drop you off in Mexico. You can find your own doc. Just so you know, I will also let it be known that you gave up your partners and boss so don't be going back to them. They won't be as nice as I am. On the other hand, if you lie to me, I will open you up with a small cut, pull out a loop or two of your guts and wait for the coyotes to show up. They will pull your intestines out and play tug a war with them as we watch. In the end they will eat your guts. It will suck to be you."

"What, that's not real! You won't do that."

"Yes, it is and yes, I will. It's an old Indian trick."

"How do I know you won't do it anyway?"

"You don't. Now talk," Bob hissed.

Freddie opened up and told Bob everything he knew. He told him about how Artie had tricked Alf and Anthony into going along with him, saying it was his uncle's orders. He had even told them that the woman, the cowboy's wife, had left him and gone back to town, so she wasn't there. The old man had lost it when he heard what happened. He was furious with Artie for being a hothead and an incompetent one at that. Not only was the attack stupid and unnecessary, but the fact that he had killed the wrong person just made it worse. The cowboy was still alive and, Artie had killed the wife instead. Rivals and problem people were fair game, but family members were to be left alone. All this was bad for business.

The old man was upset about the sheriff's raids, but he figured they had weathered that storm, and with their contact in the county prosecutor's office, they knew they had nothing to worry about. It would have all blown over if Artie had kept his head. There would have been plenty of time to deal with these hicks later.

Now it would be a tougher problem to handle. Folks were really mad about the killing, and while there was no evidence pointing towards them, the public mood was bad, and the mole in the prosecutor's office was not willing to do much. He had said that if all stayed quiet, he might be able to steer the investigators in another direction in time but not right now.

The problem the old man had was that there was a lot of paper at the ranch that was damaging. Not only were the records of the local operation there, but they had brought a lot of their paperwork from back East for safekeeping. The old man was pretty sure a bunch of hayseeds from the sticks would not be a problem, but this mess meant the cops might show up again and get lucky.

There was also the matter of the money. There was lots of cash at the ranch. The old man was taking some of it to Mexico with him, and the boys were taking some of it to Vegas; the rest they had hidden along with the papers. Freddie figured they had hidden a million bucks or more in cash.

Bob thought about all this. He had to get Artie and the others to stay. He would never get them if they went back to Jersey, so he had to keep this Freddie alive for a while. He was his only hope for finding the money and papers. He needed to find them and hide them where the Indian Springs crew could not find them. That would prevent them from leaving, and once they started poking around the mountains, they were his.

"OK, Freddie, it's your lucky day. I'll take the deal. Let me have a look at those legs."

Bob pulled out his knife and split Freddie's pants legs. He had hit both knees squarely, and they were destroyed. The only question was had the blood vessels been damaged to the point that the circulation to the lower legs was cut off. Bob was not a doc or even a medic, but he had seen wounds and knew a little about treating them. "I'm going to splint your legs and try and clean them up a little." Sitting back and looking closely at Freddie's face Bob added. "I can't do anything about your nose, busted teeth or the knot on your forehead, but I expect none of them will kill you."

The splinting did not go easily, shattered bone made the process of straightening and securing each leg to a stick splint quite an ordeal for Bob and much worse for Freddie, who finally just passed out from the pain. Bob decided to let him stay unconscious for a while. It was quieter that way. He needed to know where the money and papers were, but Freddie was in bad shape. He tried to revive him a time or two in order to question him, but he just kept nodding off. Bob decided it would be better if he went back to Mountain Camp and got some medical supplies. He needed to get Freddie stabilized.

Bob caught his horses and led them up the slope and around to his camp where he saddled Mescal and put the pack saddles on the other two. Then he grabbed up some food and took a blanket out of his bedroll and went back down the slope.

Freddie was awake when he got back to the spring. Bob tossed him the bag with a couple of cans of beans and the blanket. "Here, I'll be back tonight. You need medicine, and I'm going to get it."

"You're not leaving me here alone are you?" Freddie was on the verge of panic.

"You're not alone; I saw bear sign just up that canyon, and I know there's a lion in this area. They'll keep you company."

"A lion, are you nuts? This isn't Africa."

"A mountain lion and a bear, don't forget. If you keep quiet and still, they may not find you. There's something to eat in the bag."

Freddie looked into the bag and pulled out the beans. "How am I supposed to open these?" He asked, holding up the cans.

"With a can opener."

"Oh, sure a can opener, everyone carries a can opener," he groaned.

Bob pulled out his dog tags with the P38 can opener on the chain and held it up saying, "I do."

"Fuck you."

Bob took one of the cans and opened it about two thirds of the way and bent the lid back. "Here, have some breakfast."

Freddie was in the middle of protesting between groans when Bob swung up and rode off leading his string.

† † †

On his return from Mountain Camp, Bob had set Freddie up with a shelter. It wasn't much, just a brush lean-to with a bunch of pine boughs to lie on. He had a couple of blankets, a canteen of water, and some canned food with a can opener. Bob had redressed Freddie's legs and given him some Darvon left over from a horse wreck he'd had earlier, and these seemed to be helping Freddie with the pain. He had also given him a shot of Combiotic to fight infection. He wasn't sure what the dose should be for a person, but he decided a calf's dose would be about right. Bob didn't know if Combiotic would work on a person, but he figured it would either help Freddie or kill him. No matter, as long as he stayed alive long enough to tell him where the money and papers were stashed."

"Your shitting in tall cotton there, Freddie. You got this palace to live in and a first-class doctoring of your wounds."

Freddie was not impressed. "Fuck you, hayseed, you put me in this mess."

"Yes, I did, and I just want you to know that I called the sheriff's office and told them you had given up Artie, his uncle, and the rest of the boys. It shouldn't be long before Mr. Vechio's contact lets them know." This was a lie. Bob was not stupid enough to let the Indian Springs bunch know anything, but this might push Freddie in the direction he wanted.

"God, I'm screwed."

"Yep, and this old hayseed is the closest thing you have to a friend."

Freddie looked at Bob with pure hate, "If that's true, then I am fucked even worse than I thought."

Bob smiled menacingly, "It's true. Now tell me where the money and papers are hidden."

Freddie thought about this for a while and decided he had nothing to gain by keeping the secret, and he knew it would hurt a lot if he didn't talk. This cowboy was crazy. Freddie could just imagine him feeding some coyotes or a bear or a mountain lion his guts while he was still alive. He had dreamed about it. "OK, I'll tell you."

The next morning Bob saddled up Crestnut and trotted over to the ranch headquarters. He was leading Chango and Mescal. After checking carefully, he was sure there was no one there. Looking through the barn he found a pick and wrecking bar, which he tied to the pack saddles along with the shovel and ax he had brought from camp. He then headed for the buildings up the road to the north. Freddie had told him the money and papers were buried under the floor boards in the far-left corner from the door of the first building in the second group. That was about four miles from Headquarters.

It didn't take long for Bob to dig up what he was looking for. There were several canvas and leather satchels filled with bundles of cash and a small suitcase full of papers. Bob repacked his tools and divided the satchels and suitcase between the panniers to keep them balanced. It was a substantial load but not overly heavy. He made no attempt to replace the boards or fill the hole. He wanted Artie and the boys to find this.

Bob did not go back via the ranch headquarters but instead went west over one ridge, then up the road towards the airfield before cutting west then south to come at his camp from the west. He saw no good in following the same path, and it was, in fact, a bad idea to become predictable; besides it didn't hurt to keep Freddie confused.

When Bob returned to his camp, he stashed the money and suitcase full of papers in a crack at the back of his rock overhang and covered it with a large rock. The money was wrapped in wax paper and plastic then stuffed in the satchels. It should all be safe until the pack rats found it.

After unsaddling his horses, he led them back to the spring for a drink, hobbled them, and turned them out. Freddie was not looking good. "How are you feeling?" Bob asked.

"Not good. I'm burning up."

Bob approached Freddie carefully; he did not trust him and reached over to feel his forehead. He was very hot. Bob thought he noticed an unpleasant smell and looked down towards Freddie's legs. The wounds were seeping through the bandages, and the skin he could see below the bandages was badly discolored. Leaning over close to Freddie's legs, he gave a short sniff and nearly gagged.

"Freddie, I'm going to give you another dose of the Combiotic." With that, Bob went over to the spring and pulled up the plastic bag he had the bottle of Combiotic submerged in. The spring was no refrigerator, but it kept the bottle cool. He loaded the syringe with another dose, this time a half dose larger than the last, and rolled Freddie over giving him the shot in his hip.

Freddie moaned in pain and said, "Your bedside manner is shit."

"I'll work on it. Now get some sleep."

Bob walked back up to his camp, heated up some dinner, and watched the drive to the ranch. After a while, he felt a bit guilty and got some heated beanie weenies and carried them down to Freddie along with some lemonade mix.

The sun was setting back up in his camp, and Bob was tired; he had not slept much in the past couple of days. He didn't expect much to happen tomorrow, Sunday or the next day, Monday, but Tuesday was just around the corner, and he would be busy then. He needed a plan, and he had two days to work on it.

Sleep came early, but as tired as he was, it didn't last long. He was soon wide awake but not due to night sweats. This time it was Angelina. The dream started with her looking radiant, and it made him ache with want, but then she got upset with him and lost her radiance. She became sad, and even though she said nothing, he could tell she was upset about the way he was treating Freddie.

He tried to explain that it was the only way, but she said he was being cruel and he should stop. He couldn't take Freddie to the hospital; that would land him in jail. He couldn't just turn him lose either. Releasing him in the mountains would just lead to his slow death, and leaving him in town would lead to Bob's arrest. She was not satisfied with these answers. This is what had awakened him, and now it was keeping him awake.

By morning he decided he could no longer keep Freddie alive and in pain. That left him with two choices: put him out of his misery with a quick shot to the head or get him to the hospital. The smart thing was simply to shoot him and be done with it. This had been his plan since the beginning. He had had no intention of setting him free; he was just going to kill him when he was done with him. Truth be told, he was done with him now, but he had not shot him yet even though he should have. A deal is a deal, he thought.

Bob let out a big sigh and headed down the backside of the ridge to the spring and Freddie's lean-to. "OK, Sweetheart, I will get him help," he said to his dead wife. "You win." Once he got there, he woke Freddie up and asked, "How are you doing this morning?"

"Not good."

With this, Bob gave him some Darvon and said, "Freddie I'm taking you to town. I am going to find a doctor in Agua Prieta. Getting you from here to the car will be hard on you. Are you up to it?"

"Yes." He looked genuinely surprised. "I thought you were going to kill me."

"I was, but that changed."

"You are a mean son of a bitch. Why should I believe you? What's to keep you from dragging me out of here and killing me anyway?"

"Nothing except that would be stupid. Why the hell would I go to extra effort? If I was going to kill you, I'd do it here and be done with you. Did you eat anything last night?"

"No."

Bob rummaged through the bag of canned goods and pulled out a can of peaches. Opening them, he handed the can to Freddie. "Here, eat this. You are going to need your strength."

Bob led Chango up the slope to his camp where he saddled him and then returned to Freddie. He put a halter and lead rope on Crestnut and led him over to the lean-to. "Freddie, I'm going to help you up onto his back. I don't know if you can straddle him or not. It is either that, or you lay on your belly across his back. It's your call. What do you want to try?"

Freddie looked at Bob like he was some sort of fool. "What are you, fucking crazy? I'm not riding some nag."

"It's either that or walk, which for you means low crawl. There is no road within half a mile of here. Now what will it be?"

"I don't think I can sit."

"OK, belly it is. Before I help you up, I need to know where the keys are for the Jeep at the ranch."

"They're in the ashtray."

Bob had taken his pistol out of its holster and laid it aside. He saw no reason to tempt fate. Wrapping his arms around Freddie, he lifted him and threw him over his shoulder, then carried him to Crestnut, and laid him across the horse's back. "You're lucky I have this horse with me; he won't buck."

Bob recovered his pistol and swung up on Chango's back. In order to spare Freddie any unnecessary pain and to save a bit of time Bob was going to take the shortest route he could to the ranch drive that led from the main road to the Indian Springs Ranch Headquarters. He would leave Freddie there, near the intersection of the drive and the main road. He would then ride fast to the Indian Springs Headquarters, hide the horses in case anyone returned, get the jeep, and return to pick up Freddie for the trip to Agua Prieta.

CHAPTER TWENTY-SEVEN

"Yes, honor is important." Don Fabion

Bob had gone west on the forest road instead of east to the highway. He wanted to talk to Cruz. He thought about calling from Indian Springs but was afraid that would leave a record with the phone company. Going to see Cruz was taking a risk, but he had no choice.

He lucked out and found him loading his horse in a trailer not far from Government Trap. He would not have to drive to Cruz's house, past the Tres Cruses Headquarters, and risk being seen with Freddie in the truck.

Bob stepped out of the Jeep pickup and waited for Cruz to come over. He didn't want to leave Freddie alone.

Cruz smiled and greeted Bob, "Hola, Bob, Como estas?

"Bien, y tu?"

Cruz was looking hard at Freddie. "I am good." Then he looked at Bob, and the question was in the look.

"He is one of the bunch from over there." Bob said waving his arm towards the east. "I need to take him to a doctor in Agua Prieta. Do you know somebody there I can trust?"

"Si, I know." Cruz thought for a minute. "Why you not finish him?"

"I made a deal with him. I know it's stupid, but I made a promise." Of course, he did not tell Cruz the promise was to his dead wife in a dream.

"I understand this. You have to keep your promise for your honor."

"Si," Bob answered. He was a little ashamed. His honor was not the reason this man was alive. Angelina's kindness and compassion were the reasons Freddie was not already dead.

"I will go back to my house and call a doctor. You meet me at Malpai Mesa."

Malpai was an anglicized version of the Spanish mal pais or bad country. In the Southwest, it meant bad lands or rough country, typically made up of old lava beds. They could be fairly high and were always rough.

The San Bernardino Valley had several old calderas that had spawned the lava flows a half million years ago. These old flows now made up the malpais. It was different country than Bob was used to. There was more brush and cactus but still lots of grass. The biggest difference was the rocky ground. It seemed as if every inch of ground was covered with fist-sized or larger basalt rocks.

Cruz met Bob at the mesa northeast of Douglas. Bob filled him in on what had been happening. Cruz said to follow him. He knew where there was a cattle gate used by ranchers from both sides of the border. There was no checkpoint there. They went east towards New Mexico and then worked their way south across the old malpai until they came to the gate. Once they were through, they got onto Highway 2, and Cruz led the way into Agua Prieta.

They pulled into a small walled yard and parked. Cruz went to the door while Bob and Freddie stayed in the Jeep. Before long, a distinguished, older man came out with Cruz and walked up to the Jeep. Bob thought he looked familiar but couldn't place him. As he stepped out of the vehicle, Cruz introduced the gentleman as Don Fabian Elias, a great uncle to Angelina. He shook Bob's hand and said, "I am so sorry. Angelina was a very special woman."

Now Bob remembered he had met this man at his wedding. "Thank you, Don Fabian. She was a special woman."

"Is this one of the animals that attacked your home?" he asked looking at Freddie with hate.

"No, but he works for them."

"Please, bring him inside."

Don Fabian was not only Angelina's great-uncle; he was also a doctor. Bob thought that was a fine bit of luck. It could go hard on Freddie if Angelina's great-uncle decided to be sparing with the anesthesia, but he agreed to see to his wounds.

When Don Fabian was through examining Freddie and had put him under with some sedatives, he led Bob and Cruz to the living room. "He will lose the right leg and probably the left one also. I will do what needs to be done. What do you want me to do with him after that?"

Bob pulled out a bundle of cash and handed it to Don Fabian. "Keep him here until I am through with what I have to do. Take what money you need from this to cover your fees, then give what's left to this cabrón, and tell him to get as far away from here and New Jersey as possible. There is fifteen thousand dollars here. It should be enough for him to get away after you have paid yourself for his treatment. Remind him that I have put the word out that he helped me, and if that's not enough to get him on his way, tell him the coyotes are still waiting for their meal."

"Bob, you are too generous. You should let me lobotomize him."

"I appreciate the offer, but I made a deal with him, and honor demands I keep the deal."

"Yes, honor is important."

† † †

It was early still so Bob and Cruz stopped for an early supper in town. The cantina was fairly spacious and pretty bright with lots of windows, but at this late afternoon hour it was nearly empty. Aside from two men at the bar there was an old man playing a guitar accompanying a young boy who was singing. Cruz explained these songs were mostly corridos, stories. In this case mostly sad ballads of this northern frontera of Mexico. Other than the music the only sound was the buzz of the faulty, blinking neon sign behind the bar proclaiming the excellence of Cerveza Pacifico.

Bob and Cruz took a table away from the others that afforded them some privacy. Bob listened to the boy sing while Cruz placed their dinner order. He could not make out most of the lyrics, but he understood the boy was singing about going north in search of work and something about La Migra.

As they ate their dinner Bob filled Cruz in on what had happened so far. He did not discuss his plans with Cruz as that would only serve to put him in a compromising position.

Cruz did have some advice for Bob, however. He reminded him of some old mines with deep winzes. They would make excellent graves. Cruz also told Bob, he and Jack had been seeing to Mountain Camp. They had seen his tracks from the other day and hoped everything was all right.

"Please, tell Uncle Jack and Aunt Maria that I am fine. Don't tell them about any of this, but tell Uncle Jack that I expect the Indian Springs crew to be back on Tuesday."

"I can do this thing for you."

"Good, also tell him it won't be much longer. Cruz, when I am done, please get in touch with Don Fabian and ask him to send Freddie on his way."

"OK."

When they finished their supper and were leaving, the boy was singing something about the police in Agua Prieta and the jail in Cananea. Bob was stuffed. He had loaded up on burritos, rice, beans, chilies, and coffee, along with a couple of Cerveza Pacificos. He had been eating out of cans for a week, and a real meal was welcome.

CHAPTER TWENTY-EIGHT

"You never get tired of being stupid, do you?" Mr. Vechio

It was Tuesday morning. Bob was set up north of the ranch headquarters where he had a pretty good view of the house and drive. The reason he chose this location was that it was on the road leading to the buildings where the money and papers had been hidden. He was sure that collecting that stuff would be the first order of business. He intended to make it a costly endeavor.

It was early afternoon when the car came up the drive. It stopped and five men got out. Bob was pretty sure he recognized Alf, Anthony, Artie, and Mr. Vechio, but the driver was new. They all went into the house, and soon the driver and Anthony came back out. They headed to the barn and returned to the car carrying some tools. Bob was glad he had returned the pick and wrecking bar the day before.

It wasn't long before they were driving north and passed Bob's location. He swung up on Crestnut's back and put him up into a gallop. He rode straight for the buildings cutting off the dogleg which the car would be forced to take along the road. This shortened the distance he would have to cover by nearly half. When he got near the buildings, he saw that the car had not yet arrived. He had plenty of time to get ready. He dismounted, hobbled the horse, and pulled his Mauser out of the saddle scabbard. He had already prepared a position where he had a good shooting rest and an unobstructed view of the building's door just two hundred meters away by his pace count, an easy shot.

He settled into a comfortable prone supported position, noted there was no wind to speak of, and began scanning the area through his rifle scope. Soon the car pulled up Anthony and a man he did not recognize got out of the car and went into one of the buildings. Bob put the cross hairs on the building's door. Just then the driver came out of the door and hurried towards the car. Anthony was right behind him.

Bob felt the slight recoil and saw Anthony go down. He racked another round into the chamber and pumped it into the inert form lying in the dirt. Bob took out Anthony first because he considered him a threat. He would let the driver return with the bad news about Anthony, the money, and the papers. Bob watched as the car spun its tires in the dirt and raced back to the headquarters.

Bob policed up his brass and hurried back to his horse. He listened for the Jeep but heard nothing, so he mounted and began working his way back to his earlier position. Surely, they had heard the gunshots. When he got back to where he could observe the ranch house, he saw activity. Mr. Vechio was gesticulating frantically at the driver of the car, who had just reported what had happened. The others seemed to be searching for something, running in and out of the house and looking in the Jeep. Finally, Alf held up something from the Jeep. Ah, thought Bob, the keys.

This was going to be too easy. Alf and Artie got in the jeep and started out of the drive. He would take out Alf and the Jeep and let Artie sweat before taking him down. Then the Jeep stopped. "What now?" Bob said under his breath. He could see the old man was waving them back. Evidently, he thought better of sending them up the road, smart man.

Bob kept the house under observation for the rest of the day then returned to his camp after sunset. He downed a quick meal and took up a sleeping position that would allow him to easily check on the house without getting out of his bedroll. It was not the most comfortable place for him to sleep, but tonight he wanted to be where he could catch any activity.

† † †

He had had another bad night. He was awake much of the night and never felt as if he had really slept. Today could be difficult if he had to do much.

After checking on the horses and eating breakfast, Bob settled down to watch the ranch from his camp. He was working on his third or fourth cup of coffee and trying to stay awake when he saw people moving around the ranch house. "This is not an early rising bunch," he said to himself. All four men were getting into the Jeep. He could see that they were carrying long guns of some description, whether rifles or shotguns he could not tell at this distance.

As Artie, Alf, and Mr. Vechio drove up to the building, they saw Anthony's body on the ground. The driver had already stopped the Jeep when Mr. Vechio said, "Don't stop; drive up to the door, and we'll get inside the building."

When the jeep pulled up to the door the four men rushed into the building not knowing what to expect but with guns ready. What they saw was what Mr. Vechio had feared. "Freddie took our stash. That no good son of a bitch took our stash."

Turning to the driver he said, "Chris, take us back to the house." Then he turned to Artie and Alf, "You two come back up here and bury Anthony. Be sure to bury him deep. I don't want anybody finding him."

Artie said, "It wasn't Freddie. It was that cowboy from Tres Cruses."

The old man thought about this for a while. "No, how would he know where the stash was? Only Freddie knew it was here — Freddie and us."

Artie noticed the look in his uncle's eye, and he didn't like it. "It wasn't any of us. You know it couldn't be any of us. We would never do that to you."

"That's what I thought about Freddie, too, but it's gone," Mr. Vechio said.

Artie continued to argue. "It had to be that cowboy. Maybe he got Freddie to go in with him on it, but it had to be him. If Freddie had done this on his own, he wouldn't have stayed around and shot Anthony. He would have split as soon as he dug up the cash"

"Maybe he had just done it, and they caught him at it," said the old man.

"We left over a week ago. Why would he wait?" answered Artie.

"You may have something there." Said the old man. "Freddie wasn't the smartest guy, but he wasn't the dumbest either. Freddie would not have bothered with the account books; he would have only been interested in the money. So you figure this cowboy is good enough to get the better of Anthony?"

Alf chimed in. "Vince thinks so. He did some checking; this guy is some kind of war hero. A real badass according to Vince. I can tell you that when we hit his place, he was shooting back not hiding under the bed." Then looking at Artie, he said, "Vince warned you about him. He told you that if you kept messing with his old lady, you'd pay. Now look at this shit."

"That's crap. He's just another hick, and she had it coming."

"Fuck you!" Alf said to Artie. Then turning to the old man, he said. "Mr. V, I don't mean any disrespect here, but we are all paying for Artie's fuck up. Anthony's dead and probably Freddie too, and what about business? It's costing us a fortune every day we don't move product through here, not to mention over a million bucks that's missing. Mr. V — this is wrong. If Artie weren't your nephew, you'd never stand for this shit."

Mr. Vechio was glaring at his nephew, "Artie, did Vince warn you?" There was a long pause. "Don't lie to me; I'll check with Vince."

"Yeah, he might have said something about this guy being in Vietnam or something, but that don't mean shit."

"Maron, how can you be so stupid? Vince is a made man. He knows what's what. If he said this cowboy was a bad ass then you should have listened to him."

"Bull shit, he ain't a bad ass. He's just a country hick. Vince don't know shit."

The old man had kept his voice low until now, but Artie's stupidity pushed him over the edge. He lost it and began to yell. "Shut up, you fool. You know nothing. Vince has been around. He knows a threat when he sees one. Obviously, you don't. Because of you I am down two good men and lots of money. You're the reason we're in this mess. You're bad for business. If you weren't my brother's son, I would turn you over to this cowboy right now."

Artie started to respond but thought better of it.

"Alf, do you think this cowboy did it?"

"Yes, Mr. V, I think so. So does Vince."

The old man thought for a moment then said, "I'm sending for help. We . . ."

Artie interrupted. "No, we don't need any help. I know where this hick lives. I'll take care of him myself."

Mr. Vechio was getting exasperated with his nephew. "You never get tired of being stupid, do you? He isn't at his house, he's out here. I wouldn't be surprised if he is watching us right now. Do you think it was dumb luck that he stumbled on Anthony and our stash? Did you see those wounds? He took him down with one shot and then followed that with one for good measure. Anthony never got a shot off. He was out here waiting on them."

† † †

When Mr. Vechio got back to the ranch headquarters, he reinforced his instructions to Alf and Artie about burying Anthony's body deep and away from the buildings. He didn't want anybody finding the grave. After they drove off, he got Vegas on the phone and called in some favors. He was given a contact in Phoenix. Phoenix had agreed to come out and bring two others to assist. He assured Mr. Vechio they could handle the job. They were due to arrive tomorrow.

All this was unknown to Bob. What he did know was that it would not be as easy as he had hoped. The old man had a brain.

No doubt the old man was working on a plan and maybe sending for help. Bob would have to be prepared. He must keep the initiative and work for any advantage he could gain. He had to ensure they played his game. He could not let them dictate the rules. One option was to get to the house and reduce the numbers. He had to keep the pressure on and not allow them to regain their balance.

Bob collected Mescal and started for the ranch headquarters. He would set up just to the east on a low ridge that would give him a good view. He had already paced the distance as four hundred five meters to the back door. He had a good escape route to the east if he needed it. There were no roads to the east, and there was good cover. He could then go either north or south before circling back to the west.

It was late afternoon before he was in position, just in time, for the Jeep soon appeared coming back down the road. Bob steadied his rifle on a rest and waited for the Jeep to stop. Artie stopped the Jeep, and Alf got out and stood stretching before limping towards the house.

Bob took in a breath let some of it out, held it, and squeezed. The report of the rifle and the recoil surprised him a little as was often the case with a clean trigger squeeze, but he kept his target in the scope; half a second later he saw Alf stumble and fall. He quickly chambered another round and found Artie in his scope. He didn't want to kill him just yet so he watched. Artie shot a quick look at Alf and ran for the house.

Alf rose up a little and looked towards the house, but there was no help coming. Bob watched for a while and decided not to finish Alf. He was probably bleeding out, and the two in the house showed no willingness to help him.

Then to his surprise the door flew open, and Artie ran out towards Alf. The old man stepped out on the porch and began shooting. He seemed to think Bob was in the barn or behind a shed as that was where he was directing most of his fire. Covering fire, Bob thought. The old man has stones.

Again Bob felt the recoil, but he did not feel good about this shot. He had hit the old man, but he thought his shot was off a bit. Mr. Vechio fell but got back up and continued to shoot while Artie abandoned his rescue effort and sprinted back to the house. As Artie rushed past the old man, he nearly knocked him over going through the door. A fine boy you have there Mr. Vechio, thought Bob as he started to squeeze off a final shot.

He didn't take the shot as the old man had been pulled back through the door by the driver before he had the chance. Bob decide there was no reason to stick around so he topped off his rifle, policed up his brass, and went to his horse. Swinging up he headed south and then west to his camp.

Inside the house Artie's uncle was giving him hell. Clutching his arm, he yelled, "Boy, you are the biggest idiot I have seen in a long time. You said the shot came from the barn or shed. That cowboy was nowhere near that barn. He was way off. That bullet hit me long before I heard the shot, and it wasn't very loud."

"How was I supposed to know that?"

The old man was peering out the window between the blinds. "I think he was on that hill over there. That damn thing must be a half-mile away. Alf isn't moving anymore; I think he's dead"

"That's not my fault; I thought he was over at the barn."

"It's not your fault? Yes, it is all your fault. You don't think. If you did think, we wouldn't be in this mess. That hick, as you call him, is a real live, no shit soldier. He is kicking our asses and has already killed two, if not three of us, and winged me pretty good. My arm is broke, and all this because you don't think.

"If you paid attention to business instead of trying to be the tough guy and chasing skirt, none of this would be happening. This cowboy just might kill us all." With this, the old man took a seat. He was in a lot of pain; he was bleeding heavily, and he was feeling faint. "Artie, check out my arm. You need to stop the bleeding." Looking at the driver he said, "Chris, go upstairs and keep an eye out."

CHAPTER TWENTY-NINE

"Sucks to be you." Bob Hasett

Bob awoke a bit before dawn and went through his normal morning routine of checking the horses, eating breakfast, and cleaning up before he settled down with a cup of coffee to begin his vigil of the ranch headquarters. The sun was just over the horizon when he saw a dust cloud rising over the road leading from the highway.

He got his binoculars and watched closely as the cloud approached the drive. Would it turn up the drive to the headquarters or continue up the canyon towards the pass that led over the mountains? It turned. The cloud was now coming down the drive towards the headquarters.

Bob said to himself, 'The old man called for reinforcements." This changed things some but not much in Bob's opinion. He had more than enough ammunition. He wondered how long this would continue before the law got wind of it and stopped the massacre of all these Easterners. They had already suffered two KIA, one MIA, and one WIA. As far as Bob was concerned, they would have at least one more KIA. Any losses beyond Artie were up to them.

Four men stepped out of the car. He thought one was Vince. They were not met outside by anyone but seemed to be responding to somebody in the house. They gathered their bags from the trunk and hurried inside. Bob noted long gun cases were carried by three of them. This bunch may be a bit more skilled than the others. One of them was even wearing a safari coat like some kind of African, big-game hunter.

Bob packed his camp and saddled Crestnut. He didn't want to stay this close to the ranch house any longer. One thing for sure, this bunch was going nowhere until they had dealt with him. He would not have to hunt them; they would be hunting him. That part of his plan was working, maybe a bit too well.

He headed north into higher country. He would set up his camp at a spot he knew about three and a half miles from the ranch house. He wouldn't be able to observe the ranch headquarters from his new location, but he had a view of the road coming up the canyon on the east from the house that joined up below the mesa with the airstrip here they merged into the road that ran to the top of the mesa. From here Bob felt he had a pretty complete view of any comings and goings that might concern him. Now he had to bait them to come north.

Bob felt secure in this position. Its location reduced the chances of his being surprised to almost nothing. On top of that it was a natural defensive position. The site was nearly impossible to get to from the south due to a rock cliff of a couple of hundred feet or more in height. This cliff was actually made up of a bunch of hoodoos and still contiguous, columnar jointed tuff, giving it the look of an immense wall with deep claw marks scratched into the surface by some sort of huge bear. Some of the boulders at the base were as big as houses. The complexity of this structure provided numerous hides and hidden paths.

As for approaching from the opposite direction, that would require a hike of several miles over rough country and mountains approaching 10,000 feet in elevation. He didn't believe this crew had the skills required to pull that off. Even if they did, they would have to find him and root him out of his rock stronghold.

Bob found a hollow in the cliff face behind a hoodoo. It gave him overhead shelter and had the bonus of a decent hidden trial through a gap in the rock which led up to the ridge top. There was plenty of feed up top for his horses but no water. He would have to take them down the back side of the ridge to a spring-fed drinker every day. It was one of old Bill Foster's waters, but he couldn't imagine that Artie or Vince knew about it.

After getting his camp set up, he ate a big lunch. He was going to have to stir the nest a bit this afternoon to get the hornets buzzing. He needed to start thinning the ranks of this bunch before the new guys got the lay of the land. The longer they stayed, the more they would learn about the area, and the harder his job would be.

He guessed they would head north towards the building where he had killed Anthony or maybe check out the low hill to the east of the headquarters from where he had shot Alf and the old man. He would stay high and work his way south until he could get a shot. He needed them to come north. Hopefully, they would take the bait.

It was early afternoon, and Bob had ridden quite a way towards the ranch headquarters looking for his adversaries. He was on top of a low ridge looking to the south along the road. He thought he saw movement, but there was no dust cloud from a vehicle. He kept watching, and before long he saw them on foot, walking down the road but keeping a decent interval and scanning the country all around. There were three of them, that left three plus the old man unaccounted for.

They were nearly a mile away, but if they kept coming, it wouldn't be long before they were within range. They stopped once and waited for thirty or forty minutes before continuing. He kept watching, waiting until he had a shot. When they were about five or six hundred meters away, he began to think about his shot. Which one would he shoot first, and how close would he let them get? One of them was carrying a scoped rifle. He must have been one of the ones that arrived in the car. He would shoot him first.

It seemed so simple. It was simple, too simple. Bob raised his head from his cheek weld on the stock of his rifle and took a deep breath. It was a trap. Somewhere, there was somebody waiting for him to take the shot.

Then the walkers stopped again. This was odd. They had only traveled a few hundred meters since their last break. Of course, they are giving their shooter time to reposition, he thought. Shooter or shooters, there were four men unaccounted for. They must be bounding ahead from point to point whenever the walkers stop. This would allow them to keep within range in the event Bob took a shot thus giving them the opportunity to take him out.

So the best of them were not walking down the road. The walkers were bait. The one or ones Bob needed to worry about were still hidden. He would have to find them. This added a new level of complexity to the problem. He had the upper hand for now and knew he had to take advantage of it.

Bob stayed low and pulled back over the ridge. Catching up his horse, he went back to the north. He would continue this cat and mouse game, but wanted them extended as much as possible before he opened the dance. One thing for sure, he would not engage this bunch more than once on any piece of terrain. Every fight would be on familiar country to him and new country to them.

He repositioned himself further north about two hundred meters to the west of the road, again on the high ground but with special care given to an easy escape route while keeping undercover. He didn't know if the bounding shooter or shooters were east or west of the road, but he had a better escape route to the west, so he picked that.

It took quite a long time for the walkers to work their way up this far, but they showed up and true to form, they stopped every few hundred meters. Bob was not paying too much attention to them but was watching the country around them. "There," he said to himself "there he is."

Walking up a cow trail that ran more or less parallel to the road and about one hundred meters to the east was a lone man. He was wearing a strange camouflage suit that looked like a bush. Bob had never seen anything like it before. It was covered with strips of rags and garnished with vegetation.

The walkers were stopped about three hundred meters south of Bob. As he watched, the shooter selected a hide and took cover. He was about one hundred meters south of the walkers and the same distance to their east. If there is another, where is he? Bob thought. He should be about the same distance to the west of the walkers. Bob marked the location of the first shooter and began looking for the second. The walkers were still stationary.

Bob caught some movement in the trees along the stream bed. The other shooter was there. When he got about even with the walkers, he stopped. Bob was watching him closely through the binoculars. He was dressed like the other shooter. It was effective camouflage. Only their movement gave them away.

It was an obvious choice; he would take the one closest first and then try for the second. The walkers were not a consideration at this point. His only decision at the moment was rather to do it now or wait for their next bounding move forward. He decided to wait. If he caught them during their movement, they would not be set up. He would have the advantage of a covered and concealed position while they would be in the open, more or less.

The walkers started forward. They were looking pretty haggard. The elevation was getting to them. Good, that worked for him. He hoped the two shooters were suffering the same increased pulse and respiration rates. As they got even with him, he could hear them talking. He couldn't tell what they were saying, he could just hear their voices. Artie was in the group, and the others seemed to be shunning him a little. No wonder, he had fucked things up good.

They continued for another one hundred fifty meters. Then looking at his watch one of them signaled, and they stopped. Bob swung his binoculars back to the nearest shooter and saw him rise up and start to move forward. If he stayed in the stream bed, he would be in an open area fifty meters past Bob. That was where he would take the shot. Bob shifted his view to the other shooter. He needed to be sure of his location when he started this party.

Having located the man on the far side of the road, he went back to watching the man in the stream bottom, but he was not in sight. He had left the streambed. Damn, thought Bob, where is he? It seemed like an eternity before he heard the explosion of Quail rising only a few meters from him. "Shit!" he heard the shooter say and then the sound of him hitting the ground for cover. Bob smiled to himself, his adversary had stumbled on a covey of Mearns Quail and kicked them up breaking the silence with the loud beating of wings that startled even experienced quail hunters.

He was very close to Bob's hide. Bob had only one option: keep quiet and wait for him to move and give away his position. There was a bunch of chatter from the road walkers. They were calling out, asking what had happened. The shooter did not answer them but mumbled something under his breath about stupid. Bob barely caught the sound of his voice. That was enough. He was close — very close. The only movement Bob allowed himself was a quick check of the road walkers and the other shooter. The road walkers were agitated and appeared about ready to run. The other shooter was scanning near Bob's location with his scope. He had probobly heard the quail and was trying to figure what was going on.

After what seemed an eternity, Bob heard the sound of the nearby shooter stirring. He must be getting to his feet, thought Bob. Then it was quite again. After another long pause Bob could hear the man walking, slowly and carefully. Bob repositioned himself slightly being sure to keep some cover between himself and the far shooter. He was peering under the lower branches of an oak when he saw the man's lower legs only a few feet away. Bob had already taken out his pistol. At this range, ten to twenty feet, it was the best choice.

The shooter cleared the oak tree and was no more than fifteen feet away when Bob squeezed the trigger twice. One shot to the side and one to the head. It was done. Now he put the pistol back and started looking for his second target. He could hear a bunch of excited talking below on the road, but he could not find the other shooter. He burrowed down deeper in his position and continued to watch the far side of the road.

He caught the glint of sunlight reflecting off something under a tree and hunkered down even further. Thunk! The shot had hit the log behind him. He had dropped his head behind cover just in time. He knew where the shooter was. He just had to get a shot at him without exposing himself. Bob low crawled to a thick stand of oak forty meters to his south, being careful to stay in a small depression, and using downed logs and big rocks whenever possible for cover and concealment. He took up another prone supported position deep in the shadows of the trees and located the shooter. He was in a prone position not more than three hundred meters away and perhaps one hundred feet lower on the opposite slope. He appeared to be glassing with his scope. Bob thought, he may not know whether or not he hit me, and he has not found my new position.

Bob went through the familiar drill: take a breath in, let some of it out, hold, aim, and squeeze. Again, he felt the recoil more than heard the shot. He quickly chambered another round ready to put it into his target, but there was no need.

Bob swung his attention to the walkers in the road. They weren't walking now; two had taken off at a dead run and one with the scoped rifle was taking cover behind a tree next to the road. The one behind the tree was calling out to the shooters. After getting no response he began sprinting from one tree or boulder to the next taking cover and throwing up the occasional shot to the west of the road as he made his way back towards the ranch headquarters. He would have to take him out next. He wasn't a particular threat, but he was more dangerous than what was left of the Indian Springs crew. He hadn't run like a scared rabbit, and he knew how to move under fire.

Bob waited for him to leave his cover and sprint to the next. The runner had set up a pattern of zigzagging every ten meters or so. When he broke from cover Bob had the cross hairs on him and waited for him to zig, knowing he had ten meters before he zagged. He led him and squeezed off the shot. He dropped him with a shot to center of mass at about two hundred fifty meters. Continuing to watch the area, he saw the other two heading southeast through the scattered trees at a pretty good clip. They were about five hundred meters away, a long shot on a running target. He took it anyway. He missed. He thought he saw dirt kick up beyond and in front of his man, and he was sure he saw them both shift into higher gear and run faster.

Another day, Bob thought.

† † †

When Artie and Chris made it back to the ranch house, they were completely spent. They had been running for all they were worth. It was only two miles from where they were ambushed to the ranch headquarters, but they got lost running through the trees and had added an additional two or three miles to their ordeal.

Both men were badly beat up, covered with bruises and scratches from plowing through the trees and crashing down slopes. They each sported more than a few cactus thorns from prickly pear and cholla.

"Uncle Arturo, he has an army out there. They ambushed us. I think they killed everybody. Did anybody else get back?" gasped Artie."

"What are you two doing here? What are you talking about? Where are the others?"

"Dead, they're all dead. We came back to warn you. There must be a dozen of them out there. It was like World War Three."

"Did you see any of them?"

"No."

"Did you see any of our men shot?"

"No, but . . ."

Here his uncle stopped him with a raised hand. "Enough!"

Vince gave Mr. Vechio a knowing look. In response the old man stood up and said to Artie, "You stay here with Vince. He has something to discuss with you. Chris, you come with me."

Vince waited until the other two had left the room. "Artie, close the door and sit down. It's only out of respect for your uncle that I have not put a bullet in that tiny brain of yours. He told me I should, but that would be too hard on him. You might be a total and complete fuck up, but you are his nephew and name sake, and he loves you like a son. For this reason alone, we are having this conversation."

"What the fuck are you saying?"

"Mr. V. and I talked. He decided that if this hunt today failed, we were done with this cowboy. Not only has it failed, but we may be down three more men. On top of that you were wrong to start this war. Any man with stones would be after you for the shit you pulled. You picked the wrong man to piss off.

"Business is business and rules are rules. You broke the rules. You attacked that cowboy in his home and killed his wife. We don't kill wives or kids, you know that, and now look at this mess you got us into. On top of losing, what—maybe five or six men and pissing off every citizen within a hundred miles of here on both sides of the border, it's ruining a good business. Tell me why I shouldn't put you under."

"You can't touch me. My uncle would never stand for that. You're talking shit," he said contemptuously and started for the door.

Vince sprung out of his chair and took Artie to the floor. Before he knew what was happening, Artie was on his back with a knife at his throat. "Don't give me an excuse."

Artie saw pure rage in Vince's face. He was not bluffing. "OK, I'm sorry. Let me up."

"No, you stay right where you are until I finish, and if you piss me off again, you will join Anthony, Alf, and the others in a hidden grave. Capish?"

"Yeah."

Vince loosened his grip a little. "Your uncle and me are through with this cowboy. This war with him is a bad business, and it is bad for business. It has cost us a lot of money and some good men. Now we even owe the Vegas and Phoenix crews for their losses. You fucked up, and you're going to fix it."

"How am I going to fix it?"

"You're going to go find that cowboy and tell him all we want is the money and books. We don't care about him one way or the other. If we get what we want, he is free to go on about his business. Tell him I'll meet him to discuss it."

"What about me? He isn't going to stop until he kills me."

"That's your problem. You can deal with him after, but you don't do anything until we have our shit."

"If we catch him, we can make him talk."

With this, Vince tightened up his grip again, and the anger returned to his voice. "You are the stupidest fuck I know. Haven't you figured it out yet? This guy is one hard son of a bitch. He isn't going to tell us shit unless he wants to."

"I can make him want to. Just leave him to me."

"You don't get it. You killed his wife and from what I hear she was pregnant so you killed his baby, too. The way he is going after us makes me think he doesn't give a shit about himself. He wants us or rather you and doesn't give a shit if he gets killed in the process. You can't make him talk. You took the only thing he cared about. Now all he cares about is revenge. You do it my way, no discussion."

CHAPTER THIRTY

"Whatever is begun in anger ends in shame." Benjamin Franklin

With dawn, Bob was lying in his bedroll trying to talk himself into getting up, but he was so tired. It had been a bad night. The night sweats had come again; when that was over, he fell back to sleep and dreamed fitfully about Angelina. They were not good dreams, they verged on nightmares and left him drained. He desperately needed sleep, but the horses needed tending. He could not let up on this bunch of gangsters. If he gave them time, they might recoup. He didn't want that, he wanted them off balance.

After watering his horses, he was sitting in his camp eating breakfast and thinking of his next move. If they did not come for him, he would have to go for them. Either way was no matter to him as long as it ended. He was tired.

By midmorning, he was set up at a point where he could keep an eye on the site of yesterday's ambush. He had a good hide with a good escape route; he was ready for the next round. While glassing the area, he soon located each of the three bodies more by the presence of ravens, buzzards, and coyotes than by seeing the bodies themselves.

After a few hours, he was struggling to stay awake in the warmth of the afternoon sun when he was surprised to hear what he thought was a car horn. It was way to the south, and someone was repeatedly blowing it. As he listened, it was apparent the horn was getting closer. Soon he could see the dust of a vehicle coming up the road. When it got to the point of yesterday's fight, it stopped but continued to blow the horn.

"A white flag, the damned Jeep pickup is flying a white flag," Bob said under his breath. Soon the driver got out holding the white flag high. He began to walk up the road shouting. Bob could not tell what he was saying, but he could see it was Artie. Now what the fuck could this mean? he thought.

He could simply shoot him and be done with it, but this had his attention. It could be a trap. He would have to be careful. Bob decided he would hold his position until after Artie had passed and see if anyone was shadowing him. If there was no one else, he would slip farther north and wait for Artie to pass him again. He would play this game until he was sure Artie was alone.

Artie kept driving north blowing the jeep's horn and stopping every few hundred meters. At first Bob had held back and let Artie proceed quite a bit beyond him. He wanted to be sure there was no one on Artie's backtrail. Once he was sure Artie was not being followed, or at least not closely followed, he had swung up on Mescal and headed to the north end of the ridge were the road and jeep trial met at the airstrip drive.

Artie continued his slow progress up the road until he reached the point where the road met the jeep trail and turned back up the spur to the airstrip. He didn't know what to do here so he just waited. He couldn't go back. Vince would probably kill him if he did.

Bob wanted to get to the road junction ahead of Artie but couldn't risk being spotted. Keeping away from the road and jeep trail, Bob rode Mescal over some pretty steep country with more than its share of thick woodland. He was in a hurry and put the iron to Mescal's flanks. This was one time he was not worried about this horse's penchant for gathering country at a prodigious rate in spite of obstacles and terrain.

True to his reputation, Mescal had leapt forward at the first touch of the spurs. Soon he was stretched out dodging trees or just splitting the gap between them, jumping rocks, depressions and at least once a big boulder that Bob was sure was too high. Bob was laid out over the horse's neck with his head just to the right a little behind the horse's head. This was not only for the reduced drag but to help him clear the low branches Mescal was passing under or in some cases through. At one point they came to a deep canyon with steep sides. Bob sat back preparing to bailout and take his chances with the ground when Mescal crashed over the edge and sat on his haunches sliding down the slope. Bob kept his seat by leaning back over the horse's rump and raising his feet in the stirrups out in front of him nearly even with the top of Mescal's neck. They slid like this to the bottom of the canyon where Mescal gathered his feet under him and started up the other side.

Bob was set up when Artie arrived. Artie had choices here. He could take the old trail north, take the bend in the road that button hooked up to the airfield, or go back to the ranch house. He wanted to go back but knew he couldn't. Vince made it clear he had to stay out until he got the cowboy the message that Vince and his father wanted a sit down.

Bob watched for a few minutes and when Artie started to get back in the jeep to follow the road to the airfield, Bob fired a shot in the dirt in front of him. Artie froze. The shot came from fairly close, not like the others when the shots that killed Alf and the others had been from way off. This cowboy was a better shot than to miss at this range. What did he want?

Artie looked around and then started to walk back the way he had come. When he passed the pack trail and kept going south, another shot hit the dirt in front of him. Artie stopped again. "What do you want?" he shouted. There was no answer only silence. "What do you want?" Again, nothing. Artie turned and looked at the trail. It was not what he wanted, but he had to give it a try.

After Artie had walked no more than a quarter of a mile on the old trail, he heard Bob say, "Halt."

Artie froze. The voice was close, then he heard it again. "Do what I tell you, or you die here, and you die hard. Now put your hands behind your head, lace your fingers together and drop to your knees. Now lay down on your stomach and keep your hands behind your head."

Bob stepped out of the brush beside the trail holding his pistol on Artie. He pulled a pigging string out of his belt and tied Artie's hands tight. "Ouch, that hurts, not so tight."

Bob kicked Arty in the head and hissed. "Shut up. Don't say a word until I tell you to."

Artie said nothing. Bob jerked him to his feet, blindfolded him, and walked him up the trail a couple of hundred yards to where he had tied Mescal. Bob unfastened his rope latch and shook out a loop. He dropped it over Artie and snugged it up under his armpits.

Artie said, "I have a message," but before he could finish, Bob hit him on the side of the face with his pistol with so much force that Artie stumbled sideways and fell.

"What part of, "shut up', don't you understand?" Bob growled.

Artie was silent. He was not sure if he could answer or not.

"That was not a rhetorical question. You can answer."

"Sorry, can I talk now?"

"No."

Bob swung up on Mescal and took a couple of dallies with his rope on the saddle horn and started his horse up the trail at a brisk walk with Artie at the end of the rope.

It was proving to be quite a task for Artie to keep up, especially with the blindfold. He fell several times but managed to get back to his feet after being dragged just a few yards each time. Whenever he did fall, Bob stopped to give him a chance to gain his feet. "I must be getting soft." Bob said to himself, "Two years ago I would have drug this dirtbag through every rock garden and cactus patch on this mountain."

After traveling for a couple of hours, Bob stopped. It was not that far to his camp, but he circled a few times to add length to the trip. This was done to deceive Artie.

Bob stepped down from his horse, led Artie to a Ponderosa pine tree and tied him securely to the trunk. "I'll be back in a while. Be quiet, and maybe the bears and mountain lions won't know you're here."

"What, are you joking?"

"No, now be quiet. I won't be more than a day or two."

"You can't leave me here."

Bob grabbed Artie by the throat, "Did I say you could talk?"

"No."

Releasing his grip, he said, "Bye."

Artie was sounding pretty plaintive now. He didn't care if he had permission to talk or not. "Stop, don't leave me here. I have to piss. What am I supposed to do about that?"

"That's your problem. Piss is one of the things bears and lions key on when looking for a meal. Be careful."

Bob led Mescal to the water point, and after the horse drank his fill, Bob took him up to where the other horses were. He then went back to police up Artie. As he approached Artie said, "Who's' there? Help, untie me. A crazy cowboy kidnapped me!"

"This is not your lucky day, Artie. It's me, the crazy cowboy."

"Shit, you lied to me."

"Sucks to be you." Bob untied Artie from the tree and checked his hands and blindfold to be sure they were still secured. "Come on." Bob said as he tugged on the rope leading Artie to camp.

Artie was sitting with his legs tied at the knees and ankles, but his hands were free, and the blindfold was off. Bob let him have a little to eat. After Artie had wolfed down the beanie weenies, Bob decided it was time to find out what was afoot.

Bob was sitting across the small fire from Artie, who he had sitting with his back against the rock at the back of the overhang where Bob had his camp. He had the pistol in his hand and was thumbing the hammer menacingly. "What's your message?"

Artie was feeling a little better after eating but decided it would be a good idea not to act the smartass. "Vince wants to meet with you."

"Why?"

"He and my uncle want this over with."

"Want what over with?"

"The killing, the war you have made on us."

Bob pulled the hammer back and pointed the pistol at Artie's crotch. "This is no war. This is fire fight and a little one at that. You couldn't handle a war. I didn't start this shit; you did, asshole. All I am doing is finishing it. As far as I am concerned, it is over now. I have killed your two compadres, and I have saved you for last." Bob looked hard at Artie. "I am going to kill you. You killed the only thing in this life I loved. My wife was a good and decent person, and you took her from me."

"No, don't kill me. Talk to Vince. My uncle will make it worth your while. All they want is their money and papers back. They don't care about you. If you give them back their stuff, you are free to go."

"I am free to go now. They have nothing I want or need now that I have you."

"If you don't meet with them, they will take it out on your aunt and uncle." This was a lie, but Artie was desperate.

Bob was caught off guard by this. He thought about it for a minute, and said, "I'll think on it. I'll tell you what I decide in the morning."

"Are you sending me back?"

"Not tonight, now roll over on your stomach."

Bob tied Artie tight. He hog tied his hands behind his back and pulled his ankles up tying them to his hands. Then he threw a saddle blanket over him and picked up his bedroll. "Sweet dreams, asshole." He left the overhang. He would sleep away from the camp, just in case.

CHAPTER THIRTY-ONE

"To love another person is to see the face of God." Victor Hugo

Bob was feeling warm and content. Angelina was standing across from him with an inviting smile, holding her hands out, beckoning him to come closer. He wanted to be with her so badly it ached. This woman represented everything soft and loving in his world. Now here she was, just a few steps away. It would be good again.

He tried to go to her but no matter how hard he worked at it, Bob could not close the gap between them. Now the warmth and contentment were leaving him and being replaced by frustration. The harder he tried, the more useless it became. Panic was starting to set in.

She dropped her arms, and the smile changed to a look of concern. Bob could hear her, though she was not speaking. "You cannot join me now. I want you, but it cannot be."

Bob was getting desperate, "Yes, I can. I can join you."

Now she was stern, "No, you cannot come to me. You have too much hate inside." With this, she faded away.

Bob sat bolt upright. He was breathing heavily. The dream that had begun so well had ended so badly. It was not like a normal nightmare with terror but even worse with despair, with a complete absence of hope. He felt completely drained. Angelina's scolding look was more than he could stand.

Your name didn't have to be Freud to figure this out. He knew these dreams were all in his head, but that did not make them any less disturbing. Angelina was a kind and loving person and would not want Bob consumed by hate for anyone, not even her killer.

Was there a way around this? Could he do what he must without being consumed by hate? On the Rock he had killed without hate. But that was different, that was war, it was impersonal. This was very personal. Did that matter?

A couple of hours later he was sitting in the gray, predawn light watching Artie. He had been watching him for some time. Bob was wondering about him; had he ever been a decent human being or had he always been a shit even as a kid? Bob decided he must have been a shit, a playground bully. The kind that he had to fight every time his father was transferred to a new post.

As he sat in the cold morning air, the depression was leaving him. He had been mulling over his situation since being awakened by the dream. He had even resorted to prayer, something he rarely did. He wasn't sure there was any help to be had in prayer, but he was sure there was nothing to lose, and he needed to try every avenue he could.

He would lose the hate and anger and look on what he was doing as his duty, as his job. It would not make his victims any less dead, but perhaps it would quell this rage within him. He felt as if he was burning up from the inside out. He did not like being angry. He just wanted to be happy. There wasn't much chance of that, but he would work on losing the anger.

This was not about morality. He suffered no delusions about that. This was about survival, his survival. If he was going to live in this world, it would be easier without the rage. He could only hope that if there was a final judgment, his actions would be seen as justified. No matter, it was too late to turn back now. He had already killed and maimed half a dozen or more, and he was not done.

"Artie," he called breaking the predawn silence. The silence that would soon be broken anyway by the animal sounds, the sounds of squirrels and chipmunks gathering their winter food supply and the sound of the morning birds. Artie didn't stir.

"Artie!" he said again, but this time he added a not too gentle poke with a stick.

Artie stirred and then moaned, "Oh, my God, I'm dying here." Then turning his head to look over at Bob, he asked, "Can you untie me?"

"No."

"Please, at least untie my legs, so I can straighten them. I can't feel anything below my waist."

Glaring menacingly at Artie, Bob growled, "Feelings below your waist got you into this mess. I'm not sure your being numb is a bad thing." With that Bob unsheathed his aviator's survival knife and leaned over towards Artie. "I am going to loosen your legs a bit but not before I relieve you of your dick and balls."

"No!" Artie screamed.

Bob grabbed Artie by the hair, pulling him up to his knees and then pushing him over on to his back. This led to a loud groan from Artie, who was now lying on his back with his arms behind him tied to his ankles, which were pulled up to his waist in the middle of his back.

"That looks real uncomfortable." Bob said with no emotion.

Artie said nothing; he just groaned.

Bob then grabbed him by the belt buckle and brandishing the blade said, "Tell me why I shouldn't nut you like a calf before I give you to the coyotes?"

Artie was terrified. He believed he was about to die in a horrible manner. "Because my uncle will track you down and kill you, your uncle, your aunt., and all the rest of the crew from your ranch."

"Bullshit, what else have you got?"

Artie stammered out some inane gibber, but it meant nothing to Bob.

"Shut up, you fool. Here is what is going to happen. I am taking you back to your vehicle. You are going to drive that Jeep up to the airfield, then you are going to call your uncle on the CB and tell him I am ready to meet with them at the airfield ASAP."

Artie looked a little confused, "What's ASAP?"

"As soon as possible, I want them to get there pronto, or I start shooting off your body parts, starting with your favorites."

"What if they refuse?"

"They won't. I have their money and their books, but if they are that foolish, well, then sin loi motherfucker, up against the wall. I suggest you act your part well."

Artie was sitting in the Jeep at the far end of the airfield when the car came up the slope and stopped. Mr. Vechio and Vince looked the area over before driving the length of the airfield to where Artie was parked. "I don't see any sign of our cowboy."

"I doubt if you will, Mr. V; he is one cagey son of a bitch."

"Well, if he shows up we have to find out where the books and the money are. Are you sure Chris understands that he is not to shoot him unless it looks like he is going to kill us?"

"Yes, he understands."

"It would be a really bad deal if he got offed before we got our stuff."

"Don't worry, Mr. V, Chris understands." Both men jumped when they heard the shot and looked back to see what had happened. "Shit!"

"You don't think Chris fucked up, do you?"

"No, I think we just lost our backup man."

Zip, thunk, wssssss, "What the fuck?" yelled Mr. V as Vince pulled to a stop.

"He shot out our tire," said Vince.

"He's trying to kill us," Said Mr. Vechio.

"No, Mr. V, if he wanted us dead, we'd be dead. I think he wants to talk."

The two men got out of the car, Vince raised his hands, and Mr. Vechio raised the arm that was not splinted in the sling. With this, Artie yelled to them, "He wants you to strip."

"He what?" bellowed Artie's uncle.

"He wants you to strip. You'd better do it. He'll kill us all if you don't."

Looking at Vince, Mr. Vechio muttered, "That goddamned kid's a pussy."

"Maybe, Mr. V, but he's right about this."

Bob watched from his hide, and when he saw that they were undressing, he slipped back to his horse, swung up and struck out a lope, circling around the airfield to get in position near the Jeep. When he got there, Artie had done as he had been told and stopped the others about fifty meters from the Jeep, where they were standing with their hands in the air.

Bob said, "turn around slowly with your backs to my voice." The two men turned. "Now bend over and spread your cheeks."

"Like hell!" said the old man. A shot rang out and clipped the top of his right ear.

"The next one will be a little left of that. Now spread your cheeks." They did.

Once Bob was satisfied they weren't hiding anything, he had them stand straight and continue turning around until they faced his direction again. "Drop to your bellies, and extend your arms straight out to the side." Once the two men had done that or at least done the best they could considering Mr. Vechio's wounded arm, Bob said, "Cross your legs." They crossed their legs. "Turn your faces to the left, and don't move or talk until I tell you to."

The old man was grumbling under his breath about his ear, but he did as he was told. Vince said nothing, he just turned his head.

Bob made his way up to the Jeep leading Crestnut and dropped the reins. The horse would not move now; Bob had selected him for today because he was the most reliable and steady horse he had. If shit hit the fan, he wanted a horse he could count on.

Bob opened the passenger door and reached across to Artie, who was not hogtied anymore but still tied by his hands and feet just the same. Grabbing him by the hair, he dragged him out of the truck. Then he shook out a loop in his rope, worked it around Artie's chest and pushed it up under his arms before drawing it tight. He then went to his horse, swung up and taking a couple of dallies on his horn, he dragged Artie to the others.

Bob stayed in the saddle and positioned himself with the sun over his shoulder about fifteen meters from the three gangsters. You can sit up now, but keep your legs crossed and your hands behind your heads.

Artie complained, "I can't."

"Not you, you're not part of this parley."

The other two got to a sitting position, Mr. Vechio with Vince's help. Bob was uncomfortable with the arm in the sling. Something could be hidden in there. "It's Vince, right?"

"Yes," answered Vince.

"I want you to position yourself by the old man's injured arm but arm's length away." Vince did as he was told. "Now I want you to unwrap that dressing."

Mr. Vechio looked up in anger. "No, my arm is broke from where you shot it. He can't remove the bandaging."

With that, Bob raised the shotgun and aimed it at the old man. "OK, have it your way."

"No, no, wait. Don't kill me, you need me."

"I don't need shit. The dressing, sling, and splint come off, or you die now. Your choice."

"OK, Vince be careful."

Bob said to Vince. "Stay at arm's length, keep everything in my view, and if you come across any weapons, tell me about them immediately, or it all ends badly for you, for all of you."

"OK, I understand." Vince gave Mr. Vechio a knowing look and said to Bob, "There is a pocket pistol in here and a knife."

"Which one is easier to get to?"

"The pistol is right below the elbow, ready to pull out."

"Freeze!"

"Stand up, old man." Vince went to help him up, and Bob shouted. "No help." The old man struggled to his feet. "Now don't move until I tell you."

Bob rode around behind the old man and stepped off his horse. "Walk backwards towards me." When the old man got about ten meters from the others, Bob said. "Stop, drop to your knees, then to your stomach. Now put your good arm under you. I want to see the hand poke out all the way on the other side, and I want all your weight on that arm, comprende?"

The old man did as he was told. Bob then knelt with one knee on the back of the old man's neck and reached into the sling. There it was, a small 380 auto pistol. Bob dropped in it the pocket of his leggings. "Where is the knife?"

"In the top, by my shoulder." Bob found it and removed it as well. Once he was done, he mounted back up and had the old man rejoin the others.

Now he had Vince continue with the removal of Mr. Vechio's dressing, reminding him of the consequences if something seemed suspicious. Once all this was done, and Bob was sure the wound was real and there were no more surprises hidden in the sling, he had Vince rebandage the old man.

Mr. Vechio looked miserable. The color was drained from his face, and he had sweat beading on his face in spite of being naked on a cool, fall day. The business with the arm had been very painful, but he had not cried out. Bob thought he was a tough, old bird.

Bob had Vince and Mr. Vechio stand and pointing to the trees about seventy-five meters away he said, "Walk over there; I'll follow." As for Artie, Bob simply policed up the end of his rope, the other end of which was still looped around Artie's chest, dallied it around his saddle horn and followed the other two dragging Artie behind.

He had them proceed a quarter of a mile or so down a cow trail until he felt fairly secure, then he had them stop and sit. He dragged Artie up to them and positioned himself to cover their back trail and began, "Now let's talk. I understand you have a proposal for me." Bob said this as he sat on Crestnut about ten meters away with his shotgun trained on the three.

The old man asked, "What was that shot we heard before?"

"You mean about the time you got to the airfield?"

"Yes."

"That was me canceling your insurance policy."

"What do you want?" asked the old man.

"Nothing more, I have what I want," Bob said, pointing the shotgun at Artie.

"Then why is he still alive, and why are we here?"

"Because he said you would go over to my uncle's ranch and kill everybody there if I refused to meet with you or if I hurt him."

Mr. Vechio looked at Artie with total scorn. "He lies, and he broke the rules when he killed your wife. That never happens. We are soldiers, you and I."

Bob interrupted him, "No, I was a soldier; you are a scumbag.""

"OK, have it your way, but you know what I mean. What happens to us happens, but families are civilians and are not to be hurt." With this the old man spit on Artie. "So," he continued. "you have nothing you want from me?"

"That's right, nothing except assurance that my uncle and his people are not in any danger from you or any of your people."

"They are in no danger."

"Why did you want to talk with me?"

The old man looked tired. "You have something of mine."

"Yes, I do. The money is of no real consequence to me, although it would be nice to have that sort of pocket change. The books, on the other hand, are the only thing between me and death."

"If you don't care about the money, then give it back. As for the 'books', as you call them, I can recreate what's in them. I don't need them to keep the business going."

Bob knew that if he gave the money back and if the old man believed the books were hidden in the mountains where they would never be found, he was not safe.

"No doubt that's true, but I have left them in a safe-deposit box, and I left instructions sealed in letters with several people to open that box when I die or if I disappear," he lied. "You don't need the books to stay in business, but you do need them secure to stay out of prison or worse." He hoped this was true.

This line of talk went on for a long time. The sun was dipping towards the western horizon, and it was getting chilly. The talks were stalled, but only Bob was comfortable either physically or with the state of affairs. Mr. Vechio and Vince were starting to suffer from the cool air and were shivering noticeably. Artie was just in pure misery due to being tied and dragged. Uncomfortable as the two were they were not giving up. They kept trying to make a deal with Bob. What became obvious was that the money was very important to them, but the books were the real problem. Now Bob knew what he needed to know. He had the advantage.

"Ok, I'm done." Bob sheathed his shotgun to the others' relief. Then pulled his pistol and shot Artie in the head. "We are finished here. I am keeping the money and the books. The books will remain secure from the law unless something goes wrong with me or any of mine."

Mr. Vechio looked with surprise, shock, and maybe a little sorrow at his nephew. "You killed him." The old man was sitting with a dumfounded look on his face, like a deer in the headlights.

"You said, 'Kill him,' so I did. That's my part of the bargain; I saved you from having to do it. Leave my country as fast as you can, go back to New Fucking Jersey or New Fucking York or fucking Chicago or whatever overpopulated hell hole you come from. If you ever come west of the continental divide, I will hear about it. I will hunt you down, and I will kill you."

Vince jumped to his feet. "You can shoot me if you want, but I have played it straight with you. Listen to what I have to say."

"OK, talk fast." Bob had replaced the pistol in the holster and removed the shotgun from the saddle scabbard.

"How about we trade you the money for the ranch?"

"How about I keep both?"

"Look, you killed the ones that killed your wife and a few others. You have had your revenge. Mr. Vechio here knows you had the right to do that and will not bother you or yours anymore. If you give us back the money, we will give you the ranch. What do you say?"

Bob looked at the old man who was not paying any attention to Vince. "What do you say, old man?"

"What, what are you talking about?"

Vince explained to him what he had offered. He also added a few thoughts on the futility of trying to do business in this backwoods wilderness. They would be better off without this albatross around their necks. He worked hard to make his point.

"OK, we will sell you the ranch for the million and a quarter you have of our money."

Bob laughed, "Somebody's been selling you a line of crap. There is no million and a quarter."

"What is there?" asked Vince.

"Just over a million, maybe a million one hundred thousand. In case, you forgot I have all of it, and the ranch isn't worth that much."

"It's our money," protested the old man.

"You stole it, and if I knew from whom, I'd give it back to them, but I don't so here's the deal. I give you back three-quarters of a million, and the rest goes to local charities, in my wife's name."

The old man looked worn out. He was finished arguing. It was better than nothing and much better than being dead, a fate he was surprised he had avoided. This cowboy was the coldest son of a bitch he had ever run across. "OK, it's a deal." He looked at Vince and then at Bob. "I need a good man like you. Are you interested in working for me?"

Bob shot the old man. "No," he answered, then he asked Vince, "Was he really that stupid?"

Vince was staring at the old man. He shook his head and said, "No, but he was that arrogant."

EPILOG

Bob and Jack Barnes were sitting on the ground taking a break, leaning back on their elbows, taking in the view. Far below and ahead of them to the east across the Indian Springs Ranch were the cinder cones and open country of the San Bernardino Valley. The cattle below them were drifting down the slope at a leisurely pace but with purpose. Their horses were grazing contentedly when a red-tailed hawk circling above let out with its signature scream. Jack sighed and said, "It doesn't get more western than this."

"It certainly doesn't." answered Bob. He sat quietly for a short time. He needed to talk to his uncle, and he knew it would be hard. He had dreaded this conversation but the longer he waited the more he knew it had to happen. "Uncle Jack, I need to talk to you about something important. Is this a good time?"

Jack suddenly felt drained. A knot formed in his gut. He had known this was coming, and he hated it. Motioning towards the cattle he snapped, "These girls are lined out. Our work here is done." Standing up and gathering up the reins of his horse, he swung up saying. "We can talk on the way back to Tres Cruses. Spit it out, boy."

Bob was taken aback by Jack's hostile reaction. He knew it would be unpleasant to talk to his uncle about this, but he hadn't said anything yet. Did Jack know he was going to leave?

Jack led the way to the forest road and put his horse into a slow trot. This wasn't a conscious effort to stymie the conversation, but it was effective, at least for a while. Bob, realizing this was to be the pace rode up beside his uncle. "Uncle Jack, I've decided I have to go away."

With this, Jack reined his horse to a stop and turned to face Bob. "Why?"

"Too many memories."

"Not all the memories are bad. There have been some good memories here." Jack looked exasperated and continued. "Hell, Bob, the best memories of your life were right here with Angelina. How can you leave that?"

"I'm not leaving that. I carry those memories inside here." He said placing his hand over his heart. "It's just that everything I see, hear, or smell reminds me of her and reminds me that she's gone. It hurts."

Jack considered this for a moment. Over the past few months, he had in fact often thought about the possibility of this conversation taking place. He knew Bob was doing what he had to. Jack resigned himself to the inevitable.

"OK," said Jack. "What are your plans?"

"I don't know for sure. Maybe I'll head for Alaska. I hear there is about to be an oil boom, or maybe I'll go back into the Army."

"What about the ranch. With the addition of the Indian Springs outfit, it is more than I can handle." Jack was looking downcast. "Bob, all this is yours when I'm gone. You can't turn your back on it."

Bob fixed his gaze on his uncle's eyes and said with conviction. "Uncle Jack, you can handle all this and more. This is no hill for a climber. You know exactly how to deal with all this. Running a couple of ranches is no challenge for someone with your abilities. You don't need me to help you run this place any more than any other cowboy."

"Your Aunt will be really upset." Said Jack quietly.

Bob felt a lump rising in his throat. He had not felt this since Angelina's death. "I know I'll miss her and you and Cruz and everybody. I'll be back for visits, and I'm not staying away forever. This will always be home."